THE CURSING STONES MURDER

George Bellairs (1902–1982). He was, by day, a Manchester bank manager with close connections to the University of Manchester. He is often referred to as the English Simenon, as his detective stories combine wicked crimes and classic police procedurals, set in quaint villages.

He was born in Lancashire and married Gladys Mabel Roberts in 1930. He was a devoted Francophile and travelled there frequently, writing for English newspapers and magazines and weaving French towns into his fiction.

Bellairs' first mystery, *Littlejohn on Leave* (1941) introduced his series detective, Detective Inspector Thomas Littlejohn. Full of scandal and intrigue, the series peeks inside small towns in the mid twentieth century and Littlejohn is injected with humour, intelligence and compassion.

He died on the Isle of Man in April 1982 just before his eightieth birthday.

THE CURSING STONES MURDER

An Inspector Littlejohn Mystery

GEORGE BELLAIRS

ipso books

This edition published in 2017 by Ipso Books

First published in 1954 in Great Britain by The Thriller Book Club

Ipso Books is a division of Peters Fraser + Dunlop Ltd

Drury House, 34–43 Russell Street, London WC2B 5HA

Contents

CHAPTER ONE
THE RETURN OF THE *MANX*
SHEARWATER

Although nothing official had leaked out, the fisher-men and idlers standing round Weatherglass Corner at Peel knew there was something amiss with the return of the *Manx Shearwater*. She was coming in from scallop dredg-ing between Contrary Head and Jurby Point and instead of taking it easy on account of the weather, she was tear-ing across Peel Bay for all she was worth. A south-westerly gale was blowing and the sea was rough, but in her anxiety to make harbour she drove her bow into the steep waves until it vanished completely. Then she rose high in the air as though preparing to take a long jump for port. Even after the *Shearwater* had passed the breakwater her mast-head described a dizzy arc as she felt her way into the channel.

The eyes of the onlookers ashore turned first to the incoming vessel, then to the group of men standing on the West Quay where the *Shearwater* usually moored. Two policemen in uniform, a detective in a slouch hat and rain-coat, and the local police surgeon who was starved to the bone and remained sitting in his car smoking a cigarette. By the time the boat docked, a knot of sightseers had gathered

1

round the police party who didn't like telling them to clear off because normally they were all friends together.

Past the pier the water in the harbour was calm and the *Shearwater* settled on an even keel and slowly glided to her berth, her Diesel engine gently chugging as her skipper eased her alongside. A mooring-rope smacked the cobblestones of the quay and more men than were needed hurried to hook it round a bollard. She was a trim little craft, locally owned, which fished with the herring-fleet during the season and then in autumn turned to dredging for scallops in the rich beds off the Manx coast. Her crew of five were all on deck in stiff oilskins. They looked dazed and anxious for someone to tell them what to do next. The skipper in the small wheelhouse turned off the engine and joined them. Almost before the boat touched the side the police were aboard, walking gingerly like cats in the rain to keep their balance and avoid soiling their clothes. The detective, an Inspector in the C.I.D. from Douglas, was the first to speak.

"Nobody's to go on shore yet. Where did you put it?"

Cashen, the captain, pointed to the hold without a word. He was a tall, middle-aged, weatherbeaten man, tough and wiry, with a calm face and little to say for himself.

"There was nowhere else to put it. We laid a sack over the scallops...."

One of the deck hands, an Irishman, thought he'd better say something. Nobody took any heed of him. A long line of spectators was festooned along the quay alongside the ship and a row of anxious faces followed every movement and word of those on board.

At five o'clock that afternoon the *Shearwater* had raised a body in her dredging gear. It had lain on the bottom because the trousers had been tied at the ankles and filled with stones. None of the crew had wanted to look at it twice;

they'd wrapped it in a sail and lowered it among the shell-fish in the hold. There was a short-wave wireless transmitter aboard and the skipper had at once sent a message to Port Patrick on the Mull of Galloway and from there they had telephoned the Manx police.

"It was like this. ..."

The Irishman couldn't keep quiet. He wanted to tell someone all about it, but the detective waved him aside.

"Better take off the hatches then."

The crew looked at one another; four Manxmen and one from County Clare with a broken nose. The captain was the first to move and the policemen gave him a hand. The body lay below like a parcel in its shroud of sailcloth on the piles of scallop shells. The Irishman crossed himself.

"It isn't a pleasant sight. The fish have been at him."

The skipper spoke for the first time.

"We'll take it as it is to the mortuary, then."

The crew were obviously relieved. Two of them descended into the hold, their feet scrunching and rattling on the scal-lops. Cautiously they lifted the bundle in the sailcloth and raised it to the level of the deck, their boots slithering on the shells which were almost like quicksand.

An ambulance had drawn up on the quayside and the remaining three of the crew now carrying the wrapped-up corpse seemed in a hurry to dispose of it. They almost ran across the deck, manœuvred their burden up the lad-der to the causeway, and slid it in the vehicle, which hast-ily departed after the two policemen had climbed inside as well. It swished along the wet cobblestones, ringing its bell as though there were some hurry about it all. After the body had gone, the atmosphere grew less tense, the groups on the water-edge started to talk, and now and then somebody laughed.

The detective turned to the skipper.

"We'd better take a statement at the police-station. There's no room to do it here."

"Will you be needing us...?"

The crew stood in a compact body, their faces anxious, like schoolboys eager to get away and play. They felt they'd earned a drink and there were plenty willing to stand them a round to get a first-hand tale of the day's happenings.

"All right. But don't go far. We'll need you later on."

They'd no intention of going far! Only to the nearest pub.

"It was like this...."

The Irishman had started telling them all about it already. A lorry drew up alongside and the crew got busy helping to load-up the catch for a quick dispatch to the mainland markets. Gulls hovered expectantly over the *Shearwater*, wailing and crying for the scraps and rubbish they expected to be tipped out of the galley. The onlookers waited till the crew were free; they even gave them a hand, and then they escorted them to a tavern just off the East Quay. They looked a ragged lot as they departed, like strikers on a hunger-march. Men in blue jerseys, in oilskins, in old overcoats, idlers, fishermen waiting for boats, all eager to loose the tongues of the *Shearwater* men and get their fill of the yarn. As they crossed the bridge over the river, a reporter from a Douglas paper joined them.

"It was this way.... Let's begin at the beginning...."

Night was falling and on-shore lights were springing up in pubs and shops on the sea-front. The street lamps of the town came on, infrequent naked bulbs with reflectors which cast yellow pools below and intensified the darkness outside their orbits. The harbour lights on the breakwater and pier shone out and those of the marine parade threw long reflections like silver paths across the water. Over the river the huge masses of Peel Castle and the ruined St. German's Cathedral were just visible in the last of the daylight from the west.

At the mortuary Dr. Fallows, assisted by two policemen and with the detective, Inspector Perrick, in attendance, had opened the grisly sailcloth. Fallows was from the mainland and had set-up in Peel, it was said, for his wife's health. Previously, he had been a pathologist in a large English teaching hospital. The case in hand left him unmoved, but one of the constables had to go outside to be sick. The other looked ready to vomit at any time, too.

The report of the *Manx Clarion* was less gruesome than the surgeon's.

The body was that of a fairly tall man of early middle-age. Medical evidence showed that it had been in the water about a fortnight.... It had apparently been clad in a nylon shirt, flannel trousers and sandals. Little remained of the shirt, but the trousers were of stouter material and, when it was hauled aboard the *Shearwater*, the heavy stones which had kept the body immersed fell from the torn cloth. There were no signs of identification on the clothes, which bore certain proprietary labels of such general use as to be valueless.

There was a fracture of the cranium of considerable size, too large to be caused by accident and probably made by a blunt instrument or rock. The contents of the skull had almost completely disappeared, but the clothing had partially protected some of the organs and medical experts are of the opinion that the body was already dead when placed in the sea.

The teeth had all been extracted and upper and lower dentures were in place.

Inspector Perrick, of the Manx C.I.D., in charge of the case, is following several lines of inquiry and hopes...

"Better tone it down a bit. Still too horrific," said the editor to the reporter, so the official edition omitted all references to what the fish had done before the body was recovered.

Tom Cashen, the skipper, had been away to reassure his wife and fortify himself with a meal and the sight of his home before resuming his ordeal. He turned up at the police-station an hour later to make a statement. He was a careful man and hadn't even had a drink to keep up his spirits, although there were plenty of offers. Through his day's adventures, Tom had become quite a local hero, but he wasn't drinking in case he muddled up his evidence.

"How did it happen? Tell us in your own words, Tom."

Inspector Perrick was homely, but he knew what he wanted. A cheerful leisurely man, middle-aged, medium-built, and running to fat a bit. He was locally known as Raincoat Perrick, for when on duty he wore the same shabby outer garment in all weathers, summer and winter. There wasn't much that Perrick didn't know about goings-on on the Island. The pair of them were smoking pipes and Perrick wore his raincoat, although there was a blazing fire in the room.

"There's not much to tell. ...."

Cashen was a laconic and non-committal Manxman. One of the best skippers on the island, but a bit shy and short of the right word.

"Go on."

"You know what the dredging gear's like, Inspector?"

"Yes."

Sid Perrick knew all about that, too. The scallop boats dragged the beds with a large steel comb about a couple of yards long, attached to a hawser. Behind the comb followed a large frame like a spring mattress, a steel net made-up of rings three or four inches in diameter. As the comb detached the shellfish from the beds, they fell back on the mesh, which acted as a riddle as well, shaking out the rubbish and retaining the scallops. A fishing net attached to the steel one, made the whole into a huge bag, which from time to time was raised by a winch and the scallops inside it emptied in the hold.

The body had got entangled in the gear and was hoisted aboard.

"We knew what it was right away, lek. Now an' then, bodies from wrecks are washed ashore. But when we took a look at him ... we hurried to wrap him up and put him away."

"What time would that be, Tom?"

"Goin' on for five o'clock. I wirelessed Port Patrick right away."

"It's a busy part of the coast?"

"Middlin'. The tanrogans are pretty thick there. The boats are often around. Then there's yachts and off-shore boats always about. It's pretty busy."

Perrick nodded and removed his pipe.

"Tanrogans. You don't often hear that word now, Tom."

"It's the Manx, you know. Scallops they call them across the water."

"Had you been dredging long?"

"Maybe four hours."

"Been there before lately?"

"Not this season. The herrings are only just off. Then we laid-up a bit for painting and repairs to the gear. ...."

7

"Any of the other boats been there?"

"No. We were the first to start just there."

The door opened and the two policemen appeared. Rain had started to fall and they wore dripping capes. Both of them looked a bit white about the gills.

"We've finished, Inspector."

They took off their capes, shook them, hung them up and started to forage around for materials to make some tea.

"We need a cup. …"

"Bin a nasty job?"

"You're telling me! The doctor says he'll see you after surgery. In about an hour. He's a cool fish. Never turned a hair. You should have seen the body. It turned us up."

The bobby was an enormous figure. The idea of turning him up seemed preposterous. His mate was the opposite; thin, hungry-looking and with a long red nose. He seemed in a daze and let the other do all the talking. He was a thoughtful man and didn't like death in any form.

"How long had it been in the water?"

The thin constable hiccupped and made himself scarce. Outside, in the other room, the kettle started to boil. It was a patent one and blew a whistle as the steam emerged.

"A fortnight to three weeks, the doctor said. I don't know how he knows. There was part of it left and he seemed to know from that. I suppose it's his job."

The large bobby's eyes grew round with admiration at the powers of science.

"He also said his head had been smashed-in before he was put in the sea. He was dead before he got in the water."

The smaller policeman appeared in the doorway carrying a tray with a teapot, four thick cups, a large milk jug, and a blue bag containing sugar. He still had his helmet on. He paused as he heard his mate's final words.

"The fish 'ad been at him good and proper. ...."

"Oh, shut up!"

The younger policeman shouted it in anguish and looked ready to tip the tray and its contents on the floor in despair. Then he halted.

"I'm sorry, sir. But I won't sleep for a week after what we've seen to-night. 'orrible! I've seen a lot but never anything like this one. ... The skull was ..."

The fat constable's jaw dropped.

"You're at it now. You tell me to shut up because you can't bear it and then *you* start details more 'orrible still. What's the matter with you, Edgar?"

"Get your tea drunk and stop chivvying one another. You shouldn't be at the seaside if you can't bear seeing an odd body washed-up now and again. Come over here, Tom."

Perrick led the way to where a large framed map of the Isle of Man hung on the wall. Behind, the constables amicably helped one another to tea and started to blow on it and drink it with eager gulping noises.

"Just show me where you were exactly."

Cashen didn't even pause to find the place. A good skipper, he could read a map or a chart with the best.

"There ..."

His large finger fell on a spot about three miles out to sea from the coast, approximately midway between Peel and Kirk Michael, and at right-angles to a creek marked *Lady Port* on the chart.

Perrick scratched his head.

"Anybody might have sunk it there. We get yachts sailing those waters from all over the shop. England, Ireland, Scotland. Some of 'em don't even put in here at all; just race out from their home ports and back. ...."

Cashen put in a word. Although he didn't say much, he wasn't a slow thinker.

"But the body was weighted with stones, you know, Mr. Perrick. They'd hardly bring it far like that. Wouldn't you say it was more likely done on the Island and whoever it was took it out and sunk it off shore."

Perrick didn't lose his good-humoured smile, but there was something unhappy in it all the same.

"That doesn't really get us any nearer, does it? If the body isn't identified…"

"Not much chance of that! The doctor went all over it. Unless we get a description, we're sunk."

Perrick almost jumped. The voice of the heavy policeman came from behind him between noisy swigs of hot tea. He'd forgotten, in his concentration, that there was anybody else in the room.

"He'd got his false teeth in. Grinnin' away in his skull that the fish had…" triumphantly went on the constable.

The thin one made a choking noise and ejected a spray of tea.

"Don't. … I can't stand it."

"Get on with yer tea, Edgar. Don't let your imagination get the better of you."

Perrick broke in:

"There've been French, Scotch and English boats in here up to last week. Any of them might have done it. As I said, unless we hear of somebody disappearing and are able to fit in the body with the description, we've a tough job on."

He was right. In spite of all his efforts and over a week's hard work, he got no further. There were plenty of people missing from all over Europe, but none of them tallied with Perrick's own particular corpse.

There was an inquest and an open verdict and then the funeral of an unknown body recovered from the sea. It looked as if the case would have to go in the unsolved files.

And then, one morning, the constable from Bradda rang-up Douglas headquarters. A Mrs. Ashworth, who kept house for a man named Levis, had received back from San Remo a bundle of letters she'd re-addressed to an hotel there, where Levis was supposed to be staying for six weeks. It seemed Levis hadn't arrived in San Remo, so the hotel proprietor had returned his correspondence with a bill for twenty pounds for compensation for keeping a room which hadn't been claimed.

CHAPTER TWO
NEWS FROM SAN REMO

"Here! What d'you think you're playing at at the Post Office? I re-addressed this to Mr. Levis at San Remo a fortnight since and now it's back again. It's always alike nowadays. We pay our taxes and what do we get…?"

The postman halted beside his bike propped against the gatepost of *Thie Aash*, sighed, and turned in his tracks. A small, elderly, tight-laced woman was in the doorway talking away angrily as though they were standing face to face. He couldn't tell a word she said, only see her mouth opening and closing like that of a fish in an aquarium.

"What is it now?"

Thie Aash! House of Peace. What a misnomer! There never would be any peace whilst Mrs. Ashworth reigned there. Gossiping, brushing, dusting, scuttering, shouting, turning the place out of doors and putting it back again. She never stopped! The house stood high on the cliffs on the way to Bradda Head, with a glorious view of Port Erin Bay, the sea in front and the green hills of Man gently unrolling themselves behind. It was a large, sunny bunga-low built of stone with wide windows letting in the light and view, a green roof and a broad terrace and rock gardens. It caught the sun from every angle and they could watch it set over Ireland in the evenings. It had cost a pretty penny to build and a prettier penny to fill with its costly furnishings and modern pictures you couldn't make head or tail of.

The postman wished it were his. He looked at the calm waters of the bay, the headlands, and the hills all lit up with sunshine, with vast cloud shadows and little fields to decorate them.

"Though every prospect pleases, and only man is vile. ..."

Cubbin, the post, was a Methody and he knew of all the goings-on at *Thie Aash*. Mr. Levis and his bottle-parties, his pretty ladies, and his sinful neglect of what was right and proper.

Of course, Levis was a come-over from the mainland. In his middle forties, he'd arrived with plenty of money, earned in Africa they said, bought one of the finest sites in the South, and immediately begun to disfigure it with a sprawling edifice large enough to accommodate a dozen, instead of his housekeeper and himself. Then the carryings-on had started. Women. ... Wicked and ungodly ones. ... Bad enough coming and settling there to reap the benefit of low income tax, without making an exhibition of extravagance and licentiousness.

It all flashed through Cubbin's mind as he walked with disapproval back to the house and within earshot of the shouting Mrs. Ashworth.

"Look here. ..."

She flung down a packet she had opened on the mock rustic table on the terrace. Behind her Cubbin could see a room furnished in unpolished maple with block floors to match. He didn't like it. It had a half-naked look like the Jezebels he'd seen there with Levis.

Mrs. Ashworth was indicating an envelope with a foreign stamp, addressed to *Thie Aash* in a spiky foreign hand.

It contained a score of other smaller ones, re-addressed from his home in Mrs. Ashworth's illiterate, infantile writing to Mr. Cedric Levis, Hotel Rousseau, San Remo.

"This is the lot I've re-addressed over the past fortnight just as Mr. Levis said I was to do. What's he sent 'em back for?

"Do you hear?"

Mr. Cubbin's mind was on other things. Through the open french window he had spotted over a stone fireplace a picture of a naked woman.... Or at least that was what he took it to be, although it was like a fish standing on its tail, pale and phosphorescent, with long hair and two breasts shaped like pears. So that was what Levis had once boasted, in a pub in the Port, that he'd paid five hundred pounds for!

"You're not listenin'..."

"He's not sent 'em back. That isn't his writin' on the big envelope. Give here. What's this?"

It was a covering letter, written in violet ink on hotel notepaper. The postman pulled himself together and read it over Mrs. Ashworth's shoulder.

As you have not come to claim your chamber I am sending you back all your communications which have arrived. At the same time find account please for chamber held vacant over period reserved, and not claimed. Your early settlement will find us grateful and please also instruct me about baggage held here unopened. Always at your service....

"He didn't claim his room. He mustn't have got there."

Mrs. Ashworth said it in a hushed voice. She was imagining her employer lying with his throat cut in some dirty foreign back-alley.

"He sent on all his luggage except one small case that he said he might want on the way. I wonder if them foreigners has murdered him for his money. ... Things happen, you know, and Mr. Levis always looked as if he had plenty."

The pair of them stood there almost in attitudes of silent prayer, pondering the wickedness of the world, trying to think out a solution. A blow-fly wheeled in at the door, looped the loop, and buzzed out of the window. From the distant beach came faint sounds of laughter and screaming. Almost unconsciously the postman swotted a wasp which had settled on his bag.

"What had I better do, Mr. Cubbin? I'm sure something 'orrible's happened to Mr. Levis."

Puzzled and a bit scared, Mrs. Ashworth had lost her aggressiveness and grown weak and womanly, regarding the postman with round, questioning dark eyes. He didn't look much of a tower of strength. Tall, as thin as a rail, with big hands and feet, a large straggling moustache and troubled, kindly eyes.

"There's Ted Lowey. ... Let's ask *him*."

If Cubbin, the post, had silently prayed for succour, he couldn't have received a better reply. The answer was slowly floating past on a bicycle. P.C. Edward Lowey was on his way to Bradda Tower where, it was reported, some boys had set fire to the heather. He couldn't see any smoke, but in case his eyes deceived him, he'd thought it best to make the trip. He'd struggled on foot and on his bright new bicycle uphill all the way and now he was hot, breathless and very annoyed at the youngsters who seemed to have discovered the knack of making fire without smoke.

"Hey ... Ted. ... I say ... TED. ..."

Lowey, large, clean, always benevolent, polite and civil, patiently dismounted. He'd shoved his bike most of the way

15

up the hill and now when he could free-wheel a bit, he'd to get off, and most likely to answer some damn-fool question about rats or cats or perhaps a patch of damp on the sitting-room wall. People asked him all sorts of things.

"What is it, Mr. Cubbin?"

Cubbin, the post, was a Town Commissioner and entitled to respectful address.

"What do you think of this lot, Ted?"

P.C. Lowey turned over the mail scattered on the table with a large forefinger and read the covering letter carefully.

"Well?"

Like a pair of operatic stars singing a duet, Mr. Cubbin and Mrs. Ashworth told the bobby their tale, now one speaking, now the other, then both at once, and finally Mrs. Ashworth alone in a burst of overwhelming coloratura.

The constable listened patiently, passed his finger along his chin, found a part where he had missed with his razor, frowned as he rubbed it again, and then gave judgment.

"Looks a bit funny to me."

"What had we better do?"

"Where did he leave the suitcase he didn't send on in advance, Mrs. Ashworth?"

"He was going by air. But he'd an errand or two to do. He didn't say where. He wasn't one for confidin' in me what he was doing. ..."

They all looked at one another and nodded. Women!

"Perhaps he left it at the airport on his way."

"Like as not."

"I'll speak to the airport and then to Douglas. Can I use your 'phone? And can I have a drink of water before I do? Dry work all that way uphill pushing a bike."

Mrs. Ashworth turned impatiently to the tap in an inner room, filled a glass, and handed it to Lowey, who eyed it dubiously, wet his lips and teeth with it, and then put it down. No use trying to catch a sympathetic glance from Mr. Cubbin, who was strictly T.T., and president of the local branch of the Band of Hope.

First the airport. Lowey, when the occasion demanded, could be wonderfully sharp and crisp. He got straight to the point and a straight answer came back. Mr. Levis's suitcase was still at the airport, unclaimed in the baggage office, and they'd be very much obliged if someone would come and remove it. Furthermore, Levis hadn't turned-up for the afternoon 'plane from Ronaldsway to London on August 21st, and it had left without him.

P.C. Lowey hung-up thoughtfully.

"This is a matter for Douglas," he said at length and dialled exchange and asked for police headquarters. He told his tale and his own conclusions concisely and smartly, and there his work on the case ended. In less than a couple of hours, Levis was identified as the body dredged from the scallop-beds by the *Manx Shearwater.* Not only had he a plate riveted to his shinbone as a result of a wartime wound of which Mrs. Ashworth was aware, but his dentures had been made and were recognized by a Liverpool dentist to whom they were sent by 'plane immediately after his account was found among Levis's bills.

Once the body was given a name, things began to move.

"An arrest is, we believe, imminent," stated the *Manx Clarion* at the end of four columns reporting the new developments.

It was the way Inspector Perrick said "Ah" when the reporter questioned him which caused the hopeful comment. There wasn't much went on in the Isle of Man that Perrick didn't know. He took a police car and drove to Peel right away. He didn't even call at the local police-station, but, thrusting his hands in the pockets of his raincoat, left the car in the public car-park and made his way through a maze of narrow streets to a cottage just behind the promenade. He knocked on the door and a little elderly woman with white hair and wearing a large white apron answered it. Her sleeves were rolled up to the elbows and there was a smell of baking on the air inside.

"Good afternoon, Mr. Perrick."

Everybody knew the Inspector without his needing to introduce himself. The woman eyed him anxiously.

"Is Fenella in, Mrs. Corteen?"

"No. Not at this hour. She's at the shop. ..."

"Her uncle's?"

"Yes. She helps about the place. Can I do anything? What's the matter, Mr. Perrick? Nothing bad, I hope."

The voice with its gentle Manx singsong tones was timid and apprehensive.

"Just a few inquiries. ... Where's Johnny? Has he got a job yet? By the way, might I come in for a minute? People are beginning to watch us."

He was right. A number of curious neighbours stared hard as they approached the Corteen house and they even walked backwards after they'd passed to be sure of missing nothing.

"Come in."

A small, neat house, two up and two down, furnished simply with cheap furniture. A big living-room with a kitchen in the rear and the stairs rising between. Obviously the home of someone connected with the sea. There were old photographs of sailors on the walls, and on the high mantelpiece over the iron oven-fireplace were four glass floats picked up from the tide-line and used as ornaments, and two model ships in bottles. An old wooden sextant hanging on a nail, and behind the door two peaked fishermen's caps.

Sitting in an armchair by the fireside was an old man in a blue knitted fisherman's jersey and serge trousers. A cold pipe dangled from his loose lips and he didn't move or seem interested when Perrick entered. He was fifteen years older than his wife, had retired from the sea twelve years before, and now, helpless and senile, he sat by the fire all day, looking ahead or at the flames, only speaking when he wanted anything. At his feet, a small child of about two played with a wooden horse.

"She leaves the child with you, then?"

The old woman showed spirit for the first time.

"She's got to earn a living, hasn't she? The money they granted wasn't enough to keep the both of them. She's got to leave the child somewhere. He's a good little boy and isn't much trouble."

She bent and caressed the child, who went on spinning the wheels of the horse's feet and ignored her.

"Poor little thing. That Levis deserves all that's coming to him for what he did ... God will punish him. ..."

"He *has*, Mrs. Corteen. Levis is dead."

The woman reeled back a pace and threw up her hands. "Dead! How?"

"You'll hear soon enough. I want a word with Johnny. Where is he?"

"Johnny? Johnny didn't ..."

"Nobody's saying he did. I just want a word with him."

"He's not workin' yet. He's after a deck-hand job on one of the boats, but the season's wrong. He says if he doesn't get somethin' soon, he'll go over to the mainland for work. Like as not you'll find him somewhere on the quay ... round the boats. ..."

"Or in the *Captain Quilliam?*"

"He's a good boy, but the army made him a bit unsettled. It's a shame."

The old man made noises indicating he wanted his pipe lighting. Perrick struck a match, applied it to the bowl, and Corteen drew at it with feeble, rapid puffs. Otherwise, he didn't say a word nor take any interest in what was going on.

Perrick threw a last look round the room. The child playing contentedly with his wooden horse; the old man, stupid and senile, more like an old and tired animal; and the patient old woman bearing the burden of all the family troubles. He raised the latch and went into the street again. It had started to rain and the wind, blowing down the narrow alleys like funnels, plastered it on the front of the Inspector's raincoat. He thrust his hands deep in the pockets again and threaded his way up-town to Michael Street. This was the main thoroughfare and, at one corner, half in it and half in another lane of tall property, stood a pastrycook's shop. *J. Quilleash. Baker.* Perrick thrust open the door, a bell rang, and the smell of hot bread and spices met him.

Jonathan Quilleash was Mrs. Corteen's brother. He had just entered the shop with a tray of soda cakes and his wife took them from him and put them one by one on plates in the window. When the detective appeared, she advanced to meet him. Quilleash was a first-class baker and boss in his own bakehouse, but socially he was a nonentity. His wife did all the talking.

"Good afternoon, Inspector."

Mrs. Quilleash said it half in inquiry, half in challenge. Everything was straight and above board in their business and she wondered what the police were wanting.

"Afternoon, Mrs. Quilleash. ... Mr. Quilleash. Is Fenella in?"

"Yes. In the bakehouse. Did you want her?"

"Yes, please."

There was a hush as the baker and his missus waited for the officer to explain, but he didn't. Perrick just stood like a rock until Jonathan went to get his niece.

She entered a bit timidly, dusting flour from her hands. A delicate-looking, attractive girl, tall and slim and perhaps a bit tuberculous. She had the clear, flawless pink complexion which often goes with the type, blue eyes and fair curly hair. A long white smock hid her figure, but she was well aware of her charms. There was a slightly vulgar and uncertain sophistication about her. The style of her hairdressing, the well-manicured and polished finger-nails, the lipstick, the smile, and the way she held her head all indicated the penny novelette addict, the omnivorous reader of women's weeklies and their hints and recipes for beauty and allure.

"You wanted me, Mr. Perrick?"

Fenella's aunt and uncle watched her jealously. Her father was helpless and her mother had no control whatever over her. The Quilleashes and her brother Johnny were the only ones who could take any care of her. She had done well for herself, attended classes in typing and book-keeping, and got herself a job as receptionist in an hotel in Ramsey. Then along had come Cedric Levis, taken her everywhere in his car, bought her clothes and jewellery. Just like the novelettes she read by the dozen. To the last detail, including the illegitimate child, and, of course, the wife overseas who didn't understand him, but who prevented Levis from making an honest woman of Fenella. … He gave her two pounds a week, paid through his lawyer.

The Quilleashes strained their ears. Surely, Fenella hadn't been up to some more hanky-panky!

"Have you seen Cedric Levis lately, Fenella?"

She tossed her head.

"No. And I don't want to."

She meant it, too. A decent fellow who would inherit his father's grocery shop in Douglas and who hadn't seemed a bit put-out when she told him about the child, had been paying her a lot of attention, and she saw the chance of settling decently down and forgetting the past.

"I mean it."

"You won't see him again. He's dead. His was the body the scallop boat brought in the other week!"

Perrick had a sense of the dramatic. He liked to toss information at people like a hand grenade and watch their reactions.

Fenella Corteen turned as pale as death, groped behind her for the solitary chair in the shop, and sat down on it. She didn't seem to know where she was, her eyes open wide and staring, her rather fleshy lips moving without saying anything.

"Feeling all right, Fenella?"

Her uncle was indignant and told the detective so before his spokesman could stop him.

"You shouldn't have given her a shock like that...."

His wife intervened.

"Better see to the loaves, Jonty. Leave Fenella to me."

She took the girl in her ample arms.

"There now. It's better as it is. He'd never have done you any good. He was a wicked man. Don't take on so."

The girl flared up.

"I'm glad he's dead! I don't love him. I never did. But, to die like that and...and..."

Perrick stood sturdily before her, his hands in his coat pockets.

"And ... and ... *what*, Fenella? Shall I finish it? And just at the time when Johnny had said he'd swing for Levis. That it?"

"But Johnny wouldn't. ... He wouldn't hurt a fly. It was only his temper."

Mrs. Quilleash put her hands on her great hips.

"If you'd come back from overseas ... from Malaya ... and found while you was away a dirty scum like Levis 'ad given your sister a baby and not done the right thing by her, what would you have said, Mr. Perrick? Tell me that. What would you have said?"

"Half a dozen soda buns, if anybody's interested in sellin' anythin'. ..."

A stringy little woman with a rush shopping-bag was eagerly trying to buy cakes and hear what was going on at the same time. Mrs. Quilleash dealt with her automatically and bundled her out.

"Where were you on the afternoon of August 21st, Fenella?"

"What's that to do with it? I didn't kill him. How could I have? He was found in the sea, wasn't he?"

"All the same, tell me."

"I don't remember. It's a long time since."

"Think. When did Johnny get home from his National Service?"

"August 19th. ... But he didn't do it. I swear he didn't."

"We can check the date."

"No need to. It was the day after little Bob's second birthday and Johnny said even if it *was* a day too late, he'd buy him a present. He got him a wooden horse. ..."

"Bob is the child?"

"Yes. Who do you think I'm talkin' of? It's not his little fault he's ... he's ..."

"I know. You were telling me where you were on August 21st."

"I recollect now. In Douglas. It was early closing and I went to Douglas and came home on the last bus."

"Who were you with?"

"I met a friend. I don't see what it's got to do with you, or Cedric's dying."

"Who's the boy-friend?"

"You've got a nerve!"

Her aunt intervened.

"Tell him, Fenella, and let him get going. He's keepin' customers out of the shop. They'll be thinkin' we've done something dishonest."

"If you want to know then, his name's Fred Harris. ..."

"The grocer? I heard he was a bit keen on you, Fenella."

"Well! You'll be telling us you can read our thoughts next!"

"I wouldn't be surprised. Like me to read yours now? You're wanting me to get going so you can find Johnny and tell him what I said. You're fond of Johnny, aren't you?"

"Nobody ever had a better brother, and don't you dare say a thing against him ... or ..."

"All right. But I shall get to him first, Fenella, so you can get on with your baking. I'll be seeing you again. ... Good-bye. ... 'bye, Mrs. Quilleash. And good-bye to *you*, too, Mr. Quilleash, standing just round the corner there, listening-in, with your shadow falling right across the doorway. ..."

With a chuckle, Perrick let himself out, drew his coat around him, and made for the waterfront.

The rain had swept the place clean and driven the old-timers and gossips from their meeting-place round the weather-glass at the corner of the quay and the promenade.

They had adjourned to the fishermen's pub, the *Captain Quilliam*, called after the Manx hero of Trafalgar.

The *Manx Shearwater* was again tied-up at her moorings after a further spell of scallop-fishing. There were two of her sister ships with her. A French fishing-boat had put in for medical attention to a deck hand who had slipped and broken his collar-bone. On board, some of the crew were getting ready to continue the voyage and two carpenters in oilskins were hammering on deck. At the far end of the quay by the bridge, some partly painted overturned rowing-boats whose owners had abandoned the job. At the head of the breakwater, a knot of anglers, undeterred by the weather, huddled over the water patiently fishing.

Perrick turned in the *Captain Quilliam*. It stood in a side-street just off the East Quay and had once been a large old house. A blast of alcohol greeted him as he opened the door. The bar was full of sailors and idlers rained-off from their usual routine. Some of the crew of the French ship were among them, talking broken English. The rack behind the counter seemed to hold every conceivable kind of drink. Calvados, Drambuie, Schnapps, Vodka.... Everything. Macallister, the landlord, boasted that he could meet the tastes of every ship that put-in.... The French skipper was standing drinks of Calvados all round.

Perrick beckoned Macallister.

"We're busy making hay while the sun shines ... or while it *doesn't*, to be exact. Can't it wait?"

"I won't keep you. Is Johnny Corteen there?"

"Yes. Want him?"

"Send him outside. Can I use your private room?"

"Sure...."

Some artist had done four good charcoal sketches of Peel on the walls of Macallister's little room in exchange for drinks. The landlord had had sheets of plate glass riveted over them. Perrick was admiring them when Johnny Corteen entered.

"What do you want?"

"Sit down, Johnny."

"I'm all right as I am."

Corteen had been drinking with the rest and was half-seas over. A lad of about twenty-one or two, dressed in a fisherman's jersey and blue serge trousers tucked in rubber boots. You could see a resemblance to his sister. Well-moulded features, good healthy complexion, a turned-up, slightly impudent nose, and sensual sarcastic lips. Only where his sister was, by accident or artifice, blonde, Johnny was dark, like a foreigner. They said some of the Manx had a dash of Spanish blood from the survivors of an Armada galleon.

"All right. Stand then. I've called to tell you Cedric Levis is dead. He's been identified as the body the *Shearwater* pulled in the other week."

Corteen rocked on his heels. The Calvados had given him Dutch courage. He sneered at Perrick.

"Why tell me? I didn' do it. Good riddance for Fenella, if you want to know what I think."

"The night you came back from the army, didn't you threaten to do-in Levis on account of what he'd done to Fenella?"

"Miss Corteen to you. I won't have my sister used familiarly.... Seems she hasn't been able to look after herself while I've bin away. Well, I'm back, see?"

"Don't you cheek me, Corteen. Just answer my questions or I'll sock you on the jaw. Pity you've nothing better to do than drink away what bit of money you saved in the army. Now. It seems Levis was killed on the afternoon of August 21st. Where were you then?"

Corteen grew a bit shamefaced. He'd known and liked Perrick since his boyhood and the idea of physical violence between them seemed all wrong.

"I dunno.... I got drunk every night for nearly a week after I came home. The chaps *would* stand me drinks, you see...."

"You came home on the 19th and almost at once, after you'd seen little Bob and heard who was his father, you started to talk about swinging for Levis. You said that here, you know. Did you see Levis on the 21st?"

"No, I didn't. I don't even know the fellow. Never seen him in me life. If I had met him, I wouldn't have promised what I'd do. The dirty li'l swine."

"Were you here on the 21st?"

"Yes. Every day that week. Celebratin' after the long thirst in Malaya."

"Where did you go after closing-time on the night of the 21st?"

"I don't know. I was a bit squiffy.... One over the eight, if you get what I mean."

"Did you go home?"

"I don't know...."

Perrick stood up and faced Corteen, took him by the jersey and shook him.

"If you don't know, I'll have to tell you, then. At five o'clock on the morning of August 22nd, a constable on patrol, P.C. Walker to be exact, picked you up drunk under a hedge on the Peel Road. Out of the goodness of his heart, instead of locking you up, he took you home, knocked up your mother, and you were put to bed. Walker reported that at the station. You were out all night. What were you doing?"

Corteen rolled his head from side to side.

"I don't know. I was drunk."

"Mightn't it be that some time during the day, you met, fought and killed Cedric Levis, hid the body, and then, when it was dark, you pinched a boat from the harbour, rowed out to sea and, having weighted the body, sank it, little thinking the scallop boats would be dredging there later?"

Corteen milled around and started to look rough. Perrick seized his wrists with a powerful grip and held him.

"Don't be a fool, Johnny! Rough-house won't do you any good. I ought to arrest you on suspicion, but I'm going to let you get properly sober and then you can try to think what happened to you that night. Think who was with you, if any-body, where you went, what you did. You couldn't have been so blind as to wander around all night and know nothing of what you did."

"I tell you…"

"And I tell *you*. Don't try to leave the Island. Don't even try to leave Peel, or it'll be worse for you. I want to know where to find you when I want you. Now get going. …"

Corteen didn't join his mates, but reeled out into the street and along the quay, muttering to himself.

A loafer standing silent in the passage overheard it all and in an hour everybody in Peel knew it. Johnny Corteen had murdered Levis, on account of what he'd done to his sis-ter. They were all on Johnny's side and Perrick got some black looks as he moved about in the City. It was all over the Island by nightfall, even at Grenaby, where Archdeacon Kinrade spent a sleepless night because Annie Corteen, Johnny's mother, had, before her marriage, been maid at Bride par-sonage when the Archdeacon had been rector there. At nine the following morning Teddy Looney's old rattletrap of a taxi drew up at the door of the Corteen house. Teddy had gone in the wrong direction down a one-way street and his ears were burning from the words the bobby had said to him before he spotted the Archdeacon in the back.

Mrs. Corteen had hardly time to greet her old master before she was in tears, telling him the full tale, swearing Johnny was a good boy and innocent. And the night before, there had been so many people there talking the thing over, that old Corteen had sensed trouble, got excited, tried to get up, and had a stroke.

"I've always tried to lead a good life, parson. I always tried to do my best for the children. And got nothing but trouble. First my husband, then Fenella, and now Johnny likely to be took for murder. He's a good boy and wouldn't do anybody harm, but he was out of doors all the night that Mr. Levis was killed and he can't remember what he did. The police seem to think he *won't* remember, but I know Johnny better...."

When he got home, Archdeacon Kinrade went half a dozen times to the telephone and then returned to his study. He felt old and tired and unable to cope with the ordeal of a long-distance call to London. Finally, he drew up to his desk, took pen and paper, and began to write. He sealed the letter and then took up the telephone and asked for the hotel at the airport. He was through in a minute.

"Can you give me the steward of the Northolt 'plane to-morrow, please?"

There was a pause.

"Hullo, Archdeacon. Casey here. Anything I can do for you?"

"A favour, if you don't mind, Casey."

"Anything. Only say the word, sir."

"Could you take a letter over with you and see it delivered at once in London? I know it's asking a lot, Casey, but this is a matter of life and death...."

"Sure, sure. A pleasure, sir. Want me to come out for it in the runabout?"

"That's very good of you."

"What part of London do you want it delivered, sir?"

"Scotland Yard. To Chief Inspector Littlejohn. ..."

Chapter Three
Night at the *Captain Quilliam*

… I am sure he had nothing to do with it and all his friends here—in fact, everyone in Peel—think he's innocent. But the circumstantial evidence points so damnably in his direction. I would not have troubled you, only he is a good lad, if a bit hot-headed, and he is the sole comfort of his mother, who's had a lot of trouble. You did say you would bring your wife over to see me before very long. Would it be possible… ?

It was ten o'clock in the evening and Littlejohn and his wife had been sitting reading before the fire with the dog between them. Littlejohn had fallen asleep over a thriller and Letty was reading the latest translation of a Colette novel when the bell rang and a messenger from Scotland Yard handed in Archdeacon Kinrade's letter.

"Who's it from, Tom?"

"Archdeacon Kinrade. He wants us to go over if we can, right away. A young chap he's very fond of looks like being arrested for murder. What do you say?"

She looked at him with understanding. Warm hearted, full of compassion, in spite of all his years in the force, he

was easily imposed on. In three days they were due to leave
for the wine harvest round Bordeaux as guests of a vintner
to whom Littlejohn had done a good turn. They were going
off to celebrate Littlejohn's promotion to Chief Inspector.
But the Rev. Cæsar Kinrade was another thing altogether.
His friendship had brought something into the Inspector's
life which couldn't be counted in cash or kind.

"I don't mind. I've been a bit afraid with all that wine
and food at your age you might come back worse than you
go. We'll have to take the dog, of course."

"Of course."

Meg, their old-English sheep-dog, seemed to understand,
rose, yawned voluptuously, barked, turned round twice on
the same spot, sank down, and fell asleep contentedly.

Littlejohn read the three-page letter aloud to his wife. It
gave, in a robust, firm hand, details of the Peel dredger case.

"It's a bit awkward. I can't butt-in on the Island police,
although they're a good lot to get on with. I'll just have to
play the amateur for a bit. ... Right, then. I'll ring up the
Yard and arrange to go to-morrow. We'd better not go by
'plane with having the dog. There's an afternoon boat from
Liverpool."

Letty was already in the bedroom, sorting out the contents of the half-packed trunks, throwing out the flimsies
and adding the warmer things, substituting woollen pyjamas instead of Littlejohn's nylons. ...

The dog, confident that her interests were in good
hands, snored before the fire and now and then yapped joyfully in her dreams.

As the Littlejohns gathered their luggage on Lime Street
station, Liverpool, the following day, they became engulfed
by a crowd of travellers from the incoming Manx boat on

their ways to London. And in the mêlée, the Inspector spotted the fresh face and cheerful teeth of Sergeant Knell, who had helped him so much in connection with the murder of Deemster Quantrell. Knell was accompanied by an amazingly good-looking, dark girl, with a flawless unadorned complexion and a figure which made men turn and stare in admiration.

"This is Miss Teare.... I mean, Mrs. Knell, sir. We're on our honeymoon."

It was as much as Littlejohn could do not to ask what had held up the wedding! Almost a year ago, the banns had been up!

"I'm an Inspector now in the C.I.D., sir."

"My congratulations on both events.…"

They hadn't much time together, but Knell had a shrewd idea what was taking Littlejohn to the Isle of Man again.

"Johnny Corteen, sir?"

"It's really a promised holiday with the Archdeacon, but I might help if I can."

"Sid Perrick is in charge. What a pity it's not me. You'll find Perrick is one of the best. He'll appreciate any help you can give him. He's not proud."

The porter arrived with the loving couple's baggage and Knell and his bride were hustled away. As the Manx Inspector inverted the woman's umbrella he was carrying and waved it in farewell salute to the Littlejohns, a shower of confetti and rice fell upon him from it.…

The sea was like a millpond and they reached the Island as the sun was setting beyond the backbone of quiet hills. As the boat entered the harbour, they could see the sturdy, gaitered figure of Archdeacon Kinrade standing with the harbour master at the pierhead. His glorious froth of beard was as white as snow and his clear blue eyes shone with welcome.

He had hired a "drive yourself" car for the Littlejohns during their stay.

"I thought Looney's rattletrap was hardly the thing for a lady."

They reached Grenaby about eight o'clock and the place seemed to enfold them in its peace. "It'll get you. You won't want to leave when the time comes," someone had said to Littlejohn once about Grenaby. It was true. The rustling of the trees, the rush of the river driving its way under the bridge, the hooting of the owls and, somewhere in the distance, the loud cry of some wild thing in the night. ... The Archdeacon had talked to Letty all the way, but as they entered his parish, he grew quiet as the spell fell upon them all. All except Meg, sprawled on the floor of the car, sleeping off the surfeit of buns, biscuits and meat-pies with which a large group of admirers had stuffed her on the voyage.

They dined and it was striking nine as they finished. And now Littlejohn having parked the car and left the vicar of Grenaby to call on Mrs. Corteen for news, was making his way to the *Captain Quilliam*. Nothing like a prompt start!

The holiday season was over, the coloured lights of the promenade had been removed, and now the city ... for such it calls itself on account of its ruined cathedral ... was quiet and dimly lit. A string of lamps along the seafront, some sodium bulbs along the quay, the warm glow of curtained windows, and, overhead, the moon almost at full with high white frothy clouds slowly drifting across it. The French fishing-boat was still moored at the harbour. Her lights were on, for she was due to leave early next morning. Across at the West Quay, three ships of the herring fleet were tied-up. A light shone from the fo'c'sle of one of them, the *Manx Shearwater*, which was off early to the scallop-beds and some of the crew of which were sleeping on board. Across the sea shimmered the reflections of the lights of the waterfront. Somewhere somebody was playing a mouth-organ.

Littlejohn pushed open the door of the *Captain Quilliam* and turned to the right into the public bar. The place was full, the atmosphere thick with smoke, and you couldn't hear yourself speak for the hubbub of chatter and the shouts of half-drunken men. The crew of the French ship were having a farewell spree and spirits passed freely. They'd drunk all the Calvados and were now on whisky and schnapps. One wall was covered with the labels of various ships which had entered the port. Boats from Brittany, Scotland, Norway, Denmark, Iceland. The skipper of the French ship was unsteadily fixing his own card with a drawing-pin. *St. Yves, Tréguier.*

Littlejohn found a seat in a corner. He was surrounded by sailors, sitting on benches at marble-topped tables or lolling with their glasses against the walls or at the bar. Nobody bothered much about him, except the landlord. He wasn't known and visitors on holiday often called for a drink and a bit of local colour. The presence of another stranger only made one or two of them swank a bit more. They raised their voices and talked of fabulous things which had happened to them. The rest aided and egged-on the yarn-spinners. They were of the seagoing fraternity, a race apart from the land-lubbers, whom they liked to bait now and then.

"Can I get you anything, sir?"

The landlord, tall, muscular, calm amid it all, and in his shirtsleeves, stood before the Inspector.

"A bottle of red label."

"There's another room at the back if you find it a bit thick in here."

"I'm quite happy, thanks."

They all milled merrily around except a solitary figure in the opposite corner from Littlejohn. A stocky, elderly, weather beaten man in jersey and sea-boots, with a long moustache and huge hands scarred by old fisherman's abscesses and festers. He was drinking rum and was almost helpless. His presence seemed to throw a blight on the gathering. Men kept looking over their shoulders at him, wondering what he was trying to drown, or where he'd got the money from for his drinks.

"That's the last, Ned. ..."

The landlord placed another small rum on the table before him. The morose sailor was up in arms at once.

"Who says it's the last? I can pay for all I want, can' I? It's for me to say when I'll stop, not you. ..."

The landlord glanced in Littlejohn's direction from the corner of his eye. He knew from his bearing that there was something official about the Chief Inspector and he was putting on a good show for him.

"Not here you won't, Ned. I said that's the last. You've a long way to go home and you're leaving here in a fit state to get there."

The drunken man cast a scowling glance round the room and his eye fell on Littlejohn.

"Ah. ...A copper, eh? Tha's why I'm not allowed to buy what I want. I'll go where my company's wanted then. Can' enjoy me drinks with a blasted copper lookin' on. ..."

He downed his drink in one and, half in rage, half in bravado, dashed the glass on the marble top of the table and broke it. Then he rose, and reeled from the room.

The silence created by the sailor's little one-act drama was broken. The men round the bar started to shout louder than before.

"What's come over Ned Crowe and where's he gettin' the money for all his drinks?"

"Nice and steady, he was, once. Now he gets drunk every night. It's a mystery to me...."

"They say the Almighty guides the feet of the drunks. How he finds his way home beats me...."

Their voices petered out. They began to talk in low tones to one another, their eyes now and then glancing in Littlejohn's direction, wondering what his business might be. Two fishermen more drunk than the rest got a bit truculent about it.

"Is he from the police? He looks it."

"So what? Let 'em all come. They'll not pin anythin' on Johnny Corteen...."

The atmosphere certainly had altered. The French sailors couldn't understand the reserve which had fallen over the rest. They gathered together in a tight group at one end of the counter on the defensive.

"What is it?"

The French captain couldn't stand the silence any longer.

The drunken sailor was quick to answer.

"We got company," he said, with a dirty look in Littlejohn's direction. "The police are with us.... Don' you worry, Frenchie. It ain't you we don't find welcome. You're always welcome here, see?"

He was maudlin and reeled across to embrace the Frenchman.

"It's the same all over the world, isn' it? We sailors unnerstand one another...."

The landlord was getting afraid of a rough-house.

"I don't want to interfere, sir, but would you care to come in my room for a minute? They've been having a bit

of a party with the Frenchies and some of them have had
too much."

Littlejohn smiled and shrugged his shoulders.

"I've got to go in any case."

"Rhoda! Come and mind the bar."

The landlord shouted for someone in the next room and
a buxom smiling girl appeared and took over. There were
cheers and shouts of pleasure from the sailors as Rhoda
went behind the counter.

"It's like this, sir. I don't know whether you're police or
not. It's no business of mine. But the men there are very
fond of Johnny Corteen. He's just got back from the East
and he's a bit of a hero to them. Now, there's talk that he
might be arrested for the murder of a bounder called Levis,
who's been carrying on with his sister while Johnny's been
away. The men seem to have got it in for the police."

The landlord was anxious to please. He'd always been
on good terms with the police and that is a sound security
when you've sailors to deal with, especially foreigners who
don't understand licensing laws.

"You're right, landlord. I am a police officer, but I'm
not on this case you mention. I'm here on holiday with
Archdeacon Kinrade, an old friend."

The landlord's reserve vanished.

"Archdeacon Kinrade! That's different. I'm sorry they
were a bit uncivil in there. As I said, they've been going it
hard with the Frenchies. ... Let me get you another bottle of
red label."

He was off before Littlejohn could stop him. Obviously
anxious to put things right in the bar. He came back smiling with the beer.

"Do you want to go back in there, sir?"

He jerked his head in the direction of the bar.

"No. I must be off. By the way, who's Ned Crowe, the one who kicked up the fuss?"

"A decent enough chap. Runs a little farm and does a bit of off-shore fishing in his boat. His place is at Gob y Deigan, about four miles from here along the Kirk Michael road. He lives alone and used to come once a week to buy his groceries and things in Peel, have a drink or two, and then go home quietly...."

"And now?"

"Over the last month he's changed. He seems to have got money from somewhere, he's here every night, and he leaves with a right skinful. I'm getting fed up with it. I'll have to tell him to take his custom somewhere else. It depresses the regulars to see him there, scowling and muttering to himself in a corner. I can't think what's come over him."

"Is Johnny Corteen not here to-night?"

"No. I'm glad, in a way, because he might have kicked up a rumpus if he'd seen you. The police are on his heels, you see. I wouldn't be surprised if they'd taken him to the station. They've been questioning him a lot lately."

Littlejohn turned up his coat collar and paid for his drinks. In the lobby a couple of men from the bar were going home as well. They nodded genially and smiled at him.

"Goo' night, sir."

The landlord had evidently made peace with his customers on the strength of Parson Kinrade's being Littlejohn's friend.

"Our mishtake. We thought you was after Johnny.... Thass all ri'...."

The other sailor made a swift rubbing-out gesture with his hand to show the incident was closed.

It was chilly outside. The lights of a lot of the houses and cafés on the front and quay had gone out and the place was deserted. Somebody was playing a harmonica on the deck of the *St. Yves*. A tune from *Moulin Rouge. It's April, my dear....* A hoarse voice took it up in French.

Archdeacon Kinrade was sitting in the car in the car-park, a rug up to his chin, and his beard spread across the front of it like a bib.

"Sorry to keep you, sir. ..."

"I've only just arrived back. It's a bit too late to take you up to the Corteen place now. They're getting ready for bed, though I don't suppose they'll sleep much tonight. The police have arrested Johnny on suspicion."

"It's only a precaution, sir. Don't get upset about it. You see, if he *had* done it and skipped off through their not taking the usual steps, it would look bad. They must have a good case for the preliminary arrest."

The parson sighed loudly.

"Yes, they have. Johnny can't say where he was on the night of the murder, in addition to which, he seems to have made a point of telling everybody he met on the day he returned, what he was going to do to Levis on account of Fenella. He told them all he'd kill him. Fenella hasn't helped. She's been very vindictive about Levis. She expected him to marry her, of course. She's quite given Johnny the impression that Levis is entirely to blame. Everyone knows it was six of one and half-a-dozen of the other, but Johnny won't listen to anybody but his sister. I'm sure he believes that Levis raped Fenella. It's very awkward, but I'm sure Corteen didn't do it. He might kill a man in a fit of rage and even bury or hide the body. But to take it out to sea, weighted, and sink it among the scallop-beds. ... No. Johnny's a sailor and knows this coast and all that goes on there. Why go and drop the corpse in the very spot where it's likely to be hauled up any day?"

Littlejohn started the car and they threaded their way up the narrow streets on the main road to St. Johns.

"I'm sorry to bring you so far when you've just arrived, Littlejohn, but I had to see the Corteen family to-night. I've comforted them to the best of my ability. The old woman's like somebody in a trance. Can't believe it. As for Fenella ... she takes it all in very unseemly fashion. You'd think she was proud of having a murder committed on her behalf. She's certainly going to be disappointed. I'm sure it had nothing whatever to do with her and her sordid little affair."

They drove on, the headlamps making a tunnel of light through the overhanging trees. The village of Foxdale was in complete darkness, except for a single upper room with an illuminated blind and a car standing at the front door.

"The doctor's car. I wonder ..."

The Archdeacon sounded half asleep.

From the top of the hill, beyond the thick Barrule Plantation of pines and fir trees, they could see Castletown, with a few lights glimmering and Langness lighthouse throwing its rhythmic beam over the land and back to the water again. Now and then, Littlejohn had to swerve to avoid rabbits and a solitary hedgehog bewildered and transfixed by the lights of the car. They turned right to Grenaby.

It was more like home for Littlejohn to find his wife there. It was evident that Mrs. Keggin, the housekeeper, was already on good terms with Letty and dumbfounded by her culinary knowledge. Someone had, in the absence of the men, brought in some fresh lobsters from Castletown. Mrs. Littlejohn had cooked *Homard à l'américaine*.

"We both thought you'd be hungry when you got in. It'll probably give us all nightmares, but we couldn't resist it. ..."

They ate their meal under the warm glow of a paraffin lamp on a round highly-polished mahogany table, with Regency chairs to sit on.

At the foot of the stairs, Littlejohn paused and lifted his wife's chin with his forefinger.

"Sorry we came?"

"Not at all, if you don't have too much work to do. In fact, I'm glad we changed. And by the way, your winter pyjamas are airing in front of the kitchen fire. You'd better rescue them."

The dog was already upstairs, making sure of her lodgings and whining at their bedroom door. She descended impatiently to hurry them up and breathed a blast of *Homard à l'américaine* upon them.

CHAPTER FOUR
THE DRUNKEN SAILOR

"You see my difficulty, don't you, sir? It's not within my powers to invite you to share the job. Unless I tell the Chief that the case is beyond my capacity, he won't ask for outside help. And I can hardly do that. ... It's awkward, you'll admit."

Perrick had called at Grenaby just after breakfast to see Littlejohn. He was still smiling and unperturbed, smoking his pipe and wearing his raincoat, but he was obviously in a dilemma. He wished to make Littlejohn welcome and encourage him to help, but red-tape and etiquette made it hard going.

"Officially, we're on opposite sides of the fence, in a manner of speaking. I've got to prove Corteen guilty and you're here to prove he isn't. ..."

Littlejohn smiled and puffed his pipe with obvious relish. The sun was shining, the dog was rabbiting in the hedge— mainly flurry and joyous shouts—and Mrs. Littlejohn was picking the last of the runner beans in the back garden. Parson Kinrade was in his study answering his large correspondence.

"I quite understand, Perrick. I'm really here on holiday. I'll help all I can and if Corteen is guilty, I shall say so.

But I'm an amateur this time and I'm not trying to prize Corteen out of your grasp. If he's done it, he's yours. If he hasn't, it will still be your evidence which sets him free."

The enthusiastic and honeymooning Knell had telephoned from London on his nuptial night to tell Inspector Perrick of his encounter with Littlejohn and to bespeak the Chief Inspector a favourable reception. That had brought Perrick hot-foot to Grenaby.

"There's no definite proof yet of Corteen's guilt. Nothing, except that he threatened to swing for Levis all over the place and Levis happened to be murdered nearly as soon as Johnny got home. We daren't leave Corteen at large till he's absolutely in the clear."

Perrick picked up an apple, a windfall from the old tree in the front hedge, rubbed it on his raincoat, and bit a chunk from it.

"That doesn't stop you from asking me if you can see Corteen, sir, or anybody else, for that matter. I'm only anxious to find out who killed Levis. I never liked the man myself, but I've got my job to do."

A passer-by hailed Littlejohn like a long-lost friend. It was Joe Henn, who owned a large tumbledown house just over the bridge.

"Hullo, Inspector Littlejohn. You here agen? Glad to see you. Though I must say I 'ope you don't attract a lot of crime and violence down here like you did before."

He passed on a bit apprehensively.

"I hear Levis was a thoroughly bad egg, especially where women were concerned. Might it not be that one of them, and not Fenella Corteen..."

"Maybe...and maybe not. It's a bit difficult when you're dealing with an old hand at concealment like Levis was. He'd plenty of good-looking youngsters round his place in the holiday season. He never went short of pretty girls with all those romantic holiday-makers to go at. His fancy ways, fancy house, and the money he was willing to fling about were all bait for the unwary. And he also possessed a peculiar fascination for women. ... The sort of thing that disgusts ordinary men who often have a devil of a time making even one woman in a lifetime get fond of 'em. There must have been local women, too. A fellow like Levis just doesn't hibernate when the pretty strangers have crossed back to their shops and offices. Levis was promiscuous... always on the hunt. ..."

Perrick had a pretty turn of phrase and made people and events come to life as he told a tale.

"He kept his affairs with local women very secret. I'll bet if we could find a diary or unearth his mistresses by magic we'd get some surprises."

"Doesn't his housekeeper know what went on?"

Perrick rocked on his heels and took another crisp bite of his apple. He cocked his head at Littlejohn.

"You seem to know quite a lot about Levis already, sir, if I might be so bold."

"With an encyclopædia of island lore like the Archdeacon, you must expect it."

"Aw, I see."

Perrick shied the chewed core of his apple at the ample rump of a picking hen and laughed as she leapt in the air and scuttered cackling out of reach. He wiped his fingers on his raincoat.

"You were saying, his housekeeper, sir. No. Or at least she says she doesn't know anything. She knows nothing, according to *her*. Herself is a very righteous, self-satisfied sort of woman who likes to give the impression that she wouldn't stay a day in any house where there were *carryings-on* of any kind whatsoever. She says that if Levis did misbehave, he didn't do it under his own roof. Which may be true, may be not. He ran a fancy car and might have avoided scandal, especially with married women, by taking his pleasures in quiet places, hotels, or even in the open air and sunshine. Besides, Mrs. Ashworth has only been with Levis for a little more than three months. The previous housekeeper might have told us quite a lot of what went on in the winter season, so to speak, but she's dead. Died on the mainland while on holiday in the spring. Is there anything you'd particularly like to see or know, sir? I'm going over to Peel now. Can I give you a lift?"

"It's kind of you, Perrick, but I'd better show my wife a bit of the Island first. I'll keep in touch with you. If I should come across anything useful, I'll be sure to let you know. Perhaps I'll call and see the Corteens in Peel later and also the police surgeon. I'd like his first-hand account of the autopsy. Parson Kinrade will probably attend to the introductions. You see, it might be a bit embarrassing for you with your superiors if I'm seen with you all over the place."

Perrick looked the Chief Inspector straight in the' eyes and held out his hand.

"Very decent of you, sir. I appreciate it. We'll keep in touch."

"Just one thing, Perrick, before you go. Have you made no progress whatever with Corteen's alibi? Did *nobody* see him around on the night of Levis's murder after he left the pub?"

Perrick took out his pipe and tapped the stem on his thumbnail to emphasize his points.

"Four of them left the *Captain Quilliam* together that night. At the church in the market square, they broke up into two pairs. Two went up-town and left Johnny Corteen and another fisherman called Eddie Kermode to go their own ways. Both Johnny and Eddie were pretty badly drunk and the last the other two saw of them they were arguing as to where they should spend the night. Eddie was trying to persuade Johnny to go home with him and stay at his place till he was in a better condition to face his old mother, who is a religious woman and takes badly to Johnny's drinking ways. When we called at Eddie's place, the neighbours said he'd taken the morning 'plane to England in August last."

"You mean, he might have been involved in Johnny's mischief and bolted?"

Perrick solemnly shook his head.

"No, sir. Mrs. Kermode is a Peel girl, with an aunt in Fleetwood, on the mainland. When we went to Eddie's place and found it shut up, we called at her mother's and got a part of the tale of the fatal night. It seems that about midnight, Eddie and Johnny turned up, drunk, at Kermode's home. His wife was within a month of having her first baby and was, in consequence, a bit touchy. The arrival of a couple of drunks made her see red. She told her husband she wouldn't have his disreputable companions in her house, and neither did she want him in his state, either. There was a row, which ended in Eddie's wife going home to her mother's to sleep. And, in the way some women have when they're in the condition of Mrs. Kermode, she said she wasn't going to have her child with a drunken husband around. She was going over to her aunt in Fleetwood. They couldn't persuade her otherwise and she left by the morning boat."

"And Eddie?"

"Appeared at his mother-in-law's next morning, as sober as a judge, but too late to stop his wife from crossing because it was after nine when he arrived and the boat leaves at nine. When Eddie heard what his wife had done he was terribly upset, packed his gear, and went by 'plane the same day. We got in touch with his wife's aunt at Fleetwood, through the police there. Mrs. Kermode was with her, right enough, and the baby had been born. She and Eddie were friends again and Eddie had shipped with a Fleetwood fishing-boat and was somewhere in the region of Iceland. They've wireless aboard, but till she gets back to Fleetwood it isn't much good trying to get a full tale from Eddie. She should dock in a day or two and then we'll bring Eddie back over here. Meanwhile, Johnny Corteen'll do no harm where he is. Better be safe than sorry."

"And Corteen doesn't remember whether or not he spent the night at Eddie's place?"

"No. He doesn't remember a thing, except being vaguely wakened by a policeman in the open air and taken home. He only got properly lucid when he woke in his own bed at home next day."

Later in the morning, at Peel, Mrs. Littlejohn went to hunt for some wool.

"It's too cold to sit on the beach in a deck-chair. I'd better start knitting you a pullover in my waiting-time, and I look like doing a lot of waiting. I'll sit in the car till you and the Archdeacon get back."

It was as though a blight had fallen on the Corteen home. The old man was up, dressed, and in his chair by the fire again. He sat helplessly there, his cold pipe in his mouth, slowly twiddling his horny thumbs, firmly convinced that as people died in bed, it was safer to be up.

The child had been farmed-out with a relative and Mrs. Corteen was carrying on alone. The house was spotless. The old furniture shone from ceaseless polishing, the iron fireplace was newly blackleaded, and the hearth was white with fresh stoning. An iron kettle steamed on the hob.

There was a very old harmonium in one corner. On top of it, one or two books; a Bible in Manx, a hymn book, Bunyan's *Pilgrim's Progress*. In the other corner, a large grandfather clock with a painted dial showing the phases of the moon. Its steady ticking punctuated all that went on. Tick, tock; tick, tock.

The old lady behaved like a wild thing caught in a trap. Moving here and there without much aim or reason, completely terrified and bewildered by events.

"I'll never get over this, parson. I'm at me wits' end. I wish the Lord would take me and himself both together. It's more than I can bear...."

"There, there.... It's not all that bad, my dear. Here's a friend of mine from as far away as London to help you out...."

"Tell me what happened the night Johnny came home late, Mrs. Corteen. The night Mr. Perrick has been asking you about."

Littlejohn filled his pipe and then sat in a chair opposite the old man, filled *his* pipe, as well, and helped him to light it.

"What is there to tell, sir?"

"Was it raining when he got home?"

"No, sir. A middlin' fine night, but dark."

"What time would that be?"

"Five o'clock. The church clock struck as I brought him in through the door."

"Did you notice his boots? His sea-boots, were they?"

"Yes, sir. Nothin'.... A bit muddy, but then...well...he wasn't ezac'ly in the habit of cleanin' them reg'lar."

"Did he say anything to you?"

"No. He was sort o' fuddled. He hadn't slept off the drink. In a sort of maze, he was, and after I'd pulled his boots off I led him up to bed and he let me tek off his jersey and trousers…jus' like when he was a boy…and fell on the bed asleep right away."

"Was he in any sort of temper or bad mood?"

"No, sir. When he woke next day, he didn't seem to recollect what had happened the night before. Seemed to think it nacherall he should be in his own bed, lek."

"Did you know this man Levis, Mrs. Corteen?"

The old woman started to whimper and wipe her eyes on her apron. The mention of the man had reminded her of her own unhappiness.

"No, sir. I never set eyes on the man. When the baby was born he said it wasn't his, lek, but Fenella's aunt and uncle hired the lawyer and they made him admit it and he paid for the upkeep of it through the lawyer. He wasn't the likes that would come here."

No; Levis, with his fancy ways, his easy money, his flashy house and car, wasn't the kind to be seen in the back streets of Peel. He paid his way out of trouble until finally his money couldn't save him.

"Johnny wouldn't do it. I swear he wouldn't.…"

"How did Johnny come to know Levis and all about your daughter's troubles?"

"Well, sir, with the baby playin' in the house, it didn't take him long to ask and find out. Him and Fenella was always as thick as two thieves. Always took one another's part, even against me and their dad. She must have told Johnny everythin'. She was bitter and liked to talk about it all and how she'd been wronged."

"And what did Johnny say?"

"He took it bad, sir. He swore he'd get even with Mr. Levis. But he would never have killed him. I know Johnny. He's not that bad, sir."

"Did he know Mr. Levis?"

"He saw him, sir. He came one day to Peel and they must have pointed him out. But it seems he was in his car and got away, which was a good thing, sir, with Johnny in the mood he was."

They rejoined Mrs. Littlejohn who was sitting in the car with the windows open on the promenade. It was mild for the time of year and the sea was calm, with the waves lapping as the tide ebbed. The dog was hanging through the window, barking at the seagulls skimming over the water. The eyes of all the old fishermen and loafers at Weatherglass Corner turned in the direction of Littlejohn, whom they regarded with complacent curiosity. They felt that, on account of Archdeacon Kinrade's presence, the Chief Inspector was somehow on their side and would see right done to Johnny Corteen, whom they supported as a member of their seagoing fraternity.

The harbour and waterfront were a riot of bright colour in the thin sunshine. The beautiful cliff-bound sweep of bay, the hillsides dotted with new houses and villas, the old narrow streets sweeping to the promenade, the glow of the red local sandstone and the green background of rising land. Across the water, St. Patrick's Isle with its ruined cathedral and castle. ...

Mrs. Littlejohn raised some hanks of wool.

"It's the colour of the fishermen's jerseys. I'm going to knit you a pullover of it. ..."

The parson was thoughtful and anxious to be getting on with the business in hand.

"If you want to see Dr. Fallows before lunch, we'd better be off. He'll just about have finished his rounds."

The doctor's house was near the golf links on the main road from Peel to Douglas, about half a mile out of the city.

A large bungalow, whitewashed, with access through a door in a high surrounding wall. On the door, two brass plates. *L. J. Fallows, Physician and Surgeon. Pamela Fallows, Architect and Chartered Surveyor.*

"So his wife has a profession, as well."

"Yes. It seems she was an architect on the mainland before he married her. She gave it up after they married, but she's started again in the last twelve months. I suppose it finds her something to do. She's in partnership with another woman."

The bungalow was built in Riviera fashion, with large windows, a glass door inside a porch which broke the wind, and a long loggia facing the south. The garden was trim and full of exotic plants. Palm trees, pampas grass, bamboo, hydrangeas, fuchsia and tall cypress. Littlejohn rang the bell.

The doctor himself answered the door. A tall, heavy man, with tufts of dark hair over his ears and a large, domed bald head. He looked in his late forties, with a smooth florid face, protruding brown eyes behind round gold-framed glasses, a large Roman nose and a heavy firm chin. He wore a soiled flannel suit and a nylon shirt with his collar and tie in disarray.

"Hullo, Archdeacon. What brings you here?"

A rather thin voice for such a big frame. The parson introduced Littlejohn and told the doctor the purpose of their visit.

"Come in. ... In there. ... It's warmer than the surgery."

They entered a large room which ran down a whole side of the house. One wall was almost entirely of glass and a door in it led to the verandah. A big modern stone fireplace, rugs on the polished block floor, comfortable chairs and a large settee scattered about, with little tables and a cocktail cabinet. On the walls three large reproductions of pictures by Van Gogh, Utrillo and Renoir.

"Drink?"

The doctor was busy at the cocktail cabinet before they could reply. He was evidently seeking an excuse for a drink himself. He handed a whisky and soda to Littlejohn, brown sherry to the parson, and helped himself to a large neat whisky.

"Now, gentlemen ..."

Before they could say a word, the door from the hall opened. A woman put in her head and then withdrew it.

"Pam. ... Say, Pam. ... Come back."

The newcomer returned. She looked at her husband first, with a bored tolerant expression and a trace almost of contempt, or the resignation one shows at the antics of exuberant children or dogs.

"Pam, I want you to meet Chief Inspector Littlejohn, of Scotland Yard, who's on holiday and staying with Archdeacon Kinrade. He's interested in the case I told you of—the one about the body they found in the scallop-beds."

Even that didn't arouse much enthusiasm in the good-looking woman who had entered. She must have been about ten years younger than her husband. Medium built, on the thin side, with a wide intelligent forehead, brown wavy hair, grey eyes set well apart, high cheek bones, straight nose, firm chin and a generous mouth with a trace of a sarcastic smile. She had the preoccupied look of someone suddenly torn from interesting work and eager to get back to it. And yet within her you sensed great vitality and the power of immense concentration to achieve the ends she desired. The type who attracted and stirred men whenever she entered a room, even in the company of more beautiful and artful women.

"How do you do, Inspector…Archdeacon…"

She shook hands with them, a small firm hand with a good grip. Her eyes never rested. Here, there and everywhere, but never a straight look for long at once. She held the Chief Inspector's gaze for a second and then her eyes moved to his tie, then to his right shoulder, then to the Archdeacon. Littlejohn told his wife afterwards that he wondered for a second if his neckwear were in bad taste or his suit badly cut.

"Dora is here.…I can't stay."

"Bring her in for a drink," said the doctor irritably.

Pamela Fallows turned without a word, left the room, and returned accompanied by a small, thick-set, dark girl, with hair cropped almost like a boy, dressed in a mannish costume. She even wore a tie and a masculine cut of blouse. All smiles and energy, she shook hands all round, baring her strong even teeth, her dark eyes sparkling.

"This is my partner, Dora Quine."

An incongruous pair, yet perhaps well-matched as a team. The one eager, enthusiastic, hard-working; the other dreamy, imaginative, moody, full of ideas which her partner probably slaved to bring into effect.

The doctor's wife poured herself a whisky and soda and mixed gin and French for her companion.

"We'd better take the drinks with us to the office. We're in the midst of drawing plans for the Martin place at Lezayre.…"

It was plain that Dora Quine was not as anxious to get back to work as her partner. She wanted to know all about Littlejohn's share in the case, about Scotland Yard itself, about London, the current shows, the autumn season.

"You'll excuse us.…"

Pamela Fallows led the way out and Dora followed slowly.

"Hope to see you again, soon. Pam's got the creative instinct moving strongly just at present. She gets that way at times. Cheerio!"

The door closed. It looked as if the Archdeacon had been right in his summing-up of affairs in the doctor's household. "There's unhappiness there. He's a brilliant man who would have gone far on the mainland, but he got himself mixed up with a woman and it looked like wrecking their marriage. They have two children at school in England, so divorce seemed out of the question. They pulled up their roots and came over here to start again. It doesn't seem to be working out very well. She has her work and he has his. Maybe that will be their ultimate salvation."

The doctor was helping himself to more whisky.

"Another drink, Littlejohn?"

"No, thank you, doctor."

Fallows brought out a duplicate file of the Levis autopsy and some gruesome photographs.

"It was obviously murder, doctor? There's no chance the drags from the fishing-boat could have caused the injuries?"

"Not the slightest. The post mortem bears out the date as deduced from alternative evidence, August 21st. The man was dead when he was put in the water. I'd say the blow was a fearful one, and, as likely as not, Levis's assailant was face to face with him when it was struck. A short weapon would have needed somebody powerful to deal him such a blow. On the other hand, a long bulky piece of hard wood, say oak, could almost have been handled by a child, because its own weight would do the trick. Or again, somebody might have dropped a rock on him from a height."

The doctor was lost in his subject. You could see him, in imagination, actually witnessing the killing. His precise, clear manner of expression told of the undoubted expert.

"The body would be a fairly heavy one, I suppose?"

"I knew the man by sight and judging from memory of him and the body, such as it was, that I saw, I'd say around thirteen stone."

"If he was murdered on the island and carried to a boat, then it would need someone fairly strong to get him aboard and out to sea."

"Certainly. Unless, of course, he was killed near a beach and dragged along. That's a likely hypothesis."

"Well, thank you, doctor. It's been very kind of you to tell me about it informally. I'm only an amateur on the job; just interested because of the Archdeacon's friendship with the family of the accused. It has saved me having to bother the police and perhaps cause a bit of embarrassment."

The doctor rubbed his chubby forefinger along his smooth chin.

"The accused? Is Corteen likely to be charged with the murder?"

"I can't say that, sir. There is a faint chance he might be able to prove an alibi. In any case, the evidence is purely circumstantial."

"Many a man's been hanged on it, though."

"Certainly. But Levis, it seems, was a man who might have had many enemies. That always complicates a case."

"I guess it does."

Littlejohn picked up his hat and gloves.

"By the way, doctor, do you happen to know a fellow called Ned Crowe? A fisherman who lived just out of Peel, I gather, on the road to Kirk Michael."

The doctor paused and looked over the rim of the glass he was emptying.

"Crowe? No. Can't say I do. Why?"

"Just one of those interesting things that sometimes intrigue me. I was in the *Captain Quilliam* in Peel last night and Crowe was there throwing his money about. Everybody was surprised. He's a poor and steady chap as a rule. I wondered if he might be a patient of yours."

"No. There are two other doctors here, you know. I can't say I know him."

The Archdeacon was on the alert right away. His blue eyes shone and his large beard bristled.

"Are you *sure*, Fallows? I'm certain I read in the local paper only a week or two ago that Crowe was before the magistrates for being drunk and disorderly and when he was arrested, he said he was ill, not drunk, and you were called to say that you'd examined him on the night in question and he was drunk as a lord...."

Fallows cast an odd look at the parson.

"Ned Crowe.... Oh, Ned Crowe! That's right. I know who you mean now. Yes. That's the one occasion I met him. He was a stranger to me otherwise."

"That's funny," said the Archdeacon solemnly as they got back in the car. "Either Fallows is losing his wits or else he was lying. I wonder...."

CHAPTER FIVE
THE HOUSE AT BRADDA

After lunch, they left Peel for Port Erin, where Littlejohn said he would like to see the home of the murdered man. Guided by the Archdeacon, Littlejohn took the coast road leading south through Patrick, Glen Maye and Dalby. The parson described the places on the route to Mrs. Littlejohn. "There was once a murder here," he said as they passed through Glen Maye, as though Littlejohn might at once halt and start another investigation.

The day had become fine and clear and a stiff inshore wind had sprung up. High waves were breaking over The Niarbyl, a spreading tail of rocks beyond Dalby, and across the white-capped sea in the west, the Mountains of Mourne in Ireland could just be seen. A good road led them through lonely and magnificent country with mountains—South Barrule, Cronk ny Irree Laa, the Carnanes and Bradda—stretching away in a glorious chain to the southern tip of the Island. They climbed through wild stretches of heather, bracken and waste land, with ruined farms dotted here and there and a long succession of mighty cliffs and bays along the whole of the coast to the Calf of Man. Just past the junction of four ways at the Round Table, the car coasted down to crossroads, where the parson showed Littlejohn the turn to Bradda. They didn't go short of people to direct them to *Thie Aash*, Levis's home, which of late had become a place of morbid pilgrimage.

Mrs. Ashworth was in the bungalow with two policemen to keep her company. Since the bad news of Levis, she had refused to sleep there, as though the event had put a curse on it and one night the wraith of her master might return. P.C. Lowey was officially in charge of the house until the mystery was cleared up, but, as his many duties precluded him from making it a full-time job, a young police cadet from Douglas had been sent to assist him.

"Now then, me lad, just go see what they want," said Lowey very officially to his pupil. He was determined to keep the cadet well-disciplined during his spell of duty in the south. The apprentice, a lanky lad with a fresh complexion and a nose too big for his face, put on the flat cap which distinguished his lowly rank and hurried to the gate to meet the car which was pulling up.

"More gawkin' sightseers," he flung back over his shoulder at Lowey and then he put his hand over his mouth as though trying to take back what he had said, for he had seen the gaitered legs of the Archdeacon scrambling out of the back seat.

"Crikey! It's Parson Kinrade."

Since the investigation of the death of Deemster Quantrell, the parson had earned an unsought and rather spurious reputation for being the local Sherlock Holmes!

"What are *you* bletherin' about?" said Lowey from the terrace and then he, too, said Crikey! He had spotted Littlejohn, whom he remembered from a previous visit at a time when he had been in the Castletown force.

"Now things'll really begin to 'um," he assured Mrs. Ashworth, whose jaw dropped because she didn't know what Lowey was talking about.

Mrs. Littlejohn stayed in the car admiring the view as the small procession, composed of the parson, the Chief Inspector and the dog, made its way along the garden path, where Cadet Skillicorn joined it and, after deferential greetings, ushered it into the bungalow. P.C. Lowey met them on the threshold.

"Good mornin', gentlemen. Nice weather we're having. ..."

He fell back and prodding his pupil in the ribs with his elbow said *sotto voce*, "Scotland Yard."

"Eh?" said Skillicorn. Lowey raised his eyes to heaven and sighed. The dog was busy touring the terrace gobbling up the scraps of bread Mrs. Ashworth had thrown out for the gulls. Normally, Meg would have turned up her bulbous nose at dry crusts, but when they were put out as food for something else, she developed a sudden appetite for them.

P.C. Lowey introduced everybody to everybody else. He was fond of the Archdeacon. His father, aged eighty-eight, lived at Grenaby and Parson Kinrade signed a paper every month which testified to the ancient's continued existence and right to draw his pension from a mainland institution from which he had been retired for more than thirty years.

Mrs. Ashworth stood eyeing the parson up and down suspiciously. His gaiters fascinated her. She belonged to a sect of Plymouth Brethren which met in a house at Port St. Mary. "I don't hold with Papists," she told them at the next meeting. "And I think that old man is one of 'em."

Lowey was a mine of information about all that went on for miles around. He led the Inspector and the Archdeacon to the lounge and bade them both be seated, as though the place were his own.

"I'll look after this," he said to Mrs. Ashworth and indicated the kitchen with a large thumb. She had been packing her things and as many of the late owner's as she could safely appropriate, ready for leaving the place for good. With a sniff, she turned her back and went to finish the good work.

Littlejohn was admiring the view from the windows. The land fell away sharply to the Port Erin beach and thence a long curve of bay and clean sand swept round and terminated in cliffs which the sea was lashing and covering in foam. A small lighthouse at one end and, midway, a ruined breakwater constructed of great masses of concrete which the sea had broken up and tossed about like corks. High above, the spectacular mass of Bradda Head with the Milner Tower sprouting from the top.

"Come to investigate the crime, sir?"

Lowey stood deferentially beside Littlejohn, looked out to sea, and forgot himself.

"Well! If the ruddy fool hasn't put out to sea again on a day like this! Him an' his birds! That's Professor Tipstaff from over and he's bought a little boat to study birds in. Always chooses the roughest days to go out a-studyin' them and then they have to put out the lifeboat or somethin' to bring him in again. He's balmy.... Excuse me, sir. I was just carried away...."

In the distance a small boat bobbed dangerously round the breakwater in the direction of the open sea. Hurriedly Lowey tramped into the hall to telephone the lifeboat-station to keep an eye on it. Then he took up his task again and led Littlejohn and the Archdeacon round the bungalow. An exotic place, the home of a "fancy man"; an erotic, almost depraved taste manifest everywhere. Tortured pictures and bits of twisted sculpture, dubious novels, locked book-cases containing "Collectors' editions". Lowey indicated the latter.

"Dirty rubbish," he said portentously. "I don't think Mrs. Ashworth can read, else she wouldn't have stayed here as long as she has. As she says, the job was good and well paid and, like the late Lord Nelson, she used to apply the blind eye, so to speak. … She always shut her eyes when makin' the bed, she says."

He waved his large paw at a coloured print of naked women dancing in a ring, which hung over the bed, and blushed himself and coughed behind his hand.

"A shocking chap," he added. "My nephew's young lady came here helpin' with the spring cleaning one time and, findin' one of those book-cases open, just took a look at some of the books. For weeks after she wouldn't let my nephew come near her. Sort of brainstorm it gave her. …"

Littlejohn lit a cigarette to hide his grin.

"How long has this place been built, Lowey?"

"Six years next summer, sir," replied the bobby with precision.

"Did Levis build it?"

"Yes, sir. Put up this main part first and then had a bit of a wing added last year."

"A nice job."

"Yes. Architect done. Miss Dora Quine's first real effort. Does her credit."

Lowey exchanged a knowing look with the Archdeacon to show they both knew Dora and her skill.

"That the girl who's partner to the doctor's wife at Peel?"

"The very one, sir. Matter of fact, Miss Quine and Mrs. Fallows both attended to the extension when it was put on."

"Were both of them on the job, then?"

A twinkle showed in Lowey's eye.

"Yes, sir. Two strings to his bow, in a manner of speaking. They gave the job quite a lot of attention. One or the other down every day. Not often you get such keen supervision on the part of architects, is it, sir?"

The Archdeacon frowned.

"If you're trying to imply something, Lowey, will you kindly say it outright, instead of insinuating?"

The constable jumped.

"I thought you'd have heard already, reverend. There was quite a lot of talk about the pair of them and Mr. Levis at the time."

Littlejohn ground the stub of his cigarette in an ash tray consisting of a naked nymph holding a bowl in bronze.

"Let's get this quite clear in our minds, officer. You're suggesting, to put it vulgarly, that something was going on between Levis and Miss Quine?"

"Both, sir.…Both Miss Quine and Mrs. Fallows. Mrs. Fallows, they say, put Miss Quine's nose out, to put it vulgarly, as you say. But then, that was only hearsay. No doubt Mr. Casbon, the builder on the extensions, could tell you more. He was workin' here at the time it happened."

"Where can we find him?"

"His office and yard are in Castletown, but I think, if you're going back to Grenaby from here, you'll put a sight on him just past Mallew Church. He's doing a job at a farm on the right. Ballakilbride is the name."

"Right. What's going to happen to this place now? Has Levis any relatives?"

The constable rubbed his chin.

"They do say he has a wife over on the mainland. She might be interested. There's a brother, as well, but he's in Kenya, I believe. They wired to him and it's said one of the lawyers from Douglas is winding things up.

Mrs. Ashworth's had notice and I suppose the place will be sold before long."

"Has anybody been through Mr. Levis's papers and effects, yet?"

"Yes, sir. The lawyer, Aspinall, was down here with Inspector Perrick the other day. They put everything in a suitcase and took the papers away with them."

Littlejohn strolled from one to the other of the rooms. The lounge with a dining-alcove, Levis's and Mrs. Ashworth's quarters and the kitchen seemed to be the only ones used. There was another bedroom, a study with a bed-settee in it, and a small morning-room; all were sheeted and had apparently not been occupied for a long time. Lowey, anxious to help, opened the drawers of the desk in the lounge, and the chest and the dressing-table in the bedroom.

"You see, sir, they've taken all the papers. And, if I might say so, you can depend on them taking all that matters. If Inspector Perrick is on a job, it's done properly."

"I'm sure it is."

There was a player grand-piano to the left of the window. On the lid, two photographs, cabinet size, the only two in the place. One was of a handsome officer in colonel's uniform. A dark man with a small black moustache, regular features, a firm jaw and a sensual mouth. In ink across the bottom of the picture: *Best wishes to Cedric from Ralph.*

"According to Inspector Perrick, that's his brother, sir. The one in Kenya. His name's Ralph...."

The other portrait showed a fair, clean-shaven, smiling man with wavy hair swept back from a broad forehead, a straight nose and a cynical fleshy mouth. There was a self-satisfied, cherubic look about him and a small dimple in the square jaw accentuated it.

"That's of Mr. Levis, sir."

Littlejohn knew it without being told. The man was in keeping with the place. You could almost smell his exotic scented brilliantine and after-shave lotion. Impudence, self-indulgence, assurance with everybody, most of all with women. ... The type who *would* put his own portrait on his own piano.

From the window Littlejohn could see his wife with the dog on the beach at Port Erin below. She must have strolled downhill to the village. The cadet was drinking tea with Mrs. Ashworth in the kitchen as the Chief Inspector and the other two entered the hall. Lowey gave Skillicorn a blistering look and the pupil choked over his drink, leapt to his feet and, for lack of something else to do, sprang sharply to a salute. Mrs. Ashworth came to the kitchen door. She was sulking at Lowey for sending her about her business and pouted heavily.

"Had Mr. Levis any frequent visitors just before his death, Mrs. Ashworth?"

"No. Tradesmen, that's all. He didn't entertain much here. Did it mostly at some hotel or other."

"Which hotels? Do you know?"

"No. I knew nothing of his private affairs. I was here to look after the place for him and after that we went our own ways."

"Did he always come home at night when he was on the Island?"

"Not always. Sometimes he'd telephone that he was staying with some friend or other and I needn't wait up."

"Do you know who were his friends?"

"Not particularly. As I said, he entertained them out."

"I see. Thank you, Mrs. Ashworth."

The Chief Inspector and the Archdeacon got in the car again, ran down the hill to Port Erin, and picked up Letty and Meg. The dog had been in the sea and they had to dry her on the towel they purposely carried for her. She didn't want to leave the beach and kept barking at the waves as they broke on the sand.

Just past Mallew Church a small country bungalow was going up. There was a builder's board erected in the garden. *Casbon, Builder, Castletown.* Three workmen, squatting on a pile of bricks, were drinking tea.

"Mr. Casbon about?"

One of the men removed his fag and waved it over his right shoulder in the direction of a farm behind.

"He's just gone to 'phone the works. We've run out of mortar. …"

The three of them looked delighted about it, poured out more tea, and one of them settled an iron kettle on a brazier with a view to making yet another brew.

Across the fields a small, chubby, bothered-looking man was hurrying back to the job. He stared hard at Littlejohn and the Archdeacon and then, as he saw in them possible clients for a new house, his brow cleared and he smiled an oily smile. He had lately become a worried man. Building was declining and he looked like being out of business if things didn't buck up. He had come over from Lancashire to put up a lot of houses, make his fortune, and save income tax, and now trade had dried up on him. It wasn't good enough!

"Good day, gentlemen. What can I do for you?"

"We'd like a word with you about the extensions you did to *Thie Aash*, the late Mr. Levis's bungalow at Bradda."

Mr. Casbon's face lengthened and he eyed the Archdeacon up and down, wondering what he was getting at.

"Why? Nothing wrong, is there?"

"Not a thing. We're just interested in Mr. Levis and what he did before his death."

"You from the police?"

"Yes," said Littlejohn.

"Not much I can tell you. Levis paid well. Prompt with the cash. Different from a lot of people nowadays. Business is terrible."

"You built on an extension last year under supervision of architects?"

Mr. Casbon cast a baleful look at his workmen, who thereupon gathered together their tea things and shuffled into the house to enjoy their drink out of sight.

"Supervision, did you say? Humph! They drew the plans and drew up specifications and took their per cent of the money as it fell due, but most of the time, they was hanging round Levis. First of all, it was Miss Quine. Thick as thieves with Levis, she was. Riding about in his car, rollin' her eyes at him. But about that time, she'd no more sense than to take herself a partner, that Fallows woman. She soon put Miss Quine out of the runnin' with Levis. The three of them would be lookin' round the place for hours, but you could see Levis and the Fallows dame smilin' at one another, that sort of secret look they get when there's somethin' *going on* between them, you know. ..."

Man-of-the-world Casbon put a cigarette in the corner of his mouth, lit it, drew lungsful of smoke, and ejected it in a spray from his mouth and nostrils.

"How long did that go on?"

"Months. We were there from April to September on the extension job. It got in the end Mrs. Fallows came on her own without the Quine girl knowin'. She'd go off in the car with Levis and Miss Quine would come and find her boy-friend flown. Scandalous, it was. I don't mind a bit o' fun myself, but not with married women with children. But then Levis didn't mind so long as they was good-lookers. ..."

Casbon recited it all dolefully, without a trace of relish. In between drawing furiously at his cigarette and coughing harshly, he sighed deeply, puffed out his cheeks, and deflated them again with blowing sounds.

"Levis had a bad name with women, you know. Somehow, he attracted them. Sometimes, when we was building the house and then again when we was extendin' it, a good-lookin' woman would stop and look what we was doin'? You know how interested women are in houses goin' up. ... If Levis was on the spot, he'd invite the dame to come and see what the place was like. Before they'd been there five minutes, you'd have thought they'd been friends for life. Now and then, he'd offer to take them back to where they were stayin' in his car and before you could say Jack Robinson, off they'd go. Dangerous, you know. Can't say I'm surprised he came to a sticky finish."

"I suppose gossip about Levis and Mrs. Fallows got around."

Casbon's sad protruding eyes opened wider as he warmed a bit to his tale.

"They got a bit indiscreet. People saw them together all over the Island in his car. In the end, Dr. Fallows got wise to it."

"What do you mean?"

"Mean? Why, he came down to Port Erin, drinkin' in the pubs and generally hangin' round trying to see what he could see. He never asked any questions, but was just keepin' his eyes open. There must have been many a chap doin' the same where Levis was concerned. They ought to look farther than the lad they say they've put in jug at Peel for the murder. Women he's had his fill of and chucked aside *and* their husbands and menfolk are far more likely to have settled Mr. Levis's hash than the Peel fellow. ... Excuse me; got to be seein' to this."

The lorry of mortar had arrived and Casbon hurried to abuse the driver for taking time to bring it and to rouse the workmen to unload it. The three workers on the job reluctantly left off feeding Littlejohn's dog with bits of meat-pie and shambled away to give a hand. Having got them going, Mr. Casbon returned to Littlejohn to finish his tale.

"I haven't much more facts to tell you, but I can say this. It looks very much to me as if the Fallows dame spared no pains to get Levis in tow. ... No pains and no expense, see? My wife 'as a friend who was there when the pair of them was first introduced. ..."

Mr. Casbon paused for dramatic effect, lit another cigarette, and had to have a good cough before his voice would clear. He tapped Littlejohn on the chest.

"There's an hotel just near Sulby Claddagh, an old mansion it was, and a fellow called Greenhalgh from England ... chap with plenty of money and over here to work an income tax querk, if you get what I mean. ..."

He paused questioningly.

"I follow, Mr. Casbon."

"Well Greenhalgh made it into a real swell place and there's quite a lot of private parties held there. At one of 'em, where the friend of my missus was present, Mrs. Fallows met Levis. My wife's friend says she never left him alone all night, in spite of the fact that her own husband was with her. She just fell for Levis. Well ... if you know anything about women, you'll know they've a way of gettin' what they want."

The man of the world nodded sagely and shrugged his shoulders. Parson Kinrade had joined Mrs. Littlejohn who was looking over the new building, and Casbon felt more free to enlarge.

"If you ask me, the Fallows woman went out to get Levis with all she'd got. She even went in partnership with Miss

Quine, so's she could, in a manner of speakin', get a free pass to Levis's house. She was an architect herself and that was lucky for her. Once on the job, she worked fast. She got Levis in her clutches right away. Not that it would be hard. She was a good-looker, specially when she took a bit of trouble to spruce herself up, like. Made Miss Quine look plain, I'll tell you. A wonder the two women didn't get scrapping about it. But they just carried on. Difficult to understand, is women. Guess they're so used to competing with one another that they get used to reverses. I'll have to be off, now."

The expert in female psychology thereupon went to try to infuse enthusiasm in his workmen. Littlejohn waved good-bye to him, gathered his passengers, and they all drove back to Grenaby.

Evening was settling over the quiet interior of the Island. The sun cast the long spiked silhouettes of trees across the road. At the farms on the way to the parsonage, milking was finished and farmers and their hired men were pottering about the farmyards doing their last jobs, chatting leisurely. They greeted the parson with a wave of the hand as he passed and signalled to them through the open window. A tractor hurrying home in the opposite direction pressed Littlejohn's car close to the hedge. At Grenaby village the smoke from the cottage chimneys rose straight and high in the air, for the wind had dropped and it was still in the sheltered valley. Joe Henn was fishing for trout with a worm from the bridge. *Traa dy liooar*, time enough, as they say on the Island.

At the gateway of the vicarage a car was parked and they could see Inspector Perrick in his raincoat, pottering in the front garden, eating a windfall apple. He waved to them and joined them at the door.

"Thought I'd call on my way back from Peel. They told me you'd been seeing the Corteens and then you went to Levis's place over the Round Table. You were at Dr. Fallows's house, as well. I guess you'll have made the linkup between the Levis-Fallows-Quine people and you perhaps suspect one or the other of them of murdering Levis. That's as far as I've got, too. ..."

Perrick chuckled.

"You seem to have spies out all over the Island," said Littlejohn. "You'll be suspecting *me* next."

"Hardly, sir. But there's no doubt come into your mind to find out all about what the Fallows couple did on the mainland before they came over here. It's rumoured that *he* was the party responsible for their marital unhappiness in England. Now, *she* seems determined to return the compliment over here. I'm wondering what was the real state of affairs that made Fallows leave St. Sylvester's and a first-class job and tuck himself away on the Isle of Man."

Littlejohn smiled.

"Exactly. I was just going to telephone when we got in and ask my colleague, Cromwell, to look into matters on the spot."

Mrs. Keggin, the housekeeper, appeared impatiently at the door, accompanied by the dog, who had already left the car to forage for her tea.

"Are ye going to stop out there all night? Tea's laid and spoilin'."

"Come and have a bite with us, Perrick," said the Archdeacon.

"Mebbe I will, sir. I've had a bothering and fruitless day. We've been all through the papers we took from Levis's desk and there isn't a single letter to give us a lead. He must have destroyed all his correspondence. ... One thing we found.

Levis had been divorced. He kept it dark, presumably to be able to tell women who became a nuisance to him that he'd a wife over the water. He's left all his money, a tidy sum, to his brother who's out in Kenya, with the exception of five thousand pounds. And who do you think gets that?"

"I haven't a notion."

"Old Mrs. Corteen! There's a codicil mentioning his only child, Fenella's boy. It also says that Fenella is unfit to handle money. It looks as if Levis had a sense of humour and a conscience, after all. Let's eat, sir, shall we? I've been so busy, I haven't had a bite, except a hard apple, since breakfast."

CHAPTER SIX
CLADDAGH HOTEL

A fine, sunny morning; more like spring than autumn. After breakfast, Littlejohn telephoned to Scotland Yard and spoke to his colleague, Sergeant Cromwell. Judging from the joy and exuberance in Cromwell's voice on hearing from his chief, Littlejohn might have been absent for years at the ends of the earth.

"St. Sylvester's, sir. Of course. That's an easy one. Sergeant Grebe's courting one of the sisters there.... Yes, Grebe. You remember, the one who got shot in the thigh in the Isle of Dogs affair. He fell for the sister who looked after him. He'll be only too glad to go and inquire. Fallows? Dr. Fallows. Right, sir. I'll 'phone back this evening."

"Not before, old chap. I'll be out all day. I'm taking Mrs. Littlejohn sightseeing to Ramsey."

The Archdeacon was staying at home preparing his sermon for Sunday.

"On your way, you'll pass Sulby Claddagh, where the builder fellow, Casbon, said Levis met Mrs. Fallows...."

"I'll call, parson. There's no telling what we might pick up in their old haunts."

They took the road over Foxdale and, at Ballacraine Corner, struck the T.T. course, through Glen Helen, Kirk Michael and Ballaugh.

"There's Peel again...."

From the road near Kirk Michael they looked back and could see the little city, with its promontory thrusting the castle and ruined cathedral towards the sea. A small train, emitting a lot of smoke and steam, bustled and whistled into Michael station. Beyond Ballaugh, at Sulby Glen station, they found their way, as directed by the Archdeacon, to Sulby Claddagh. There the Sulby River turned from Sulby Glen and ran through green water-meadows in the direction of Ramsey.

The Claddagh was like an amphitheatre of flat land, surrounded on two sides by trees and bushes and dominated on the other by the crumbling, green peak of Cronk Sumark, Primrose Hill. A good road ran through the fields and Letty and the dog got out to walk as Littlejohn started off for the large house at the end of the valley. Here it was that Greenhalgh, a come-over, had bought a Georgian mansion and converted it into an hotel and road-house. Situated in a quiet spot, but not far from the main road and transport, the *Claddagh Hotel* had become popular among the smart set and many holiday visitors for its comfort, its cuisine and cellars, and its dinner-dances. Regardless of cost, Greenhalgh had gutted and modernized the old place and widely advertised it.

Littlejohn parked the car, crossed a bridge over the stream, and found himself in a large garden with well-kept lawns and formal flower-beds stretching to the hotel. To add an atmosphere of continental brightness to the scene, small tables covered by gaudy parasols had been spread along the terrace. The only people about were an elderly man in tweeds and a large woman in a tight dress drinking coffee in a desperate effort to enjoy the last of the fine warm weather. They eyed Littlejohn up and down, sizing him up as a possible new guest.

Before the Chief Inspector reached the main door, four dachshunds appeared followed by a tall man in flannels and sportscoat and a woman with bare arms and a voluptuous figure in striped rayon. They seemed to be arguing. When the woman saw Littlejohn, she said something sharply to her companion, turned, and walked into the hotel with an animated stride and a provocative swing of the hips. The man approached Littlejohn.

"What can I do for you, sir? My name's Greenhalgh."

He looked like the owner of a roadhouse. Tall, nonchalant, with a military moustache, bilious brown eyes, large alcoholic nose, and fleshy mouth. A man ready to provide anything you could pay for. Littlejohn handed Greenhalgh his card. The man's eyebrows shot up.

"Scotland Yard! You on the Peel murder, sir? Didn't know they'd got so far."

He had a soaked, husky voice and a sniff which made him sound to be drinking deeply.

Littlejohn didn't explain his connection with the case. To pretend to be officially on the job was the only way to get information. Greenhalgh kept eyeing the Inspector up and down with his watery protruding stare. There were heavy bags under his eyes.

"Come inside."

Through the large main doorway into a thickly carpeted hall. The place was a mixture of ancient and modern. Two suits of armour in corners, swords crossed over the inner doors, modern electric lanterns illuminating the hall and staircase, and over the large open fireplace near the entrance, an impressionist picture, presumably hung there to baffle everybody.

"Come in my office...."

A small cubby-hole under the stairs, with a hatch through the wall to the adjoining bar, whence Greenhalgh presumably refreshed himself as he worked at his accounts. A desk, a chair, a metal filing cabinet, a typewriter, and little else. Greenhalgh offered the chair to Littlejohn and sat on the desk himself.

"Drink, Chief Inspector? I'm just going to have one myself."

He tapped on the hatch and two glasses of whisky and a syphon were thrust through by a feminine hand embellished by bangles and a wedding-ring.

"Say when...." He passed his cigarette case to Littlejohn.

"Good health!"

It seemed to be their slack period at the hotel. There was hardly a sound in the place except the barking of the dogs which now and then seemed to start fighting among themselves. The solitary window of the room faced the Claddagh and Littlejohn could see Letty throwing stones in the river for the dog, which splashed and paddled around in high glee.

"What did you want, Inspector? Surely we have no connection with the Peel affair."

"The murdered man came here sometimes, sir?"

Greenhalgh nodded, emptied his glass, tapped on the hatch, and received another.

"Yes, come to think of it, he did!"

"Did he just drop in casually or...?"

"We hold a dinner-dance here almost every evening in the season. People come from all over the Island. Levis came quite a lot. He liked dancing."

"Did he come alone, or with a party?"

Greenhalgh leered and took another nonchalant drink.

"Well.... He usually brought a partner. Sometimes a different one every week; sometimes the same one for a week or two. ... Then he'd have a change. He was fond of the girls, you know, and was a chap for plenty of variety."

"Did he stay here or leave after the dance?"

"Sometimes he stayed if it got late or if he'd shipped more drink than was good for him in a fast car."

"And then his partner would stay as well?"

Greenhalgh gave another alcoholic sniff and fixed Littlejohn with his bulging eyes.

"Now, now, Inspector. No insinuations, if you please, old chap. If Levis stayed, you could hardly expect him to chuck out his guest and tell her to walk home. Of course they both stayed, but they occupied separate rooms. I've my reputation to think of."

Judging from his appearance, thought Littlejohn, the owner of the *Claddagh* would usually be too far gone to bother about any such thing late at night.

"I've my reputation to think of. They're a bit particular over here and word soon gets round if you're being irregular. No week-ending here, sir."

"I'm not suggesting it, Mr. Greenhalgh. Do you remember whom Levis *did* bring from time to time? Anyone in particular?"

Greenhalgh eyed Littlejohn's half-empty glass with displeasure.

"Come on, Inspector. Drink up and have another."

"I'm quite all right, sir, thanks."

Greenhalgh tapped on the hatch again and received almost automatic service. This time, in merry mood, he caught the hand which passed the glass and kissed the finger-tips with mock gallantry. The hand moved across his cheek gently in the direction of the ear and then, having located it, gave it a hearty box; then it was withdrawn.

Littlejohn never saw the owner of it. Greenhalgh sniggered. He was ripe now for intimate questioning.

"Did Levis ever bring anybody particular to the dances?"

Greenhalgh, his mouth full of whisky, gesticulated to show that something good was coming in the way of scandal.

"He brough' quite a lot of pretty girls...but mos'ly holiday-makers he'd picked up. Gave 'em a goo' time and then dropped 'em. But there were one or two he stuck to for a bit. The li'l Quine girl, f'r instance. Small kid, not bad-lookin' and then not good, if you get watta mean. Snub nose. But vivacious, full of life, a real goo' pal.... S'wat I mean. A goo' pal. Levis brought her a time or two.... Then he met another and dropped li'l Quine. Doctor's wife, name o' Fallows, Pam Fallows, from Peel. Met her here at a party...."

Greenhalgh became a little incoherent as his glass grew more empty. He kept regarding Littlejohn's remaining whisky with distaste.

"Have a li'l more drink, eh?"

"No thank you, sir. I'm driving a car and have to be careful. The police must set a good example."

Greenhalgh guffawed.

"Yo're tellin' me! Where was I? Oh yes. Fallows. Pam Fallows." He beckoned Littlejohn to come closer.

"They met here and she fell for him right away. At first, Levis didn't seem smitten, but soon he'd got it as bad as she had. She seemed to *grow* on him. Not much of a figure. Not my sort. I like 'em lush an' bonny meself.... But she was a clever one. Intellecshule, if you get me. Sophishticated and p-p-poised. Just what Levis wanted."

"They came here often?"

"Quite a lot. Stayed overnight a time or two. Quite respec'ble, but drunk too mush wine, so couldn't drive safely. *Or so he said.*"

Mr. Greenhalgh thereupon winked.

"How did it end?"

"Her husband called one day and asked about her. I wasn't in, but my missus saw him. Bit cut up, he was. My wife said he got to it gradually. Said it was a nice place and his wife had said she came with friends. He hadn' bin himself.... That sort o' stuff. Levis was mentioned and the missus had no more sense than to tell him they'd been together. He looked awful at that, I believe. Bit short o' savvy of the missus to say it, but you know what women are...."

"And that ended it?"

Greenhalgh gestured excitedly and drew nearer than ever to Littlejohn. He blew a blast of whisky across the desk.

"Not by a long way, sir. It finished Mrs. Fallows. But then, it had finished before that. Levis was here with another girl before the doctor came. And this girl was a smasher, believe me, a smasher."

The hotelier thereupon beat on the hatch again, was served, and drank morosely.

"Smasher. Don't blame Levis for brushin' off Mrs. Fallows. When he came in with the girl, everybody's eyes turned on her. Dark as night, she was. Tall, slim and graceful, black hair and a face you'd never forget. Classic, sir. Classic. Pardon me...."

Greenhalgh hiccupped.

"Wonnerful complexion. An' believe it or not, *no make-up*. A nacherall beautiful complexion. Made some of the painted dolls look sick, I can ashure you, Inspector."

"A holiday-maker again?"

Greenhalgh waved frenzied hands.

"Not at all. Native. An' that's what beats me. I've seen the gal somewhere an' can't remember where. But this is the point. She was a country girl. Not Levis's class at all.

Innocent. That's what she was. Innocent. No airs. Didn't even know how to enter a room properly. Came in as if she was takin' a walk down the road on her own, instead of tryin' to impress."

"Did they come often?"

"Twice. Once a week and then Levis didn' come any more. We wondered what had happened to him. It seems he was at the bottom of the sea. Pore Levis. Down among the dead men, sir."

"This girl—you've no idea where she came from? Did anyone here know her?"

"They were all like me. They thought they ought to know her, but couldn't put a name to her or say where she came from. Levis, of course, didn' say. They were here the night the police came, but they weren't booked because they were guests, you see."

Littlejohn looked hard at his fuddled companion.

"What is all this about, Mr. Greenhalgh? Police; guests; what are you getting at?"

Greenhalgh tried to sort himself out.

"Simple. It was Sunday. No drinkin' allowed whatever by Manx law on Sunday unless you're stayin' in the hotel. This Sunday, the police called to see all was right. A few guests had got drinks and they took their names because they were dinner guests, not stayin' in the place, yer see. I got fined, and so did those they booked."

"What about Levis?"

"I said he was stayin' here the night, didn't I? *And* his partner."

"Had they checked in?"

"Yes."

"*Before* the dinner-dance?"

Greenhalgh looked put-out.

"You tryin' to trip me up? All the same, Levis is dead, so I might as well tell you. Most always Levis booked two rooms when he booked his table for the dinner. You see, it was just in case he got too squiffy to drive home."

"I see. It was part of the game, was it? He was *never* fit to drive home. Is that it?"

"No need to sound so shirty about it. He booked *two* rooms. I saw to that."

"Adjacent ones, I suppose."

"Well.... Do you want him to take one in the attic and the other in the cellar? Besides, it showed Levis's sense of what was right, if you ask me. He didn' want to risk his partner's neck by drivin' under the influensh of alcohol. Which reminds me, what about another drink?"

"No, thanks, sir. And this trick of Levis's was played on the girl you describe as dark and innocent?"

"Not the first time. He took it easy on the drinks. She didn't take much and he drove her off that night. But the last time we saw him, he regaled her on champagne and suggested he wasn' fit to drive her home. Besides, he'd told the police they were stayin' at the hotel, hadn't he?"

"What name did she give in the register?"

"Levis wrote it in. Smith.... Miss Smith, Douglas. *Smith*. Now I ask you. It wasn't up to me to call Levis a liar as he signed the book, but I'd me doubts. Ve-e-ery grave doubts, sir."

"Which police force made the raid?"

"Raid? It wasn' a raid. Just a check-up. This is a decent place. No raids here, sir."

Littlejohn got up from the table and looked through the window across the Claddagh. The sun was shining, a party in a car were unpacking a basket ready for a picnic, and

Mrs. Littlejohn was drying the dog with a towel after her revels in the river.

Levis had brought a nice girl, according to the views of the half-tipsy Greenhalgh. A nice girl who had taken Mrs. Fallows's place in his affections, if you could call them such. He'd brought her once and had behaved himself. Then he'd brought her again and been up to his old tricks. After that Levis had disappeared. He'd been murdered and fed to the fishes. …

"You didn't say which force called and *checked-up*. Was it the Ramsey police?"

"Yes. Cost me ten quid of a fine. All in a day's work, sir. I've seen to it that it didn' happen again, so you won't bear it against me, will you, Inspector?"

"It's no business of mine. But have the police been round here about Levis's death, Mr. Greenhalgh? Has Inspector Perrick or anyone else been questioning you about his movements prior to his disappearance and murder?"

Greenhalgh looked owlish and surprised.

"No. Why should they? I didn't have anythin' to do with it. I lost a very good customer in Levis, but that was all. No, the police haven't been here. You're the first, sir, and, if I may be permitted to say so, I'll hope you're the last. Don' wanter get mixed up in things of that sort. Bad for trade."

Heavy footsteps echoed in the hall and the door slammed.

"Greenhalgh! GREENHALGH! Where the hell are you?"

The hotel-keeper sprang to his feet and rushed into the hall.

"Greenhalgh! Where the hell's that taxi? It's three quarters of an hour late. Did you order it, man?"

"Yes, Colonel. Should be here any minute."

"It had better be, Greenhalgh. Don't want to miss our 'plane...."

Littlejohn slipped out after Greenhalgh and left him sorting out the travel problems of the large man he had seen on the terrace. He and the equally large woman with him seemed to be the only guests at the *Claddagh Hotel*.

The Chief Inspector gathered up his family and he drove them to Ramsey through the fine avenues of trees on the Lezayre Road. Ramsey always reminded him of a Breton fishing town. Even the styles of the residential houses resembled those of the villas of the middle-class French. Palm trees, hydrangeas, pampas grass in the gardens, neat lawns, a quiet, respectable air. And the tall houses of the town and waterfront, lacking only the names of well-known *apéritifs* across their white gable-ends.... The sky was clear, the air like wine, and the sea of the vast lovely bay sparkling and blue in the noon sun. Mrs. Littlejohn went to look at the shops as her husband made his familiar way to the police-station. The Inspector there knew him well from a previous case and was delighted to see him again. Until Littlejohn mentioned the raid on the *Claddagh Hotel;* then the Inspector got a little bit official.

"I'm sorry, sir, I can't give you the names of those we didn't prosecute. They were staying the night in the hotel and were allowed drinks. The register was checked, of course, but the names weren't taken. You wouldn't do it on the mainland, would you?"

The officer sounded a bit hurt.

"Of course not. I just wondered, that's all.... Thank you for your help, Inspector."

"Sorry, sir, we can't do more."

"Levis, the man murdered in the Peel case, was there. I thought someone might remember the name of his companion at the hotel."

"The point was raised, sir, in the investigations of Levis's murder, but the two officers who called that Sunday night didn't recollect her. Sorry again."

"Don't worry, Inspector."

Littlejohn made his way to the quay on which he'd arranged to meet his wife. He was very thoughtful. Apparently the Manx police had anticipated everything and each new line he started turned out to be, in fact, an old one. Another blank! The dog, leaping to greet his reappearance, wakened him from his reverie and he brushed Levis aside as the beauty of the waterfront took his fancy.

Chapter Seven
The Return of Eddie Kermode

L ittlejohn had decided to take things easy the following
day. There was something soporific and relaxing about
the quiet atmosphere of Grenaby. It seemed quite out of the
world and you felt time didn't matter. *Traa dy liooar.* ... Time
enough. Littlejohn ate his breakfast in bed at nine o'clock
and then lit his pipe and settled down to smoke and listen
to the rush of the water of the Silverburn driving its way
under Grenaby bridge, and the swishing of the wind in
the trees outside the bedroom window. On Moaney Mooar
farm nearby, the Englishman who rented the shooting was
already about, wasting cartridges. He was a poor shot and
always fired both barrels of his gun in rapid succession and
scared all the birds of the parsonage rookery.

"You're wanted, Tom. ..."

Mrs. Littlejohn appeared, spoke in a whisper, and
looked ready to tell the caller that her husband was asleep.

"Who is it?"

"Inspector Perrick."

"Again! All right, I'll come. ... Or, on second thoughts,
Letty, send him up."

"Here? But he's come to take you out. It seems Kermode, or somebody, has arrived from England. Mr. Perrick says you know all about it."

"In that case, I'd better get up. No peace for the wicked!"

Littlejohn slid out of bed, put on his dressing-gown and slippers, yawned loudly, passed his hand through his thinning hair, lit his pipe, and made for the bathroom. From the landing-window he could see Perrick, wearing his raincoat, munching an apple, chatting to the Archdeacon.

The Chief Inspector scowled at himself in the mirror and then started to lather his face.

So Kermode was back. That would probably mean the release of Johnny Corteen. Littlejohn knew those little close-knit seagoing communities very well. A fisherman would swear black was white to save a pal from a landlubber. And in any case, Corteen was probably the last on a long list of possible murderers of Levis. There were deeper waters than those of the noisy, drunken young brother of the girl Levis had seduced. Dr. Fallows, Pamela Fallows, Dora Quine, were all involved in an intrigue of jealousy and hate. And the beautiful dark girl, the stranger Greenhalgh had mentioned, what new fields did she open?

Littlejohn dried his razor and washed himself vigorously.

At the back of his mind lurked an uneasy feeling about his reception by the Ramsey police the day before. In the previous case in which he'd collaborated with them, they had been the most courteous and helpful colleagues. Now...it seemed they resented his unofficial entry in the Levis affair. He couldn't quite make it out. Perhaps he was just being a bit touchy, or feeling his position as an outsider, an amateur interfering.... He wouldn't mention it to Perrick, yet. It might seem small-minded or get someone into trouble....

Perrick had no more news when Littlejohn joined him, except that he was on his way to Peel to meet Kermode.

"I thought you might like to see him along with me, sir. He got in by the last 'plane from Blackpool yesterday. His ship docked in the afternoon."

Eddie Kermode was waiting for them in the police-station at Peel when they arrived. A short, stocky, dark sailor of around thirty. He had the thickset, powerful frame of a small gorilla.

"It's only for the sake of Johnny I've come over so quick. Who's going to pay my expenses, I'd like to know…" he was telling a sergeant, who looked puzzled about the financial aspect of the problem.

"Hullo, Eddie. Good of you to come so quickly."

"Good day to you, Mr. Perrick. It's only on account of Johnny being in the gaol that I've come. What do you want me to say? The police at Fleetwood said it was important."

"Yes. You know there was a murder the day before you left the Island, Eddie. A man called Levis. …"

"I knew him. A little rotter. And they've been sayin' that Johnny did it on account of Fenella. Well, that's a lie."

Kermode eyed Littlejohn up and down uneasily.

"This is Chief Inspector Littlejohn from Scotland Yard. He's helping us on the case."

"Is it that bad, then? Does he want to question me, lek?"

"No. We just want to know exactly what happened on the night of August 21st."

"That's easy. Johnny and me had too much of the drink that night. We was drunk when we left the *Captain Quilliam*. I must have invited Johnny to stay at our house, his mother being terr'ble upset on account of his takin' too much of the drink. When we got home, my wife sobered us good and proper with her tongue. She told us both what she thought of us ezzac'ly, packed-up, an' off to her mother's, and lef' us with the place to ourselves."

"You were sober enough to remember that, Eddie?"

"Sartainly. After my wife had finished with us, we was both sober. But then, we started again. ...."

"What do you mean?"

"I got mad, Mr. Perrick. I told Johnny that no woman was goin' to tell me what to do in my own house. So I got out a bottle of rum an' we had some more drinks. Johnny took worse than me. I could recollect what we was doin', but Johnny was helpless. I put him on the sofa to sleep it off and settled myself in the chair by the fire."

"What time would that be?"

"About two. What with quarrellin' with my wife and drinkin' again, it took us quite a while to settle down."

"How came it, then, that Johnny Corteen was found by the police outside Peel and under a hedge at five in the morning?"

Kermode scratched his head.

"Easy, Mr. Perrick. Johnny an me fell-out later on. I woke around four and there was Johnny unlockin' the house door and on his way out. The noise he made must have wakened me. He was still drunk and very contentious with it. He set off, not in the direction of his own home, but makin' for the country. I follahed him, tryin' to get him to come back, but he wouldn't hear sense and kep' on walkin'. ... In the end, after arguin' a bit, I left him. In fac', I told him to go to hell, and went home and slep' till daylight. You know the rest. I found my wife at Fleetwood, we made it up and are back on the Island again. All I want is to see Johnny out of gaol. ...."

"What time did you leave Johnny?"

"Half-pas' four, or thereabouts. It wanted a quarter to five when I got in home again."

"You're sure?"

"Sartin. I was sober by then. The police must have come upon Johnny within a quarter of an hour after I left him."

"Right. We'll want a signed statement from you, Eddie, but what you say seems to put Johnny in the clear. Thanks."

Perrick picked up his hat and together he and Littlejohn went into the street.

"I guess I'll go back to Douglas now and see about releasing Corteen. Care to come, sir?"

"I think not. I'll see him when he gets back to Peel, perhaps."

"Very well. Have a good day at Ramsey yesterday, sir? The police there told me you called...."

Perrick's voice grew a bit mournful.

"You know, sir, if you want to know anything, I'll always do my best to help. Ramsey didn't know you were on the case unofficially and were a bit surprised when you walked in there. You'll have to excuse them if they weren't as helpful as they might have been...."

"I've no complaints, Perrick. Inspector Lace was his usual courteous self."

"They told me you'd been asking about the raid on the *Claddagh Hotel* and who was with Levis that night. It's most annoying that the men who did the job didn't take the names of *all* who were there. That means we've missed a very important clue, I think. However, no use crying over spilt milk. We'll find out some other way. I'll let you know any developments. Good-bye for the present...."

The police car vanished down the narrow street and Littlejohn was left to his own resources. He filled and lit his pipe thoughtfully. It was obvious Perrick didn't need much help! Here, there, and everywhere, he seemed to be on the track of Littlejohn as well as the killer of Levis! An example of what the Archdeacon called Manx curiosity, their love of knowing all that happens and of good gossip ... *a li'l cooish.*

Littlejohn thrust his hands in the pockets of his coat and with his pipe between his teeth walked down to the promenade. With the exception of a few belated holiday-makers religiously taking the sea air, there was nobody about. The tide was coming in and the clear air set off sharply the ruins of the cathedral and castle on their islet. The sun, shining on the local red sandstone, cast a pink glow over them. The Inspector was seized with a whim to walk round the river and wander over the ruins, and he started in that direction.

On the way to Peel Island, Littlejohn passed groups of sailors and longshoremen taking the air and gossiping. The riverside was busy. Two herring-boats were tied up for repairs to their scallop gear and a blacksmith was working on the dredging harrows. Another French boat had put-in and the crew were cleaning her down; there was washing hanging from a line across the deck.

Littlejohn turned in at the *Captain Quilliam.* The landlord greeted him and he ordered a glass of whisky. Some ten or a dozen men were already standing at the bar, drinking their morning beer or rum and talking to the captain of the French boat and his mate. They were discussing the main local topic, Levis's murder. They gave Littlejohn sidelong looks and seemed less cordial than the other night.

"... And Johnny Corteen still in the Douglas prison. We all know Johnny wouldn't hurt a fly. And the murderer still at large. Why don't they arrest them as was more likely to have done it than Johnny? What are they waitin' for? Is it because the others are moneyed folk and are local nobs, or what?"

Littlejohn drank up and left the place. On the way out the landlord tapped his elbow.

"Don't heed them, sir. They're a bit sore about Johnny being kept in gaol. It'll blow over."

"You can tell them he'll be out by to-night and they'll be able to get him blind drunk again. ...."

He wandered along the waterfront watching the rising tide, crossed the bridge, and walked along the West quay past Peel Hill, to the castle gates and paid his threepence admission money. He didn't feel like making a thorough and systematic tour of the ruins. Just a quiet round of the place and to admire the view across the harbour.

He passed through the guard-room of the castle, strolled past the round tower and turned to the cathedral. There he descended to the crypt and then, standing in the centre of the ruins under the tower, amused himself by translating laboriously from the Latin, an epitaph on a brass plate screwed to a tomb.

In this house which I share with my brothers the worms lie I, Sam, by divine grace Bishop of this Isle, in hope of resurrection.

Stay, reader: Look and laugh at the Bishop's palace.

Died May 30th, 1662.

"Lookin' at the bishop's grave, sir? Bishop Rutter, they say. The lines are supposed to be witty to them as can read them. ...."

Littlejohn turned and found, almost at his elbow, a tall, wiry, middle-aged man with a kindly face, leathery skin and sharp grey eyes. He wore a fisherman's jersey under a blue reefer coat, and a peaked cap on his head. Littlejohn had seen him before. In fact, the gossips had made a point of trying to impress the Chief Inspector by saying they knew Tom Cashen, the man who found Levis's body, very well.

"Mr. Cashen, isn't it?"

"Yes, sir. I suppose you'll be wondering what I'm doing here. I followed you round for a quiet word. ..."

The man was obviously forcing himself to speak. Shy and reticent in his talk, he would not have approached Littlejohn except for something serious.

"*Captain* Cashen, is it, by rights?"

The man laughed.

"*Admiral*, if you must stand on rank, sir. I'm Admiral of the Fleet at Peel, for which I receive a salary of five pounds a year. Not that it's much of a job now, with only four of us in the herring fleet. In days when the harbour was full of craft—nobbies and nickeys—and 2,000 hands manned 'em, it was somethin' like a post and they couldn't shoot the nets without the Admiral said so. ..."

"Well, *Admiral* Cashen, what can I do for you?"

"I suppose you know, it was me and my boys that found the body of Levis. I'm skipper of the *Manx Shearwater,* the boat you see tied up just past the steps there on the West quay. ..."

"Yes. ..."

Littlejohn paid close attention. Tom Cashen was a man who only spoke when it was necessary and every word counted.

"I was thinkin'. ... I was thinkin', first of all, we've got to get rid of the suspectin' feelings that are all over the town. Everybody knows Johnny Corteen and everybody knows he didn't kill Levis. But we want to find who did and get the matter settled, lek. The police aren't too popular in this because they arrested Johnny and that's why I'm here with you in a quiet spot. I'd likely be unpopular, too, if I was seen. But I jes' want to put a suggestion to you, sir. ..."

He paused, wondering if he might be taking liberties.

"Go on, Tom."

The easy address did it. Cashen opened out.

"It's this way. Everybody's busy sayin' *who* did it, but they haven't said *how* he did it. The man was killed on land. Or so you'd think. And he was rowed out to sea and sunk. If we hadn't happened, lek, to be dredgin' in that part, there the body would have been till it rotted away or the fish completely ate it."

"That's right."

Cashen tapped Littlejohn's chest with his cold pipe.

"*Where* was the man killed, sir? And *when?*"

"You tell me, Tom."

"As to *when*, lek as not, he was murdered by day. The nights was pitch dark around the time it was done, and you'd find it hard to tell one man from another. If it was done by day, would you, sir, have rowed it out an' dropped it in the full light for everybody to see?"

"No, Tom, I wouldn't."

"No. You'd have hid it and took it out, maybe at dusk, maybe at first light, so's you could see what you was doin', lek, and where you was goin'. ..."

"Well?"

"Where was the body hid, sir?"

"Go on."

"Will you kindly follow me, sir?"

Cashen led the way out of the ruins across to the mound of turf which rose in the centre of the islet and when they had climbed it, pointed with his finger northeast over the great curtain wall which surrounded the fortress. Before them lay a superb view of the Isle of Man. A background of rolling hills ending suddenly where, in the Sulby Valley, the ground levelled to the curraghs and fens. In the foreground, a long stretch of coastline from Peel city to Jurby Point, with Jurby church making a solid white landmark on the cliffs. Beyond that, the northeastern slope of the coast to the Point of Ayre. Littlejohn's eye followed the changes in structure; the red sandstone cliffs of Peel, the white beaches dotted here and there and, midway, a break in the colour where the softer stone changed to rock. Cashen was indicating this spot.

"You see the place there on the coast where I'm pointin'? Where the sandstone cliffs change to darker rock? Get it? That's the Gob y Deigan, sir. Manx for Devil's Mouth or Devil's Hole. There's cliffs there covered on the top with turf and down below the Lynague Caves, some of the biggest on the Island."

They looked across the sunlit water in silence for a minute.

"I might 'a brought my glasses, if I'd thought, sir, but that's a first-rate spot to hide a body. The caves are cutoff at high tide, which is the time when you can take a boat in them and row out to sea. I've been thinkin' somebody might hide a corpse there till dusk and row out and dump it. Besides, as the crow flies, it's the nearest land to the spot where we found the body."

"Now we're learning something, Tom. That sounds a good bet as to what happened...."

"Not only that, Inspector. The road, the main road from Peel, passes within a quarter of a mile of Gob y Deigan. At a twist called Devil's Elbow, there's a valley leads down to the shore. You sartainly ought to put a proper sight on those caves and the whole place, sir."

"I feel like going without delay...."

Cashen hesitated. He'd something on his mind and was seeking words to express it.

"Tell you what, sir. We're sailin' for scallops in the *Shearwater* in less than an hour. Why not come along with us? We'll show you the ezzact spot where we found the body and then, as we'll likely anchor and stay the night aboard, I'll row you ashore. That'll cover the track in reverse of whoever rowed from Gob y Deigan to sink the body. You'll unnerstand it a lot better if you see it all from the sea."

Littlejohn was delighted. This was just what he wanted!

"Thanks, Tom. I'll be glad to. But first, I'll 'phone my wife and ask her to pick me up on the road near Devil's Elbow at… when shall we say?"

Cashen consulted a large watch.

"It's half-past twelve, sir. We'll sail on the tide at about one. We'll be havin' a bite of food on board instead of waiting for dinner here and if you'd care to join us… I could have you ashore again about five."

"With pleasure. I'll just telephone to Grenaby and then I'll see you down at the quayside."

At ten past one, the *Manx Shearwater* put out to sea with Chief Inspector Littlejohn aboard.

CHAPTER EIGHT
TROUBLE AT *CURSING STONES*

The *Manx Shearwater* sprang into life with the starting of her 66 h.p. Diesel, controlled from the wheelhouse. They hoisted no sail. The gossips at Weatherglass Corner, and a smaller group of sightseers at Munn's Corner, puffed their pipes and waved farewells as the trim little boat left the river, passed the breakwater, and made for the open sea.

Littlejohn stood by the skipper as he manoeuvred into deep water. It was as much as the small cabin could do to hold the two big men. In front, the wheel, a small binnacle, and the controls of the Diesel in the hold below; at their backs, a compact radio set; and in one corner, a radar *Echo-Meter*, which in the herring-season was used for detecting the shoals passing between the bottom of the vessel and the sea-bed.

"It's a bit lonely for Manxmen in the fishing now. Only four of us among a lot of Scots, Dutch and Scandinavians. In the old days, Peel harbour was full of nobbies and nickeys, local owned, lek. Under the command of the Admiral, like I was tellin' ye. And plenty of prayin' an' hymn-singin' on account of good catches.... All that's gone...."

Cashen seemed to find his tongue in the comfortable presence of the Chief Inspector. They might have been shipmates all their lives.

The skipper turned the *Shearwater* due west.

"First, you can be puttin' a sight on the Island from out at sea; then we'll turn to Gob y Deigan."

They had aboard a crew of five and the skipper. Cashen handed over the wheel and showed Littlejohn over the boat. The sea was calm and it was easy moving about on deck. They inspected the engine and then went for' ard.

"That's where we put the body, sir."

Cashen removed the hatches from the hold, disclosing the large gloomy space below deck for stowing the herring or scallops according to the season. It was empty except for the dredging tackle, which the crew started to haul up.

The Chief Inspector followed the skipper down to the fo'c'sle. A narrow cabin, shaped like a flat-iron, with bunks in the bulkheads. An enamel teapot on a table covered with oilcloth, an iron stove with a pipe rising through the roof, sea-boots piled in one corner, provisions and cans of milk and food in a rough wooden cupboard with the door open. ...

The youngest of the crew descended to prepare a meal.

When Littlejohn got back on deck they were out at sea, due west of Peel. The whole of the west side of the Island was now visible from the Point of Ayre to the Calf, with Peel Hill and Corrin's Folly, a memorial tower over an eccentric grave, seeming near. The wild coastline from Contrary Head to the Mull Peninsula to the south; the red cliffs and the long stretch of the Ayre beach ending in the Point lighthouse, to the north. Cashen stood at Littlejohn's elbow and pointed out the landmarks, as the Inspector looked through his binoculars. ... Jurby Point, Cronk ny Irree Laa, South Barrule, Bradda, and the rolling range of the Island hills behind the changing coastline.

"The Cronk ny Irree Laa there, means Hill of the Risin' Sun, and in the old days the custom used to be for the herrin' boats to haul in the nets and sail for port when they saw the sun risin' over the top of it. ..."

He pointed to a spot at sea west of Calf Island.

"The *Mooir ny Fuill*, the Sea of Blood, where there was once a terr'ble great loss to the Peel fishin'-fleet. ..."

"And now we'll make for the scallop banks. Tanrogans, we call them over here."

Cashen waved his hand to the man at the wheel and the ship began to bob as they turned again towards land.

"We bring Cronk-y-Voddey trees in line with Gob y Deigan in the south an' Jurby Head in line with Rue Point in the north to get our bearin' for the fishin' mark, where we found the body. ..."

On the way back to land, they ate stewed steak and beans and drank dark tea, Littlejohn sitting on a box on deck to avoid missing the view and the strong sea air.

"I wish to God I hadn't to leave and start detecting again, Tom," he said to the skipper.

Cashen laughed.

"We'll be fishin' here for weeks yet. Come along with us when you've finished the job. Try a rough day, sir."

"That's a bargain."

The dredging tackle was assembled on deck ready for business. The man in the wheelhouse made signs that they were getting above the tanrogan beds. Cashen beckoned Littlejohn aft where the gear was hanging over the stern ready for the word. The winch spun and the hawser slid rapidly across the deck; with a splash the huge sea-bottom comb and nets vanished. Before Littlejohn left the ship, the winch was reversed and hauled aboard the dripping catch of shellfish. Bits of timber, old iron, stones too large to slip the mesh, seaweed, two tin cans, bottles... and then two or three score of fan-shaped shellfish. The latter were sorted out and flung in the hold, the rest jettisoned.

"Threepence apiece, or thereabouts, to us; more than a shilling a time, they tell me, in London markets."

Cashen contemplated the tanrogans reproachfully, as though they might be responsible for the price they commanded on the mainland.

"This is where we found the body, sir."

Nothing whatever to indicate that they were sailing over the fatal spot. The sea calm, the white wings of accompanying gulls flashing in the sun, one of the crew whistling shrilly as he sorted out the rubbish from the gear. Another *Mooir ny Fuill*, a Sea of Blood, but nothing to show it.

Two of the crew were lowering the small boat from the deck and tying a rope-ladder to the rail. Cashen himself took the wheel for a minute, stopped the engine, and brought the boat about to quiet water. It was three o'clock. Littlejohn watched the skipper speak a word or two in the mouthpiece of the radio and then Cashen emerged on deck.

"Just a word to the wife," he said. "I allis pass the time o' day with her over the set when we're out at sea. The virtue in it is that herself can't back-answer me."

The boat was lowered; Littlejohn and Cashen climbed in and the skipper took the oars. With strong, slow strokes he shot the little craft from the side of the larger one and soon they were skimming across to Gob y Deigan.

Littlejohn examined the shore they were approaching, through the binoculars Tom Cashen had lent him. Most of the coast thereabouts was rocky and consisted of high cliffs, topped by turf. Sometimes the rocks plunged right into the water itself; at others the slope was more gentle and gave access to fine little beaches of golden or white sand. For the most part, the cliffs were of red sandstone, but at one spot a splash of dark rock broke the regularity, as though from somewhere inland a long spur of granite were ending in an outcrop. This granite breach tumbled roughly into the water, split by a stream flowing down a gully and cleft by fissures and a number of large caves. This was Gob y Deigan, Devil's Mouth.

Littlejohn turned his glasses on the spot which Cashen described to him. The grandeur of the coastline, the massive caves of Lynague, the stream tumbling down and its water still flowing like a separate little river far into the sea, where it finally lost itself in the lighter blue of the ocean. On the beach, secured in a narrow cove backed by a cave smaller than the rest, was a boat, barely large enough from where Littlejohn was watching it, to hold a solitary passenger.

Out at sea, they were still busy on the *Manx Shearwater.* The rattle of the winch and the grinding of the dredging gear as they flung it overboard and drew it in again sounded across the intervening space and flung back echoes from the rocky shore.

"There's a boat there, Tom."

"Yes, sir. There's a farm above and I reckon its theirs. They make out with a bit o' fishin' now and then. Plenty of crabs, lobsters, and blockan round them rocks an', if you care to go further, the tanrogan beds, where you can, mebbe, hook up a shell or two if you're lucky."

Cashen was obviously anxious to get back to his ship and his trawling. He put Littlejohn ashore, pointed out the way to the road above, and then pushed off back to the *Shearwater.*

"I'll be seein' ye, sir, as promised. Don't forget. Next time come for a full day an' a night's trip.…"

The tide left a clear path along the beach and the water line was already below the caves of Lynague. Littlejohn scrambled among the rocks and reached the boat, now high and dry on the sand. It was a small affair, large enough for two, stoutly built and freshly painted in white. Neither the boat itself, the shore, the caves, nor the rocks gave any tangible evidence of dirty work. But here was the perfect set-up for a crime of the kind the Chief Inspector was investigating. Caves in which to hide a body, shingle with which to weight it, a boat in which to row it out to sea and from which to sink its ghastly cargo.

Littlejohn stood and watched Cashen on his way back to his ship, propelling his little boat with powerful steady strokes. Tom waved to him and he waved back. He waited until the skipper had reached his destination, saw them haul him and his boat aboard, heard the rumble of the gear as the dredger sank to the sea floor and the ship moved again with its hawser taut astern. Then he turned to find his way to the road where his wife should be waiting with the car.

The best way back lay alongside the stream which tumbled down a gully to the beach. This fissure, covered in long water-weeds and rushes near its mouth, and crossed by a bridge carrying the Isle of Man Railway, gradually widened as it reached soft land and near the road formed quite a deep glen with small trees hanging over the water. Close to a bunch of these, out of sight of the road, stood a structure like a caravan without wheels, a kind of summer-house or cabin in which holiday-makers or week-enders might spend a quiet spell facing the sea. The shack was in good order, clean and painted, but locked-up. There were no traces of recent use and any footprints which might have been made had been washed away by rain or overgrown by the grass of the site.

Littlejohn walked round it, tried the door, and finding it fast, climbed on the beading which ran round the bottom of the cabin and looked in through the window. There was no sign of habitation. A couple of bunks, a small table hinged from one side, a lamp screwed on a bracket, a mirror hanging on the wall, a few paperbacked novels on a shelf.... Nothing more. The place had been cleaned up and secured.

The Chief Inspector mounted higher in the little glen until finally he reached the level of the road, where the stream ran through a field and then disappeared in another fissure mounting higher inland. Mrs. Littlejohn and Meg were sitting in the car. Letty waved through the open window. She had parked at a spot where the road widened and was carried by a bridge across the gully. A short distance farther on, the highway twisted in a vicious curve round the Devil's Elbow.

There was a farmhouse in the last field, a small shabby place surrounded by windswept trees in tortured postures. The breeze from the sea blew the smoke from the chimney flat across the roof. A wide iron gate gave access to it from the field and around it a few hens were picking and paddling in the mud. The door faced Littlejohn, and was protected from the elements of the rough exposed coast by a stout porch. This door suddenly flew open and a gesticulating figure appeared. His cries were lost in the wind.

Littlejohn halted in his tracks and faced the shouting man. He wore a fisherman's jersey, dark trousers tucked in gumboots, and a cap. The figure, strong, stocky and aggressive, seemed familiar and as with obvious haste and rage the man opened the gate and made for him in a stumbling run, the Chief Inspector remembered him.

It was Ned Crowe, the drunken sailor of the *Captain Quilliam*!

When Crowe recognised Littlejohn he became even more angry. His bellowing rose over the singing wind.

"What the hell do you want? What you doin' on my land? Get to 'ell out of 'ere. ..."

Littlejohn turned and walked towards Crowe in an equally aggressive manner.

"Hullo, Crowe. I've been down to the shore. No harm in that, is there? I understand people picnic here and go down regularly in the season."

"Well, it ain't season now and we don't want no trespassers. You ain't been down to the shore. You come up from it, but I sighted you rowin' in from the *Shearwater*. What game are you up to?"

At close quarters Littlejohn could smell the rum on Crowe's breath. He was obviously carrying on in private what he did in public in Peel.

There seemed to be nobody else about the farm, not even stock. Littlejohn wondered what Crowe was doing there, all on his own, steadily getting drunk for some reason or other. At the end of the overgrown main track from the farm to the road stood a decrepit signpost. *Teas.* But nobody had taken tea there for many a year by the look of things.

"I've just been looking over the spot where the murder happened. Your shore's the nearest land to where the body was found."

It temporarily took all the fight and stuffing out of Ned Crowe. He looked to shrink in his clothes, licked his lips, and shifted his eyes from Littlejohn's face to the ground. Then he bucked up.

"An' what might that be to you? You ain't got the authority. This is a Manx police job. They don't want no foreign comeovers poking their noses in Manx affairs ... ."

"Who said so, Crowe?"

"It's said all over Peel. You ain't got authority. You're committing a trespass. Get off my land or I'll get my gun to you."

"So you keep a gun? Is that your boat, too?"

"No business of yours. ...."

"And the caravan, there. Is that yours, too ... or did it belong to Cedric Levis?"

At the mention of the name, Crowe completely lost control. He lowered his head and rushed for Littlejohn, his arms flailing, his eyes wild. He seized Littlejohn's left arm in a grip of iron and raised his fist to strike. The Chief Inspector, almost a head taller than Ned Crowe, released himself with ease, and thrust the farmer away.

"That will do, if you don't want to get hurt, Crowe. Now, take yourself off. If you've any complaints to make about my being here, tell the police. And next time I call, I'll expect a more civil reception."

Crowe stood for a moment, clenching and unclenching his huge scarred fists.

"I'll make you pay for this. You'll see. An' don't you come anywhere near here agen, else I'll pepper ye with gunshot. Ten years since, when I was in me prime, I'd have killed you. ...."

He turned and shambled off without another word and stood at the gate glowering until Littlejohn reached the road.

"Whatever were you doing with the man from the farm?" asked Mrs. Littlejohn, as her husband joined her.

"A reception committee from Ned Crowe. He doesn't seem to like me. He talks about my having no authority to investigate the case or question him. Strange talk from a simple farmer. I wonder who's been putting ideas in his head."

"I thought he was going to murder you. One minute he seemed to be talking quietly, the next he was trying to beat your head in. ...."

They both grew silent.

"Are you thinking what I am, Tom?"

"Yes. Sounds rather like a second edition of Cedric Levis, doesn't it? When I mentioned his name, the old Crowe got mad. I wonder if Levis *did* own the caravan down there and they quarrelled. And all Crowe's rum drinking is an attempt to ease a guilty conscience."

"The name of the farm is certainly appropriate. Before you came I asked a man I gave a lift to from Peel, what the place was ..."

"Yes?"

"It's called, in English, *Cursing Stones Farm*. The man said that there used to be a mound in the far field with two round stones on top of it. In the centre of each stone was a little hollow and if you wished anybody ill, you twisted your thumb in it against the sun and cursed him with a prayer of cursing. The stones have been gone for many years. The man was seventy and he said they went when he was a boy."

"Queer."

"Yes. And he said the field where you and Crowe had your argument was once called *Magher ny Ruillick*, the field of the graveyard."

"Good heavens! Let's get going."

"I feel like a cup of tea. The next farm along the road has a sign out. Shall we try?"

"So has *Cursing Stones Farm*, but I don't think we'd be welcome. ..."

The next holding, *Ballacurry*, TEAS, was more hospitable. It was little more than a croft, but a neat, clean cottage and the woman, although a bit put-out at the arrival of guests out of season, gathered together some bread, jam, soda-cakes and tea and put the visitors in her small parlour.

She fetched a bowl of buttermilk for Meg. The place was full of old-fashioned furniture which left barely room in which to whip a cat round. It was little used and smelled damp, and to relieve it, Mrs. Kelly, the farmer's wife, a comely, solidly-built, large-boned woman, brought in a cylindrical oil-stove which gurgled and gulped out heat and smoke. From the walls, photographs of family groups, weddings, christenings, studio portraits of frozen-looking country people in their best clothes, and pictures of young men in army, air-force and naval uniforms, closely watched the Littlejohns over tea.

From the window, Littlejohn could see the *Shearwater* still busy dredging across the wide bay. It would soon be dusk and the sun was beginning to fall over Peel, the town and castle of which were plainly visible from where he stood. In the farmyard at the side of the house, the farmer was gently piloting a cow in calf to the water trough.

Facing the window stood an ancient piano with a silk front and projecting tarnished brass candlesticks. As Littlejohn raised his eyes to it over his teacup he spotted, with a slight shock, a snapshot in a frame. A group of people, including two sailors in reefer jackets and peaked caps. A festive family gathering.... In the middle, sitting on chairs, Mrs. Kelly, their hostess, and the lanky farmer, her husband, who was still attending to the cow outside. On Mr. Kelly's left, stood Ned Crowe, smiling self-consciously, and beside him, with one of the sailors close to her and obviously in thrall, a lovely, dark-haired girl, tall and proud-looking, with a happy smile. The rest of the party looked like farm-hands.

Littlejohn called out for the farmer's wife.

"Come and have a cup of tea and a *li'l cooish*, Mrs. Kelly."

The woman arrived a bit surprised.

"What do you know about the *li'l cooish*, sir?"

"A good gossip, then. I'm interested in this photograph, Mrs. Kelly."

He had it in his hand and indicated Ned Crowe.

"I've just been over to see Crowe. I got a poor reception."

The woman sighed.

"Not the only one. He's taken to the drink. Him and my husband has had a fallin'-out. I can't think what's come over him. Maybe it's on account of Margat. He's not like the same man."

"What about Margat? Is that Manx for Margaret?"

"That's right. Her mother died when she was born and Ned brought her up himself. Thought the world of her, he did. It was Margat-ven, Margat-girl, all over the place with him. Worked like a slave to bring her up. Sent her to good school at Ramsey and saw she grew up lek a lady. The farm was a nice place then. He worked hard on it, did fishin' as well, and they made teas for a little extry. Ned's sister that died came to live with them. A lady, she was. ..."

"Is this Margat on the picture?"

He indicated the dark girl.

"That's right. My Juan was sweet on her at the time. That was six or seven years since, when Margat was round twenty. My two boys is at sea. One an engineer in the navy and the other a steward on the Steam Packet. ..."

"You've done well for them, Mrs. Kelly. And didn't Juan and Margat make a match of it?"

"Naw, sir. He met a girl he liked better in Liverpool, an' they got married. Margat thought he wasn't good enough, I guess, an' he soon got over it, thank the Lord."

"Is she still on the farm?"

"She was till about August this year. Happy as a pair o' skylarks her and Ned was. He bought a pony for her and she'd ride around the country and she was in with all the nice ones at Ramsey an' Peel. Then somethin' happened. Ned took to drinkin' more than he should and they must have quarrelled. One day she offs an' must have gone to the mainland to seek work, because she hasn't been about here since and Ned's taken it terr'ble bad. Look at him and his farm, now. Just ruins. As if the curse has come on them, the Eye, as you might say."

"They were good neighbours once?"

"The best...."

Mrs. Kelly began to sob and took a bit to get herself under control again.

"What do you think happened to make them quarrel, Mrs. Kelly?"

The woman blew her nose and hesitated. She gave Littlejohn a queer look.

"It's not my business, I'm sure, but I think it must have been some man Ned didn't like and they quarrelled about it."

"You know the man?"

The woman began to knead her handkerchief into a ball and her lips set firm.

"We don't want any trouble, sir. We're not the interferin' sort at Ballacurry."

Littlejohn paused, drank his tea, and then looked straight at Mrs. Kelly.

"Was it Levis, the man who was murdered?"

The woman turned white and made a gesture with her hands like someone fending off evil. Littlejohn saw that she gripped her thumb between her index and second finger and held it tight in the form of a crude cross. She was full of the old superstitions.

"Yes, I think so."

Hardly a whisper.

"Tell me about it."

Mrs. Kelly gulped.

"You can't stop people talkin'. My husband heard things at Ramsey Mart when he went and they said things at the Chapel, as well. Levis was well known for his carryin's-on on the Island. My husband knew a farmer at Bride who said he'd tek a shot-gun to him if he saw him round his gel again. Well, Levis, he started runnin' around in his car with Margat. My husband saw him at *Cursing Stones* when he was in the top fields. Levis had the caravan down the glen for two summers and they said at the Chapel there'd been wicked goin's on there. He must have seen Margat when he was around, though they did say Ned Crowe kept her away from the glen because of Levis. But there's no stoppin' that sort of thing, try as you will, is there?"

"How long was this going on?"

"Not long, as far as I know. Two or three weeks, an' then Margat went. Like as not, her and her dad had quarrelled. Nobody seemed to see her leave the farm, but one of the sewing-class saw her at the airport as she was meetin' her sister from over. Margat was goin' on the aeroplane to Liverpool."

"Has she any relatives on the mainland?"

"Her mother's sister lives there. Near London."

"What part of London?"

"I can find out. She went to school with me and I was her bridesmaid when she was married at Kirk Michael to a soldier from London in the first war. She always sends me a Christmas card."

Mrs. Kelly rummaged in a drawer of the large sideboard which half-filled the room. Eventually she drew forth a card and passed it to Littlejohn.

Greetings and Good Wishes for Christmas
and the New Year from
Mr. and Mrs. J. B. Swanson,
    Glen Maye,
      Breck Road,
        East Croydon.

Littlejohn made a note of it on the back of an old envelope. He took the photograph in his hand again.

"May I borrow this for an hour or two, Mrs, Kelly?"

The good woman looked puzzled.

"I'm going to ask you to have a *li'l cooish* with my wife over another cup of tea, whilst I just run on an errand. I won't be long."

Mrs. Littlejohn, used to her husband's ways, fell-in without a question and he left them over cups of fresh tea.

Twenty minutes later, the Chief Inspector was turning his car into Sulby Claddagh and making for the *Claddagh Hotel*. There were one or two cars in the park; a few clients had called for afternoon tea. Mr. Greenhalgh was in his office.

"He's doing his books," said the woman with unctuous curves and straw-coloured hair, with a knowing roll of the eyes.

"What again, Inspector! Glad to see you. What'll you have?"

Greenhalgh emptied his own glass, tapped on the hatch, and waited expectantly for Littlejohn's order.

"I've just finished tea, thanks, Mr. Greenhalgh. I've something to show you."

Greenhalgh held up his hand until the almost sacramental performance of passing through the next potation was completed. He was half drunk already.

"Good health. Sure you won't? Right. Spill the beans, sir."

Littlejohn showed his host the photograph borrowed from Mrs. Kelly. He pointed his finger at Margat Crowe.

"Know the lady, Mr. Greenhalgh?"

The watery eyes of the tipsy man almost shot from their sockets and rolled down his cheeks.

"Well, I'll be damned! Quick worker, Inspector. That's the late lamented Levis's beeootiful partner of the night the p'lice called to check-up. Not a raid, I do ashure you, sir. Jus' a check-up. Do you know her telephone number, Inshpector, because, if you do, I'll be very mush obliged?"

Chapter Nine
The Frightened Fisherman

When Littlejohn arrived back at Ballacurry, he found his wife reluctant to leave the good company of the Kellys. The farmer had joined the party and stood, a shy man of few words, by the door of the room as though ready to run away at any moment; but he never did.

"Here's himself back again," said Mr. Kelly when the Chief Inspector appeared and the dog, frenzied at seeing him again, bounded to greet him.

"We're still gossiping, you see...."

The farmer found his tongue.

"My gough! Did ye ever see the lek when two women get talkin' together?"

"You're not so bad yourself, Mr. Kelly. He's just been telling us about Ned Crowe and Margat, Tom."

"It's true what I bin tellin' ye. Frettin' for his girl's what's made Ned as he is. Somebody ought to bring that gel back to him afore he dies of the drink."

Littlejohn filled his pipe and lit it.

"That might be a good idea, Mr. Kelly. We'll see what we can do. You think it was some quarrel about her affair with Levis caused her to quit?"

"Aye, that's it."

"Can you remember exactly the date she left the Island?"

Kelly scratched his topknot of iron grey hair.

"Aw, ask the missus. I'm no good at the dates.'

Mrs. Kelly was making rapid calculations.

"It was the day I give the tay at the sewing-class at the Chapel. Mrs. Mylchreest... the one who saw Margat at the airport... had come back the day afore. August the twentieth! That's it."

Kelly heaved a loud sigh of relief and admiration.

"Wonnerful memory herself's got!"

Littlejohn sat thoughtfully down in the armchair beside the wheezing oil-stove.

"That was the day before Levis met his death. He was due to leave for Italy the afternoon he was killed. Could it be he planned to take Margat with him?"

Mrs. Kelly made shocked noises.

"As lek as not. A bad man, he was, for sure."

"They may have arranged to leave the Island separately and meet in England to avoid gossip. And someone heard of it and killed Levis...."

Kelly scratched his topknot again.

"You wouldn't be suggestin' that Ned Crowe...?"

"I don't know. I wish we could talk to Ned without his getting so heated."

"He was terr'ble fond of that gel. Margat, me villish, Margat, my sweet, you'd hear him callin' all over the place. She reminded him of his wife...."

"I must try to think of a way. Meanwhile, can you tell me if Levis brought any other women to this caravan he kept here? Anyone you know?"

The Kellys exchanged glances.

"One or two, he brought. We're not the sort who go skeetin' through windows at what passes, but Levis would stop in his car nearly opposite our gate. We couldn't help seein'. ...."

"Anyone you knew?"

There was another silence.

"Better tell him, missus. If you don't, someborry else will."

"The only one we knew out of the one or two as came with him was the doctor's wife from Peel. Missus Fallows; and the doctor such a nice man. A proper shame!"

"Did they come often?"

"Once or twice. One day, I think the doctor see them there. He comes this way to some of his patients. He goes as far as Michael along this road. I see Levis there and Missus Fallows. I think the two of them had been swimmin' in the sea. Shameless, it was, and her in nothin' but a swimmin' costume and him the same. A married woman! It was a hot day and they kep' on their swimmin' suits and was crossin' the field to Ned Crowe's, as lek as not for milk for some tea, when I see the doctor's car pass. An' the doctor never drew up, but he couldn't miss seein' them."

"When would that be?"

"Just after the T.T. races; about June."

"Before Levis started running around with Margat Crowe?"

"That's right."

"Does the doctor come to you when you need him?"

"Aye. A good docther, too," chipped in Kelly. "One o' the good ole sort. Come any time. I recollect one time he helped me with a cow as was difficult in calf. Proper good with his hands and as strong as a horse. You wouldn' think it, seein' him, quiet and on the fat side, but he handled that cow jes' lek she was a baby, movin' her about the cowshed floor himself."

Littlejohn was thoughtful as they drove back to Grenaby. He didn't seem to see the sun setting red over Peel or hear the winch of the still busy *Manx Shearwater* hauling in the scallops off Orrisdale Head. He spoke first as they breasted the hill at Foxdale.

"You can take your pick, Letty. I never saw such a crowd of suspects. Ned Crowe, Dr. Fallows, Mrs. Fallows, Johnny Corteen, and Lord knows who besides. When you get a man like Levis, fooling with women all over the shop, you drag in all kinds of people. And my hands are tied. I'm the amateur on the job, this time. I ought really to tell Perrick, but we must have something more concrete before putting him on the trail...."

Littlejohn needn't have bothered, however, for Perrick was waiting for him at Grenaby. There he sat in his raincoat, in the Archdeacon's study, balancing a cup of tea on his knee and eating a piece of apple pie.

He rose quite unabashed as the Littlejohns entered.

"I was just going. I asked the parson to tell you we've released Johnny Corteen. I took him back to Peel and called here on the way home to Douglas. You've been taking a sea-trip, I hear."

Littlejohn showed no surprise. He was getting used to the omniscience of Perrick and it was becoming amusing.

"Yes. Tom Cashen took me out to the spot where he found the body and then he rowed me over to Lynague caves. Quite a place!"

Perrick took a swig of tea and carefully put his cup and saucer on the mantelpiece. Then he took a big bite of pie and vigorously chewed it before replying.

"You're thinking like I do. The body was hidden there before bein' rowed out to sea?"

"Yes. Perhaps in Ned Crowe's boat."

"You've asked him about it?"

"Well, no. As I walked from the caves to the road, I met Ned. He was very annoyed seeing me on his land. In fact, he threatened to take a gun to me."

"Did he, indeed!"

The Archdeacon, who had been standing by the window listening and saying nothing, interfered angrily.

"I must speak to Crowe. He and I were good friends once. His wife came from my parish and I married them years ago. She died when the girl was born. I don't know what's come over Crowe."

Perrick ate the last of his pie and wiped his fingers on his handkerchief.

"He's got a bit under the weather since his girl went to the mainland to get a job. She probably got tired of languishing on that tumbledown farm. I don't blame her. He educated her above her station as a crofter's daughter. It'll blow over. She'll start pining for the li'l Island again when she's been in London for a bit, and one day she'll come home. They all do."

"You seem to know all about it, Perrick."

The Archdeacon's eyes sparkled at the detective.

"It's my business, parson. The local police are better gossips than any woman. They tell me all that goes on. The port constable at Peel reported about the Chief Inspector's little fishing trip. Munn's Corner was all a-buzz with it. Well, I must be off back to Douglas. We'll keep in touch, Inspector. Nothin' you want to tell me, sir?"

"I'm afraid not, Perrick, Today's been more like a picnic than work."

"Did you get a good tea at Kelly's, Ballacurry?"

"Excellent, thanks. I saw the bobby going by on his motor-bike as my wife and I went in the farm. I suppose he passed it on."

"That's it, sir. As I once said, there's not much goes on over here that the police don't know. Good evening, all."

"You ought to have Perrick at Scotland Yard, Littlejohn," said the Archdeacon after the police car had left the road in front of the old vicarage.

"Yes. He's a good chap. It won't be his fault if the real culprit isn't brought to judgment."

And he went on to tell the parson all they had learned that afternoon. They were interrupted by the telephone. It was Cromwell ringing-up as promised.

"Before I answer it, sir, could I ask a favour? Could you find room for another lodger in the vicarage? I want my assistant over here with me. On holiday, of course, like me."

"Of course."

Cromwell was full of beans and Littlejohn could hear his voice as though he were shouting from the next room.

"We've got the dope you wanted, sir. Sergeant Grebe jumped at the idea of going over to St. Sylvester's to talk to his pretty nurse. He got a lot of news through her. Your end of the tale's all wrong, though. Dr. Fallows was a very decent chap. It was his wife caused the bother. Yes, his *wife*. Couldn't leave the men alone. Sort of disease with some people, isn't it? Nymphomaniac, the nurses at Sylvester's called her, according to Grebe, but you know what nurses are. Get exaggerating a bit, now and then, in their highfalutin professional way. It was all very simple. She got flirting with first one and then another, but finally got properly mixed-up with one of the psychiatrists. Dr. Fallows caught them together and it seems he saw red. Socked the psycho on the jaw and laid him out cold. Quite a scandal, but they managed to hush it up at Sylvester's."

"And Fallows left for the Isle of Man?"

"Funny thing about it all was, that Fallows was crazy about his wife. All her carryings-on didn't seem to change him. He stuck to her, chucked up a fine job, and took her away into private practice, presumably where he thought she couldn't get into mischief. What a hope! Women'll get into mischief anywhere … even on a desert island."

"Hullo! What's suddenly made you a cynic?"

"Oh, nothing. Mother-in-law's just getting on my nerves a bit. Slapped one of the kids yesterday. I had to tell her if there was any slapping to be done, I'd do it. Then, of course, the wife started to cry. Said she didn't want any domestic bickering."

"I'll tell you what, Cromwell, come over here till it blows over."

"What? Me? Come over to the Isle of Man? I've never been there in my life and I'd like it. But you're only joking, sir."

"Dead serious. Listen, old chap …"

The address in East Croydon. Margat Crowe. What was she doing in London? Why was she there?

Littlejohn gave his colleague full instructions.

"Before you suggest bringing Margat back home to her father, get to know why she left the Island. Was it through Levis, or what? Then come over here with her to Grenaby by the morning 'plane the day after tomorrow. Don't tell anyone you're from the police. Explain it to the Assistant Commissioner, but ask him not to mention it to the Chief Constable here. I'm not butting-in officially. There's a good man on it in Douglas and I don't want to steal his thunder. Do your best. …"

"You bet, sir!"

Mrs. Littlejohn had been telling the parson about Cromwell.

"We'll be very glad to see him, Littlejohn. He can sleep in the attic. Quite a nice room with grand views."

"Please don't let it be known he's from the police, sir. It's not fair to Perrick to fill the Island with Scotland Yard men when he's so competent himself."

"I understand. And now about Ned Crowe. Can I help? If he won't talk to you, he may do so to me. If you'll drive me to Peel after an early dinner, I'd like to call on the Corteens now that Johnny's back. Perhaps we might meet Crowe there. I'm sorry to hear he spends a lot of time at the *Captain Quilliam*."

"That suits me, sir."

Someone had shot some partridges and the housekeeper had cooked them for the evening meal. They followed it with blackberry fool, according to Mrs. Littlejohn's recipe, and topped it off with Manx cheese. The lamp on the table spread a warm glow over the room; the logs spluttered on the fire and threw out a comforting heat; the dog snored on the rug, yapping in her dreams. Over the fireplace, the Hoggatt picture of the little fields of Man seemed alive even in the dim light and shone like a benediction.

"I don't feel like moving. ..."

Littlejohn inwardly cursed Levis and Crowe, Fallows and his wife, everybody connected with crime. Here, everything seemed different.

The Archdeacon was putting on his overcoat and muffler.

"It's a nice night and all the stars are out. You'll enjoy it."

At Peel market-place they parked the car and parted.

"See you here, then, in an hour. ..."

Time seemed to stand still in Peel. In the town there was hardly a soul about. The footsteps of those at large echoed and were magnified in the narrow streets. The lights shed pools at the bases of their standards and beyond the periphery it seemed darker than ever. If you looked upwards, it was like seeing the stars at the top of a chimney, so close were the buildings in the old quaint alleys.

The waterfront was deserted. The promenade lamps shone across the water and met the coloured reflections of the navigation lights at the pier and breakwater. The tide was in and the waves splashed gently on the shore. A boat rode calmly out of the harbour, the light steady at her masthead, the throb of her engine punctuated by the ringing of the bridge telegraph. Aboard, someone was shouting in Dutch.

The *Captain Quilliam* was full, as usual. The crew of the French vessel, which had put in for repairs, were strung-out at the counter drinking rum and apple-brandy, which the landlord kept specially for such occasions. They spoke Breton and one of the Manxmen was comparing it with native Manx.

"If ye want to curse a man bad, ye say '*my hiaght mynney mollaght ort*', my seven swearin's of a curse on ye, see? Wad would ye say in the Breton, now? *Compris?*"

The Frenchman shrugged his shoulders and laughed.

"Curse, eh? *Nom de Dieu*, hein?"

"There, what did I tell ye? He says *Modha-doo*, black dog. I told ye they spoke the Manx...."

"Aw, shurrup, Clever-Dickie from Foxdale!"

They started to quarrel among themselves.

In another group they were busy getting Johnny Corteen drunk.

"Fill up agen, Johnny-boy. ...You don't get Manx ale in the prizzen, eh?"

"I've got to be home sober to-night, else the old lady'll be in tears. I promised to be sober in future."

"Just a little one for the road. Jus' a li'l *jough-a-dhorris* an' then we'll see ye to your ole mother's own dhoor."

Corteen had spotted Littlejohn.

"Come to tek me back again, eh? Perrick says I'm free, and nobody's goin' to stop me. ..."

Littlejohn sat in his corner drinking his beer without a word. It had got round that he was responsible for Johnny Corteen's release and everybody was anxious to make him welcome.

"Aw, come on, Johnny. The Inspecther from London's seen to it they set you free. He's your friend."

"Is that so? I never even seen the man till now, but Perrick told me what you look like. Perrick's the man got me free, jus' as Perrick's the man put me in. Asked all the questions when I was in the prizzen, too. What did I see when I was asleep on the Peel Road the night they say that rat, Levis, died? Did I see anybody? Anybody walkin', or on a bike, or in a motor-car? O' course I didn', an' I tole him so. I was ashleep, wasn't I? Don' remember nawthen. An' with that, he says, 'Johnny, you're free, my bhoy,' he sez. An' he ups and drives me back to Peel. Perrick's my frien'. Good ole Perrick. ... I'm goin' home. ..."

He made for the door unsteadily and his mates shambled after him to see him off.

The door opened first, however, and a lanky, gangling, pale-faced fisherman entered, pushed the crowd aside, and made rapidly for the bar. He was so loose-limbed that he looked half-drunk already. He wore a navy blue suit, a jersey under his coat, and a bowler hat. He had been on his way to do some courting.

"Give me some rum, Rhoda. Quick. ..."

The buxom girl at the bar stared at him in amazement. He looked like a ghost come to spoil the fun. One of the

French sailors had been flirting with her in sign language and had got to the stage of slipping his arm round her waist across the counter.

The crowd around the door had returned to the bar, eager to learn what had happened.

"Has she giv'n ye the go-by, Ernie? Has she got herself another chap?"

The newcomer downed his drink and pushed the glass back.

"Another...."

"My! Ye mus' have got it bad, Ernie-bhoy...."

The fisherman gulped down his second tot and found his tongue.

"So would you have got it bad if you seen what I seen. I was jus' comin' down the broo by Creg Malin and in the steepest part, lek, I has to jump for the side on account of a car dhrivin' like the devil himself. Mus' have been doin' sixty. Sixty, down the hill there...!"

"Well, that's not frightened you all that bad, has it, Ernie?"

"Naw. But there was another ahead of me, see? Another who didn't get out of the way fast enough. The car caught him full an' tossed him lek a mad bull. I shouted but it was too late. There he lay, flat on the road, all bashed about."

There was a roar of sympathy. Somebody ordered Ernie another rum. Littlejohn sat waiting for the sailor who, with characteristic Manx skill, was making a drama of his tale.

"Who was it, Ernie boy?"

Ernie emptied his third glass and his colour returned. His eyes sparkled.

"Ned Crowe! Poor Ned comin' here for his nightcap, peaceable and quiet. Next minute, whoosh...jus' a bundle in the road...."

"You didn' leave him, Ernie, did ye?"

"Naw. I yelled me head off as I ran to him. A bobby arrived from nowhere and now Ned's on his way to Noble's 'ospital in Dooglas, unconscious, lek as not dead. ..."

"Didn't I tell ye ...? There's the evil eye on the Peel Road. ..."

They'd forgotten Johnny Corteen in the excitement, and there he was, back again, standing in the doorway, pointing an accusing finger at Littlejohn, as though he could do something about it.

"The police was axin' me about goin's-on at Peel Road, but it'll need more than them to settle the black witchcraft that's there."

Then he halted and a dead silence filled the room.

Inspector Perrick, hands in the pockets of his raincoat, stood in the doorway looking as black as night.

CHAPTER TEN
NO ALIBI

Perrick strode to where the loose-limbed sailor was draping himself over the bar, seized him by the arm, and spun him round.

"What the hell are you doing here? The police have been looking for you all over the place. And put that stuff away. We don't want you drunk before we get your statement."

He angrily snatched Ernie Quiggin's half-empty glass from his hand and, with a gesture of disgust, splashed the contents on the floor.

"I thought you'd done with me, sir; honest, I did. ..."

"You should have stayed at the station till they said you could go. Now, come on with me. ... ."

Perrick's bright eyes fell on Littlejohn, and his anger evaporated. For the first time the Chief Inspector felt he'd caught his colleague out of countenance. Perrick had always tried to be as unperturbed as Littlejohn in the face of events and now he had, for a minute, lost control.

"Evening, sir. I didn't expect to find you here."

"I came to see Johnny, but he'd already drunk himself *hors de combat* by the time I arrived."

"Care to come along, sir?"

"Thanks. We'll pick the Archdeacon up first."

"Oh; is he here, as well? Right, sir...."

The Frenchmen watched the whole affair with ironic smiles. First the scared sailor, still more frightened by the terrier of a man in a raincoat; and then the pair of them nearly kowtowing to the big smiling man who'd suddenly risen from his corner....

The skipper of the *Robert Surcouf, St. Malo*, shrugged his huge shoulders. A powerful, bearded, villainous-looking man, with piggy eyes and a broken nose. He was in a foul temper. The propeller-shaft of his boat had broken and he'd limped into Peel under sail. Now it would take two days to repair and that would only be a temporary job, according to the local blacksmith, who had said he'd patch it up enough to see him to his home port, where they'd have to fit a new shaft.

All the Frenchman wanted was a bit of peace in which to get drunk and people kept upsetting him. He spat on the floor and ordered more rum.

The Archdeacon was sitting in the car, a shawl draped round his shoulders.

"You here again, Perrick? Was there ever such a man for work?"

"We've got a lot more since I last put a sight on you, sir. There's been more violence in Peel."

They told the parson what had occurred and then the quartet made its way to the police-station.

It took them the best part of an hour to get a proper tale out of Ernie Quiggin. The rum had befuddled him and he kept pausing to sort out his thoughts.

It amounted, for the most part, to a refined version of what Littlejohn had already heard at the *Captain Quilliam*. Quiggin had been on his way from where he lived at St. Germain's to do a bit of courting in Peel.

"I hope someborry's let Nessie know where I am. There'll be sich a scawl if herself's kep' waitin' for me. ..."

"Never mind that, Ernie. What did the car look like? Did you get a sight of it?"

Perrick was putting the questions and the thin constable was taking them down in good longhand and pausing patiently for the answers.

"Aw, one of the li'l Austins ... or mebbe it was a Morris. One of the li'l cars you see so much of these days."

"Have you seen it before? Was it a Peel car?"

Quiggin thought hard. You could almost hear the wheels turning in his head.

"Maybe. I didn' see the numbers. It was thravellin' too fast. There's so many of 'em around. Even the police have them."

The scribbling policeman looked up and sighed. It was like getting blood out of a stone.

"An' then, there's others like it. The doctor, f'r instance. It was like his. ..."

"Which doctor?"

"Docthor Fallows. He's just got a new one. ..."

There was a significant silence. The clock struck nine-thirty and the policeman hastened to say it was a quarter of an hour slow and lost half an hour every day.

"And what time would it be when this happened, Ernie?"

"I toul' ye afore. Just after eight. I heard the town clock strike eight a li'l while afore."

"That checks right. The police were on the spot at twenty past eight. So it must have happened about a quarter past, if what you say is true, that a constable arrived almost as soon as you gave the alarm."

"Maybe it was, though it seemed nearer eight than that. I'll give it to ye, though."

Perrick turned to the attendant bobby.

"Ned Crowe was pretty regular, was he, in his habits of calling for his drink in Peel?"

"Of late, yes, Inspector. He got to the *Captain Quilliam* reg'lar about half-past eight or nearabouts."

"H'm. News reached Douglas at about eight-thirty and I set out right away and got here before nine. That seems to work out right. Very well, Ernie, sign the statements and then you can go and make your peace with Nessie. We'll want to see you again."

"Any news of Ned Crowe, Mr. Perrick? He's not dead, is he?"

"No. He's unconscious, though, and it's touch and go."

Outside, Perrick took Littlejohn's arm in the dark.

"Perhaps you're thinkin' the same as me, sir, that it wouldn't be a bad idea to call and see Dr. Fallows and get to know how he spent the night. He's not free from suspicion yet on the Levis count. His wife and Levis, you know. ... There's been funny goings-on around *Cursing Stones* and it's quite likely Ned Crowe knew a bit too much about somebody. He's had a lot of money lately, and maybe he's come by it by keeping his silence. I'm not even suggesting that Dr. Fallows did run him down, and if he did, it might have been accidental in the dark. ..."

"If you're going there, Perrick, I'd like to come with you."

"You'll be very welcome."

The doctor was at home when they got there. A maid who looked fresh from the country let them in.

"Is Dr. Fallows in?"

"Yes, sir. He's just finishin' the surgery. He's had a busy day and didn't get started till after eight. If you don't mind waiting, I'll tell him you're here."

She looked scared after Perrick had mentioned his name and rank and seemed eager to get away. The doctor came at once from the room he used as a surgery. Outside, a brick lean-to served as the waiting-room. There were still people to be attended to; you could hear them coughing and shuffling as they waited.

"I've patients in. Will you be long?"

The doctor looked tired and drawn. His face was dead pale and his spectacles were dirty. He might have been up all the night before by the looks of him.

"We won't take long, sir."

Perrick did all the talking.

"Come in the consulting room, then."

He spread out his arm wearily in a gesture of ushering them in, but Archdeacon Kinrade held back.

"You'll excuse me, doctor. I'm only keeping the Chief Inspector company. This is no business of mine and you won't want the three of us. I'll just stay here in the hall until they come back. It's quite comfortable."

Fallows didn't seem to be listening. He just left the parson to his own devices without a word.

The surgery was stuffy and smelt of iodine and ether as well. A desk, a lamp with a green shade, cabinets of instruments and medicines, a hypodermic and a stethoscope on the desk, and on a small table a kidney-dish and a scalpel; the dish was bloodstained. Fallows must have been lancing a boil or something as they'd interrupted and in his haste hadn't thought to clear up the paraphernalia. The alcoves on each side of the wide fireplace were crammed with medical books on shelves; there seemed to be hundreds of them.

"We won't keep you, doctor. I understand you've been out to-night."

"Yes."

"What time?"

"I was called out urgently at half-past seven, just as I was in the middle of surgery. I didn't get back till after eight."

"Where did you go, sir?"

"St. Germain's. It was a false alarm. I was very angry. It's the first time in my experience anybody has called me out for a joke or a bit of malevolence. I've heard of it being done to a fire-brigade but not to ..."

Perrick, his eyes glinting, couldn't wait for the sentence to finish.

"A false alarm! What do you mean, doctor?"

"Somebody telephoned. There was an accident at St. Germain's and a man was unconscious in the road. I hurried there and could find nothing. I asked at the nearest house to the spot described, Ballahaslitt, but nobody knew anything about it. It was a cruel hoax, especially as I was in the middle of surgery."

"So you came straight back, sir?"

"Yes. Why?"

"Past Creg Mallin and down the hill to Peel? About eight o' clock?"

The doctor rose from his chair impatiently. Outside, you could hear the patients coughing louder than ever, perhaps to remind Fallows that he ought to get a move on.

"What is all this about, Perrick?"

Hitherto, it had always been Mr. Perrick or Inspector. Now, you could feel Perrick grow tense at the sudden shedding of respect.

"Let me ask the questions, doctor. You were in your car?"

"Of course I was. You could hardly expect me to walk. Will you get to the point? My patients have been kept long enough already."

"May we see the car?"

GEORGE BELLAIRS

"What for?"

"*I want to see the car.*"

Fallows took out a bunch of keys and flung them angrily on the desk.

"Go and look at it yourself, then. I haven't the time. The key's on the ring and the garage is, as you know, down the slope under the waiting-room. Annie will show you. And now, I'll thank you to leave me to my patients. ..."

He glanced at Littlejohn, who had said nothing hitherto, and half shrugged his shoulders as though they both couldn't understand what Perrick was getting at.

The garage was half underground and overhead was the waiting-room, reached by four stone steps and a door at the top of them. Above, they could hear the patients shuffling and moving their chairs with impatience. Now and then someone coughed or spoke louder than the rest.

The car was a small one, as described by Ernie Quiggin. The garage was only just large enough to hold it, all the same. The place was neat and clean. Tools on shelves on the walls, spare tyres hanging from pegs, petrol tins, a bench.

Perrick was busy examining the car. He pointed without a word to a dent in the left front wing. That was all. They looked right round the car and closely examined it for other traces of the accident. Nothing.

Back in the house, Perrick tapped again on the surgery door. Inside, voices and then the closing of an outer door. Fallows appeared.

"You again! What is it now?"

Perrick entered the room without any formality. He threw the keys back on the desk.

"Where did you get the dent in the left mudguard of your car, doctor?"

"What dent? I know of none."

"When did you last examine the car?"

"I don't know. I'm a busy man. I'm in and out of if all day. I know of no damage to it, though. It was new three months ago and as far as I know…"

"There's a dent, right enough. Did you knock anyone down on your way home to-night?"

Fallows looked dumbfounded.

"So that's it! No, I didn't.…"

"A man was knocked down just outside Peel at the time you were passing there to-night, doctor. He's now in hospital in Douglas, unconscious. Are you sure…?"

"Quite sure. I couldn't have done it and not known about it. Why pick out my car?"

"A car resembling yours was seen there and was responsible for the accident."

"Who was injured?"

"A fisherman-farmer called Ned Crowe!"

Perrick watched Fallows closely.

The doctor had been pale, but now he turned almost yellow.

"Crowe? But this is preposterous!"

"What do you mean?"

"Nothing."

"Come, sir, you were going to say something."

"I've nothing to say."

"Very well, doctor. Let me ask you another question. Where were you on the afternoon of August 21st?"

"August 21st! What date's that and what has it to do with the accident to-night?"

Perrick advanced a step nearer.

"I'll tell you, sir. Ned Crowe farms the land at Gob y Deigan. We believe that on August 21st a man named Levis was murdered there, hidden in the Lynague caves until dusk, and then his body was rowed out to sea, weighted, and sunk."

"What has that to do with me, may I ask?"

Littlejohn felt sorry for Fallows. Under the ruthless questions and the successive verbal blows of the efficient Perrick, he was losing countenance and nerve. His wide forehead was bathed in sweat, his fingers jerked, and he kept licking his dry lips.

"I'm sorry, doctor, but this has to be said. Cedric Levis was a friend of your wife's.... I might almost venture to say her lover...."

Fallows suddenly sprang at Perrick and grasped him by the lapels and shook him. The Inspector quickly recovered, seized the doctor's powerful wrists, and without effort flung him back.

"I wouldn't, doctor, if I were you...."

"Don't you dare mention my wife. You're exceeding your duties. I shall speak to the Governor about this. I'll..."

Perrick's voice was almost gentle.

"Look, sir. All Peel knows about your wife and Levis. *You* also know. Why, otherwise, have you kept inquiring all over the place if this one or that one has seen them together? Then, Levis was murdered. Can't you see, it's to your advantage to provide an alibi? We just want to know where you were when Levis was killed. The inference is, it happened between noon, when he left his home, and five, when he should have caught a 'plane to the mainland, on August 21st. Where were you then?"

Fallows sat down in his swivel chair. His patients were forgotten, although they were talking loud enough next-door.

"I don't know."

"You can't answer like that, just off-hand. Look at your diary, man. Try to think."

Almost listlessly, Fallows opened a drawer and took out a book bound in red canvas. He thumbed the pages absently. Littlejohn saw August 21st appear.

"It was my free afternoon. I went for a run on my own for a change. I'd no patients to see. I've no alibi. Nobody can help me. So, you see, Perrick, I'm all ready to be arrested."

Fallows slumped down. He looked years older.

"Well. ... What are you waiting for, Perrick? Isn't it usual to warn people that what they say will be used in evidence? Get on with it."

Perrick picked up the hat he'd earlier put on the desk.

"We're not going to arrest you, doctor, but you'd better think where you were on the date in question. Also, I hope for your sake Crowe recovers. I'll say no more."

Fallows was on his feet again.

"Wait! Are you suggesting that Crowe knows something about my connection with Levis ... or that he saw me at Gob y Deigan the day Levis was killed, and because of that, I ran him down in cold blood?"

"You've put that construction on it, doctor, not me. All I'm saying is, we've got to make routine inquiries of everybody connected, or who might be connected with the murder of Levis and also with the accident to-night. I'm not accusing you of anything, far less arresting you, but I do urge you to think carefully of your movements on the day I mentioned and also, if you did accidentally knock anyone down in the dark to-night, make a clean breast of it and make our work easier."

Fallows opened the door.

"Leave me to my patients, Perrick. I've said all I'm going to say. I have no alibi for August 21st. You can please yourself what you make of that. As for to-night's little tragedy. ... You seem intent on mixing me up with that, as well. Do your damnedest, Perrick. ... Good night. ..."

He slammed the door on them and left them in the hall to see themselves out of the house.

Perrick looked at Littlejohn and shrugged his shoulders.

"What do you make of that, sir?"

"Very strange behaviour. The man's overwrought about something. I was watching him as you spoke to him. He knows something he's not telling. I'm sure he's mixed up in the Levis affair. If not directly, then he's shielding his wife. Better keep an eye on the doctor. ..."

"Trust us, sir. What about to-night's accident?"

"If Fallows knows nothing about it, then someone was trying to involve him in it. If the false-alarm story is true, then somebody is trying to incriminate Fallows. If, on the other hand, the doctor did knock down Crowe, it will need a lot to make me believe it wasn't deliberate and connected with the other murder."

They took Perrick to his own car at the police-station and then Littlejohn drove back to Grenaby. On the way he told Archdeacon Kinrade of the painful interview with Dr. Fallows.

"I can't believe it! He's not that type, Littlejohn."

The Inspector replied gently.

"Now, now, parson. Don't try classifying men into murderers and non-murderers. If you'd dealt with as many as I have, you'd change your mind. Anyone can commit a murder if provoked sufficiently. ..."

"There's just one thing, though, Littlejohn. You say the doctor can't... or won't... give himself an alibi for August 21st. I may be able to give him one."

"You, sir!"

"Whilst I was waiting in the hall for you, I occupied part of the time turning over the pad by the telephone, seeing if I knew the names of the people written in it. It's a call-book, presumably used by whoever answers the 'phone, to note down places the doctor must attend."

"Well? And you looked at August 21st?"

"Yes. It bears one entry. Beside each entry is the time the message was received. The only entry for the date in question is *Eairy Cushlan*, and the time taken, 10.30."

"And what does *Eairy Cushlan* mean?"

"It's a farm in the wilderness between Peel and the Round Table. That's the cross-roads high on the moorland, a junction for Port Erin, Colby and Foxdale. It's not far from Grenaby, really. You ought to go to *Eairy Cushlan* to-morrow and see what it's all about."

"You're quite a detective, you know, Archdeacon. I don't know what I'd do without you. We'll go to *Eairy Cushlan* first thing in the morning."

"One other thing I did. I took the liberty of using Fallows's telephone to ring up Noble's Hospital. Crowe has a good chance. The skull is fractured, but they have operated to relieve the pressure and short of the unexpected, he should pull through. You realize, don't you, that if this accident was deliberate, someone is going to have some explaining to do when Crowe comes round?"

CHAPTER ELEVEN
EAIRY CUSHLAN

"*Kynnas-tha-shu. ... Cre'n aght ta shiu jiu?*"
Two old Manxmen saying how-do-you-do!
"Morra, morra, an' how are ye, are ye, for all?"

Littlejohn and the Archdeacon had started, good and early, for *Eairy Cushlan* with Meg in the back seat.

They turned from Grenaby into the uplands of the interior, climbed through Ronague, skirted South Barrule to the cross-roads at the Round Table, and thence coasted gently down the Dalby-Peel road.

There was a bite in the air which smelt of the sea; the sun was shining. As the road climbed, the land deteriorated until at length there wasn't even feeding for sheep. To the left, the ground rose, dark and peaty, and then fell sharply to the sea in high cliffs. From the crossways they could see a small house in the middle of a croft, the thin grassland of which looked like a little emerald in the vast background of turf.

"That's *Eairy Cushlan*, Littlejohn. It means Cosnahan's Upland. ... Take the track there. ..."

A partly metalled road leading from the main one taxed the springs of the car. About a mile away, a patch of windswept trees, then a square of gorse on top of a sod hedge, and in the stockade thus formed against the wind and weather, *Eairy Cushlan.*

The farm was dead still. Not a dog to bark, or a child to shout. Even the few hens scratching and picking around worked in grim silence, as though the poor land called for intense concentration in finding bits of food. The cry of a distant curlew and the wailing of the gulls on the shore nearby only accentuated the quietness. The place seemed charged with a grim sadness, as though hope had gone and despair moved in.

The old iron gate of the overgrown farmyard had been moved from its hinges and Littlejohn drew up the car before the gap. It was no use going further; the road ended there. A mere track led away into the wilderness. The Archdeacon indicated the path.

"Leads to *Lag ny Keeilly,* the Hollow of the Cell, the remains of a little chapel and a graveyard where they buried the old Manx kings. ... And on the way, you pass the *Chibbyr Vashtee,* The Christening Well, said to be good for consumption; *Chibbyr* means a well and *Vashtee* means Christening. ..."

The parson seemed to be talking simply to break the oppressive silence.

The farm was almost a ruin and built of rough stone. Two up and two down, a few miserable outhouses for pigs and poultry, and a small cowshed with a loft above, reached by stone steps running up the outer wall. The two men got out of the car.

"*Kynnas-tha-shu.* ..."

The old man sitting at the door in a rocking-chair and smoking a clay pipe, had watched them so quietly and unmoving that they hadn't noticed him. Now, on seeing the Archdeacon he had burst into lively action. The parson was equally excited.

"Well, well, well. . . . If it isn't Billy-Bill-Illiam! *Cre'n aght ta shiu jiu?* How are you to-day?"

The other old man was hale but shaky on his legs. He must have been in his eighties, too. White hair, a fresh face, thick set, with a large moustache. His skin was wrinkled like an old apple and his voice quavered a bit.

Gurra-mie-a, Pazon. . . . Thanks, parson. Aw, middlin', I am. Very indifferin'. . . . Limpin' with the rheumaticks. . . ."

Littlejohn stood at the gate smoking his pipe. It was like being in a foreign country. Two old men talking the old tongue of their boyhood.

"Come here, Littlejohn. . . . This is William Joughin, the last of my boyhood friends. Billy-Bill-Illiam we called him then. Billy, son of Bill, the son of William. Aw, man! It's grand to put a sight on ye. . . . And what are you doing here all alone, William?"

The ancient cupped his hand round his ear. He was a bit deaf. Parson Kinrade repeated it louder.

"I thought ye'd have heard. . . . It's goin' round the houses at Peel all about it. I'm livin' with me daughter, Kirree. Her and her man, Tommy Keigh, bin farmin' here. We're leavin' the place."

"I don't wonder, William."

"Aw, poor hungry land it is, that'll ate up all the manure an' lime ye might be puttin' on it. Intack land, it is, torn from the moor and always strugglin' to get back to the wild. We're movin' to Ballaugh to-morrer. Ye're just in time, Cæsar. Are ye here on sick-visitin'?"

"Is somebody ill, then? Is your brother, Juan, still alive?"

Billy-Bill-Illiam looked surprised.

"Naw, Cæsar. Juan's dead these years. His body's gone to dust an' his *keeigh* gone to rust, as we used to say."

"His *keeigh* . . . his plough, Littlejohn. That's a sad thought. Forgive two old men talking a language you don't understand. We haven't met for twenty years. Where's Kitty, William? Is it she's been ill?"

"Aye. All the old folk is gone, but me. *My vannaght lesh yn marroo*, as we used to say ... my blessings with the dead. Is it in you're wantin'?"

He indicated the door.

"Yes. Is Kitty in?"

"Kirree! Kirree!"

The old man called his daughter in a shrill pipe. They could hear someone descending the stairs noisily, for the carpets were up. A striking woman in her early thirties appeared. Bright coppery hair, tall and slim, with blue eyes and a clear complexion. She was dead pale.

"This is Cæsar Kinrade, Kirree, my boyhood friend and Archdeacon of Man, my gel. D'ye hear that, Archdeacon of Man."

"I hear, daa. Pleased to meet you, sir, I'm sure."

"And this is my friend, Mr. Littlejohn...."

"Pleased to meet you. It's a fine dog you've got there. Our Bess has moved over to Ballaugh with the stock."

"Your husband's there now, Kitty?"

"Yes...."

Her father corrected her.

"He's gone to the lawyer. A terrible man for lawin' is Tommy Keigh. Takin' the law of everybody that's within reach of him...."

Kitty blushed and looked better for it.

"He's on'y seein' to the lease. To hear my dad talk you'd think Tom was proper litigious."

"Aren't all Manxmen? But that's not what we called for. Have you been ill, then, Kitty?"

"She has, that. Terr'ble bad. Nearly died on us, didn' you, *my chree?*"

"Not all that bad, daa."

"You *was*. Nearly lyin' in the sheets, she was. ..."

The Archdeacon interpreted that to Littlejohn as lying in her shroud!

"Oh! You'll get lave, dad! Have it your own way."

Old Billy-Bill-Illiam was in his stride.

"All but dead. An' her own doings, at that. Workin' too hard on this hungry land. Give herself a miscarriage, that's what. ..."

The girl fled indoors as Old William warmed up to details.

"Now, in my young days, we'd soon have had her right. The wise woman would have bin givin' her the lucky herb, lek, or Charlie Chaise, the herb doctor, would 'ave come an' stopped the blood. But there doesn't seem to be no lucky herb around these days and the blood-stoppers is all dead."

"Get on with your tale, William. What happened?"

"Kirree was tuck bad at ten o' the mornin'. Liftin' the hay, she was ..."

"What date was this?"

"Jus' a week after the great Lammas gales ... the *Gaalyn yn Lhuanys*. It usually comes on the twelfth of August ... this year it was two days behindhand, on the fourteen'. I recollect it plain, becos it blew the stones off the roof and Kirree lifted 'em back. 'You'll be injurin' yerself,' I told her, an' I was right, Cæsar, though it tuck a week to show."

"She took bad on the 21st of August, William?"

"That's right, pazon."

Littlejohn and the Archdeacon exchanged glances.

"And you sent for the doctor?"

"We did. We was skeered, Cæsar, an' Kirree that modest, lek, not wantin' to be a trouble. Tommy tuck out the machine ... that theer tractor ... an' lek the wind to the telephone by Dalby. The doctor was here in half an hour. Kirree'd bin dead but for him. Aw man, the grand he was, Docther Fallows. ... He's good all through, *innagh an' gloo.* ..."

"The warp and the weft of a man, you mean, William. Yes, I guess he must be. How long was he here?"

"It's my half-holiday, says the docther, but I'll not leave her till she's safe. Ye see, pazon, he dursen't move her, else he'd have had her down in the 'ospital. Eleven o' the mornin' he was driving up the road there, and eight in the everin' leavin' us to go home. An' Kirree safe to us."

"And he was here all that time, William? He didn't go back to Peel?"

"For why? With the gel lyin' at death's door, do you think? Naw, Cæsar. He worked away and sat by her till one, an' then Tom gives him a collop of beef between two thick slices o' bread, and a cuppa tea. Then, the docther walks round the yard like a man in a *jarrood*, a daze, lek, smokin' one cigarette afther another; then up to the bedroom again till three. 'Kirree,' he sez, then, 'Kirree, you'll be all right.' An' she was, but he didn' leave her till eight, when she fell asleep peaceable, lek. Three times he sent Tom down to Peel to the druggist's. ... An' he came twice every day for three days and then once a day for a week. Then las' week, he says, 'Kirree, you won't need me any more. Off you go with your husbin' and yer daa to Ballaugh, an' if ye want childher to bless ye both with, don't be heavin' stones and things around when they're on the way. ...'"

Old William paused and then added in wonder:

"An' all that paid-for by the gover'ment ... free, lek, under the health service. Aw, a grand man is Docther Fallows."

They drank a cup of tea with Kitty and the old man, ate a soda cake or two, and then left them.

"Good luck at Ballaugh to ye both," said the parson by way of benediction.

Old Billy-Bill-Illiam waved them out of sight.

"I'll be purrin' a sight on ye, Cæsar. Come down to the port some everin' afther tay, an' we'll get a boat and have a li'l sail and a *cooish* about the old days agen...."

At the main road, Littlejohn drew up, filled his pipe and lit it.

"I reckon I did all the talking, but then it came easier to me, a garrulous old man, and probably they told me more that way. It certainly gives Dr. Fallows an alibi till evening on August 21st. Do you think we ought to go and tell Perrick?"

"Perhaps better not, sir, till we've something more concrete. What about tackling Fallows himself? Face him with the facts and see what he says?"

"You know best. I'm an amateur, Littlejohn."

"You wouldn't have thought so to hear you with Billy-Bill-Illiam! Why, he didn't even ask what you wanted to know for! It just came out in the course of conversation."

"Ah! But when he gets quiet and thinks it out, he'll be bothered. His curiosity will grow till he can't bear to think about it and he'll make some excuse for seeing me, either at Grenaby or Peel, just to quiz me about things."

They discussed Fallows.

"I wonder, parson, if the doctor thinks his wife murdered Levis and he's trying to shield her. Remember, our report from Sylvester's says he was still devoted to her in spite of the way she behaved. He may not have faced her with his suspicions and simply be trying to draw the scent from her to him. When Perrick and I interviewed him, the doctor more or less told us to think what we damn well liked; he wasn't making a statement. I think I ought to have a good talk to Fallows and try to get him to tell a proper tale."

"Meanwhile, what would you say if I spoke to his wife, Littlejohn? She might tell her own side of the story if she's faced with the fact that the doctor is risking arrest for her sake."

"You can try, sir. No harm in that. Your venerable age and your cloth might be more conducive to confession than the official ways of a pair of policemen. Shall we go to Peel, then?"

"Yes; but just a minute."

The Archdeacon climbed from the car and took a last look at *Eairy Cushlan*, forlorn in the middle of the moor, its chimney smoking with its last fires.

"Poor *Eairy Cushlan*. I remember when I was a boy, it was a trim, prosperous little croft run by a fisherman-farmer who tilled it in his spare time, supporting a little family. 'For them by day the golden corn we reap; by night the silver harvest of the sea,' as the old fisherman's hymn goes. Now the farm's on its last legs, between the sheets already, as Billy-Bill-Illiam says."

"There'll be no more tenants?"

"No. It won't pay. You can see how it looks now. In two years the moorland will have swallowed up the cultivated land, and in as many more the house will start to tumble down. It needed a Scotsman to put it properly and realistically. Stevenson might have been thinking of our old ruined crofts when he wrote about it...."

The old man sounded to be talking to himself.

"Now, when the day dawns on th
brow of the moorland,
Lone stands the house, and the
chimney stone is cold.
Lone let it stand, now the friends are all departed,

The kind hearts, the true hearts,
that loved the place of old."

The Archdeacon took off his shovel hat and waved it at
the lonely house.

"Good-bye … *Eairy Cushion* of old. …"

Littlejohn let in the clutch and they descended to Peel.

Chapter Twelve
The Unwanted Alibi

Dr. Fallows had just arrived in for his lunch and he was annoyed when Littlejohn presented himself. Mrs. Fallows was taking a snack in her office as she drew plans for some new architectural venture, and her husband was eating his grilled fish on a tray in the dining-room.

"Really, Inspector, this is becoming too much!"

"Don't let me disturb your meal, doctor. I'm sorry if it's inconvenient just now, but it's important."

Dr. Fallows pushed his tray away from him.

"Make it snappy, then. I'm busy."

"Why are you trying to draw suspicion on yourself, then, for the Levis murder?"

Fallows was drying his lips on his napkin and was too dumbfounded at first even to lower it. Littlejohn could just see his startled eyes through his powerful glasses looking at him over the top of the stiff linen.

"What do you mean, Inspector? And what business is it of yours anyhow? You're not officially on the case. I can't see why you need to meddle."

"If I don't meddle, you and your family are heading for disaster, sir. You see, I know you were nowhere near the scene of the crime at the time it occurred. You were at *Eairy*

Cushlan practically until dark from eleven in the morning on the day of the crime, which, I think, occurred before five in the afternoon."

"How do you know that?"

Fallows was mentally seeking some reply to the argument and was too flustered to find one.

"I've spoken to Mrs. Keigh, your patient."

"I protest! You've no business pestering my patients. It's unethical, to say the least of it."

"Don't be foolish, doctor. If I tell Inspector Perrick the result of my investigations of this morning, you'll have a lot more awkward questions to answer. Who are you protecting in this matter?"

"I've nothing to say."

"I'll have to do the talking then, sir. You think your wife is responsible for the crime and you are prepared to take the blame."

Fallows rose angrily to his feet and pointed to the door.

"Get out and leave me alone! I've had enough bother with the police as it is. I'm ready to take what's coming to me and I don't need your help."

Littlejohn, instead of following the doctor's orders, put his hat on the table, sat down and lit his pipe.

"Listen. Do you persist, even if your wife isn't implicated? Are you going to insist on being a martyr, in taking up the attitude of self-sacrifice instead of being sensible? Nobody will thank or admire you for it. On the contrary, you're hampering the police in their investigations. I tell you this as a friendly gesture. I've no standing in the case, as you say, but I'm anxious that the right person shall pay for the crime."

Fallows opened his mouth to speak and then snapped it shut again.

"I've nothing to say."

"You were aware of your wife's association with Levis. You followed them and watched them. But were you aware that all that was over before Levis was killed, that your wife had gone the way of the rest, been brushed-off, and that Levis had found another woman to pester with his attentions?"

Fallows sat glaring, but made no reply.

"You knew quite a lot of what happened in Levis's affairs, didn't you? You knew she'd arranged to meet Levis on the day he was murdered...."

Littlejohn was making a shot in the dark, but it found a mark.

"Who told you that?"

"Never mind. Levis was leaving the Island to go abroad for quite a long spell. He wasn't taking Mrs. Fallows with him. In fact, I think he was taking someone else....Just excuse me. May I use your telephone?"

"I won't stop you. Telephone if you like."

It didn't take a minute using his authority. Scotland Yard came on the line at once.

"Please ring up the Hotel Rousseau, San Remo....Yes, San Remo...right away. Priority. Ask if a man named Levis, who had booked with them around August 21st, reserved one room, or two rooms, and ring me back right away at this number. Peel 65432...."

Littlejohn returned to the doctor, who was helping himself to whisky. He didn't invite the Chief Inspector to join him.

"Have you finished with me?"

"Not quite. Now, sir, I want the truth, please. Did you know your wife went to Gob y Deigan to meet Levis that day?"

No reply. Fallows drank deeply, added more whisky, and drank again.

"Look here, Fallows. You've two children."

"Keep them out of it! In fact, leave me alone."

"Not till I've finished."

Surgery hour was approaching. You could hear patients entering the lean-to waiting-room, banging the door, shuffling chairs as they sat down.

"You followed your wife to her rendezvous several times, but on the day of the crime, you were held up by a dangerous case. You knew all the same, though, that she was at Gob y Deigan that afternoon. You knew that Levis had broken with her for another woman, and you thought Mrs Fallows had avenged herself and killed him. You're quite wrong, you know."

"I'm not!"

The two words were said spasmodically, before the doctor knew he'd uttered them. He looked embarrassed and closed his mouth tighter than ever.

"Which means that somebody has told you your wife was involved in the death of Levis. You weren't present. You're very reluctant to accept an alibi, but I'm thrusting it on you, and if you persist in your present attitude, I shall produce the necessary witnesses to the Island police to prove you're lying."

"What are you trying to do?"

"Clear you of guilt and, if it's possible, your wife as well."

"It isn't possible. ..."

Again the impulsive reply.

"Which means that your wife's either told you, or someone else has. I don't think Mrs. Fallows has confided in you. You may not get on well together. ..."

"Leave my wife out of this!"

"Impossible. As I was saying, it's not likely if she's committed the crime, she'll let you take the blame. Someone else has told you."

"I don't want to discuss it. It's my surgery time. I must go."

Littlejohn stood between the doctor and the door. Their eyes met.

"Say what you've got to say and leave me to my patients."

"Just this. I believe Ned Crowe has been talking to you, doctor. When I mentioned his name on my very first visit, you pretended you didn't know him, when all the time you did. Has he been blackmailing you?"

"No. He's not that sort."

"I thought not. But he told you he'd seen your wife at Gob y Deigan about the time Levis was killed. He threatened that if Johnny Corteen were charged with the crime, he'd tell all he knew. And last night, after I'd been round his place and he began to get scared, he sent for you. ... Don't interrupt. It wasn't a false alarm at all you went out for. You went to *Cursing Stones Farm* in response to a telephone call. He met you there and said he was going to the police to testify about seeing your wife on the spot at the time of the crime. So you waited until he'd got on his way and then you ran him down. ..."

It fell like a bombshell. Fallows's eyes opened wide, he staggered, and then made for the whisky bottle again. Littlejohn was there first, however, seized the bottle and held it. The two men faced each other.

"You're not drinking yourself out of this, doctor. Besides, you've patients to attend to. ..."

"You're ... you're not arresting me, then?"

"You can thank God that Quiggin was on the road as well and, in swerving to avoid him, you didn't hit Ned Crowe hard enough. He's going to get well, but when he's able to, he'll talk. You'd better make a clean breast of it all."

Fallows slumped in a chair, held his head in his hands for a minute, and then suddenly looked up.

"I'd better tell you all I know. I don't know how you've found out, but you're devilish right. I did run down Crowe and I'm ready to take what's coming to me, now or in due course."

"That's nothing to do with me. I'm not on the case. It's Perrick's business. What I'm concerned about is to clear up this stupid idea of yours in covering your wife and to get on with the case. Why did you do it?"

"The day after the body had been identified, Crowe came here. He said he knew all that had happened and if anybody was accused who wasn't guilty, he'd tell the police. I asked him what he meant."

Fallows paused. There were beads of sweat on his forehead and his lips and hands trembled.

"You see, I knew the body was Levis's from the start. I examined it when it was found. There was a gold cufflink hanging from the sleeve of the shirt. Not much but enough for me to make out the pattern before I destroyed it. It was one of a pair my wife had bought him last Christmas when they were friendly. I saw it in her drawer before she gave it to him. I knew it was Levis all the time, and I was glad. I didn't mention it to a soul. Let them find it out themselves! I'm a doctor, not a detective."

"And so …?"

"I wondered what had happened and whether my wife was involved. I may as well tell you, we don't get on. You seem to know. We rarely speak to each other except for decency in front of others or the children. We ought to have separated long ago … but … I …"

"But you love her still?"

Fallows took it on the chin without a word.

"Yes. And besides, there are the children and, after all, I'm a doctor. That's an honour in itself and in our profession … well … one has a standard."

"No need to explain, sir. I understand. What about Ned Crowe?"

"He said he went down to Gob y Deigan that day. About four in the afternoon. He'd seen Levis going there and wondered what he was at. He'd also seen my wife go down the glen."

"Ah! You know who the girl was who'd displaced your wife in Levis's affections?"

"I knew that, too. It was Crowe's daughter. But she was off the Island at the time. Crowe told me. He was half drunk when I saw him the first time. He said he was alone. He was maudlin. Said Margat had left him alone and he didn't know what would become of him."

"What did he say about your wife, doctor?"

"Where was I?"

"Ned Crowe went down spying on Levis and Mrs. Fallows. ..."

"Yes. He went to the top of the cliffs and saw down below; Levis lying on his face and my wife bending over him. Crowe said she'd killed him and he was going to see that nobody else suffered. Then, last night, he said he couldn't keep quiet any longer."

"And you did your damndest still to shield your wife?"

"Are you married? Wouldn't you do the same? After all, whatever she's done to me, she's the mother of my two boys. Is it likely I'd see her hang? And now, you can tell the police here and I'll say I did it and she found the body when she went to meet Levis."

"I won't let you do that. I shall produce the people from *Eairy Cushlan* to prove you were there all the time."

"Why can't you let me alone! I don't want to live any more. I might as well take the rap. Keep out of this. It's *my* business. The local police will never find out unless you tell them."

"Don't be a fool! Whatever the local police do, I'm not giving up this case until the real murderer has been brought to justice. Is your wife in?"

"Yes."

"Then she's probably opening her heart to my friend the Archdeacon. People have a habit of doing that to him. We must have the truth from her. Haven't you spoken to her about it?"

"I tried to, but it started a row right from the start. She got on her high horse, saying I was rubbing in her affair with Levis and trying to be the injured husband. I've tried since, but she won't speak about it."

"My view is that she went there to meet Levis and found him dead when she got there. How long was she there with him, do you know?"

"Only what Crowe told me. He said as soon as he saw her going to the shore, he crossed the field and went to the cliffs. He said she must have come up behind him and killed him right away."

"She probably found him there and thought she was sure to be accused if she gave the alarm. So she crept away and kept quiet."

"I wish to God I could believe it."

"We must ask her…"

The telephone bell rang in the hall.

It was Scotland Yard. Levis had booked two adjacent single rooms for himself and Mrs. Levis at the Rousseau, San Remo.

Littlejohn returned to Fallows.

"That was London who've been speaking to the hotel at San Remo, where Levis was going the day he was killed. It looks as if he was taking Margat Crowe with him, *as his wife*. It was either another of his tricks, or else he'd got it seriously at last and intended marrying the girl."

"The swine! I'm glad he was murdered. He was married already."

"No, he wasn't. That was a tale he told to protect himself. He'd already divorced his wife on the mainland."

"I might have expected it! Perhaps he was involved in unsavoury affairs over the water, just as he was here. Someone might have come over specially to kill him for something."

"It's quite possible, doctor, but why choose Gob y Deigan just at a time when Levis was leaving the Island, and why should a stranger from England choose just the right moment to kill him? I mean, when so many other suspects were in the vicinity."

"I see no reason why not. Opportunity is a grand thing when you're out to kill a man, and opportunity presented itself with a vengeance when Levis went alone to the cliffs at Lynague. Only, unfortunately, my wife was there at the time and unless you either keep quiet about it or solve the case, she looks like being in trouble. Added to that Ned Crowe will tell the truth when he recovers consciousness."

"Perhaps he might tell something we don't expect; something that will give us all a surprise. He may know more about the murder than we think."

"I hope to God he does! I'll leave no stone unturned to keep my wife out of this. In fact, I'd have another go at killing Crowe if I thought he was going to involve her in a sordid shady court affair."

Fallows flushed an angry red as though already in the act of doing violence to Ned Crowe.

If the doctor hadn't had a good alibi, Littlejohn could well have thought him capable of committing murder for love of his unfaithful, sneering wife. *Crime passionel!* Littlejohn looked at the doctor who stood like an animal at bay, trying to get out of his dilemma by hook or crook. A baggy old suit, heavy pale face, bald head with thick grey tufts of hair over his ears, and the hair grown long at one side and brushed across the bald crown to hide its bareness. Brown, almost innocent-looking protruding eyes; you might almost have said he was pop-eyed. And the powerful glasses which gave him a look of Pickwickian benevolence.

Yet Fallows had felled a rival for his wife's affections with a blow and put paid to a promising medical career. He had left a distinguished post on the mainland and taken his wife away to general practice in the Isle of Man in the hope of winning back her love. And then Levis had come along. Dr. Fallows wasn't the stock theatrical type of jealous husband, but he'd shown initiative and acted passionately and violently when goaded. He'd even run down Ned Crowe in a rage, lest his wife should suffer.

"I'm sure she is quite incapable of violence!"

There he was; at it again! Fallows's faith in his wife was past comprehension!

"She can't bear suffering and violence. She's too intellectual and sensitive for that. She's been a good mother. I reckon I'm not much of a man to live with all one's life. I've been too immersed in my job and neglected her."

"Don't take *all* the blame, doctor. It's not fair to think it's all your fault. ..."

Littlejohn shouldn't have said it; he ought to have known better. It only made Dr. Fallows madder.

"What the hell's it got to do with you? What do you know about our life together? I tell you, most of the blame's mine."

The door suddenly opened and Pamela Fallows entered followed by the Archdeacon.

"What blame?"

She overheard it as she entered and strode straight to her husband. Her cheeks were flushed and instead of shifting and wandering all over the place, her eyes were fixed straight on him.

"What blame?"

She repeated it quietly. His hand was resting on the edge of his desk and she clapped her own over it almost violently. Fallows looked surprised, but didn't move.

"He's just blaming himself for making a mess of your lives, Mrs. Fallows."

If Fallows wouldn't speak up for himself, Littlejohn would!

"We'll discuss that later, Leonard. Just now, I'm thinking of what Archdeacon Kinrade's been telling me. Is it true you are trying to take the blame for the murder of Cedric Levis?"

"I'm not taking the blame from anyone. I did it."

"Don't be foolish, Len. You know you were out on a case nearly all day. You hadn't come in at half-past three when I went to meet Cedric. He was leaving the Island with another woman and I wanted my letters back. He told me to meet him at our old rendezvous at four o'clock. When I got there, I found him dead on the beach. You couldn't have been there."

Fallows faced his wife angrily again.

"Why didn't you tell me this before? We could have found a way out of it together. Instead of which, Ned Crowe saw you bending over the body. He's unconscious in hospital after ... after what I did to him to keep him quiet."

Littlejohn intervened again.

"He'll recover very soon. ..."

"Please keep out of this, Inspector. If he recovers, I'll get away with it, but my wife won't. ..."

"I didn't kill Cedric, Len, and they can't do anything to me if I didn't. Can they, Inspector?"

"The law has a way of finding out the truth. We'd better get busy discovering who did do it. Did you see anyone around when you left the body, Mrs. Fallows?"

"No. As soon as I saw he was dead, I was so frightened I ran back to the road and drove home like mad. I didn't look to left or right. I only wanted to get away. But I don't think anyone else was there. That is ... I suppose Crowe was spying somewhere but I didn't see him."

"And the letters. Did you get them?"

"No, Inspector. Cedric's coat was on the ground beside him. He must have been carrying it on his arm. The letters weren't in the pockets; I had the presence of mind to feel in the coat before I ran. They weren't there."

"Did you expect them to be, with a cad like Levis?"

Pamela Fallows made no reply to her husband's taunt.

"How did Levis get to Gob y Deigan? He didn't walk. His car isn't in the garage. He must have used it to get there and yet nothing's been seen of it. Whoever killed Levis removed all traces, including the car. I wonder what he did with it?"

Fallows wasn't concerned with the case any more.

"Will you swear to me you didn't kill Levis, Pam?"

"Of course, I didn't. You didn't think I did, did you?"

"No. I just told the Inspector you weren't cruel and insensitive enough. No; I never believed that."

"All the same, I think it was very sweet of you to try to take the blame and shield me. Thank you, Len."

"Don't, for God's sake, thank *me*. I'd do it again. I'd kill anyone who dared accuse you. I'd ..."

Fallows was going off the deep end again!

"Don't the pair of you think you could get out of this difficulty better if you pulled together?"

The Archdeacon looked from one to the other as he said it.

"I'm grateful, sir, but I don't need your help in peace-making. It's my fault. I've been too immersed in my work. My wife's still young and wants to enjoy life. I've been a bit of a bore, I know. I'll try in future ..."

"Oh, Len, stop it! It's all my fault."

"Don't start quarrelling again, you two. Perhaps the parson and I had better leave you to thrash it out between you."

"Thanks, Chief Inspector. Since I found Cedric Levis dead, I've been scared stiff. I've had enough *fun*, as they call it. I've longed to ask Len for his protection, and to tell him all about it, and ask him what to do."

They weren't a romantic couple, Fallows in his baggy suit and owlish spectacles, and his wife with tears in her eyes, a shiny nose, and a smudge of tracing ink on her cheek. They were too old and disillusioned to play a passionate scene of reconciliation, but as the parson and the Chief Inspector left them, the harassed husband and wife looked ready to make a fresh start if they were given a chance, and Littlejohn had made up his mind to see that they got it.

CHAPTER THIRTEEN
DORA QUINE

"Pam rather made a fool of me with Cedric Levis and I see no reason why I should try to shield her in anything connected with him."

After leaving Dr. Fallows and his wife at Peel, Littlejohn and the parson drove to Douglas.

"It might be a good idea to find a bit of background about Levis from Pamela Fallows's partner. He threw one over, it seems, in favour of the other. Let's get a woman's angle on it," the Chief Inspector said.

Dora Quine was in her office in a block on Prospect Hill, just near the House of Keys. A large room, with plain-wood chairs, two drawing-desks, and the usual odds and ends of an architect's profession; drawing-boards, measuring-staves, filing-cabinets, and lights with green shades. When Littlejohn knocked and entered, Dora Quine was checking some plans with a girl clerk, the only other occupant.

"Could I have a word in private with you, Miss Quine?' said Littlejohn after greetings had passed. Dora Quine seemed quite pleased to see him.

"Just take a walk along the promenade for a quarter of an hour, Carrie," said the young lady. It was a good and forthright solution. Outside, the Archdeacon sat in the car, smoking his pipe and reading the news of the North in the *Ramsey Courier.*

Dora Quine drew up a chair to the fire and told Littlejohn to do the same. She lit a cigarette and he his pipe. They might have been friends for years. She wore a smart green smock over her costume. It suited her. Away from Pamela Fallows with her dominant personality, Dora Quine was quite attractive. Small, well-built, dark, with regular features, a straight nose and a good complexion tanned by the sun and wind, she might, had she been an inch or two taller, have reminded you of those comfortable, plump, classical beauties beloved of the Lord Leighton school of painters. There was nothing melancholy about her, however. No *Last Watch of Hero!* She seemed to enjoy life thoroughly. She poured out a cup of tea from a pot on the hob for the Chief Inspector and, without asking his preferences, added a dollop of Swiss milk from a tin to the dark fluid.

"We've just brewed it."

"I hope you'll forgive this intrusion, Miss Quine, and also any personal questions I might ask you. I've no authority whatever for doing this. In fact, you might think I've a devil of a cheek. But it's second nature to me to want to tidy up a case properly, and I'm curious to know who killed Cedric Levis."

"So am I, Mr. Littlejohn. I don't mind what you ask and I'll try to answer. What do you want to know?"

"You were, I believe, friendly with Levis at one time."

Dora Quine laughed. It might have been a huge joke.

"Who told you that?"

"Things get about here, don't they?"

"I'll say they do. Yes, I once had the honour of having my name in Mr. Levis's notebook and, I think, my telephone number, as well. I was one of his lady friends. He wanted it to go farther, and that's why we parted company."

"Not because Pamela Fallows cut you out, then?"

"You don't believe in wrapping things up, do you, Inspector?"

"I warned you, Miss Quine. I'm trying to get at what I want to know in the quickest possible way. I hope you don't mind."

"Not at all. No. It was more or less all over between Cedric and me before Pamela ever came on the scene. I wasn't in the least heartbroken when they took up together, though, I must say, I didn't approve of their carryings-on. Leonard Fallows is a bit stuffy, but he didn't deserve *that*, and he's been better about it than Pam ever deserved."

"Did he ever talk to you about it?"

"He used to ask me where she was whenever I met him about the place. I knew what he was thinking. I once told him quite plainly that I wasn't his wife's keeper, even if I was her partner."

"And their carryings-on? What do you mean by that?"

"Pam Fallows and Cedric Levis were alike in one thing. They spared no expense or pains to get their own way. Levis met me, for example, at a dance at the Villa Marina here. He bore all the signs of being smitten at once. So he had a wing added to his already adequate bungalow at Bradda and got me to do the job, just so that he could have me around and take liberties ... or so he thought. He got to calling here for me and taking me to Port Erin to his place on one pretext or another ... studying plans, surveying the site, helping him to make up his mind on this or that scheme. On the way, he'd want to stop for lunch somewhere. Then it got to slipping an arm round my waist in the car, inviting me to dinner-dances in the evening, buying a lot of wine, and then suggesting we stayed the night at the hotel, because he felt it wasn't safe to drive home after so much alcohol. I left him there and drove home myself in his car. After that, I brushed him off. I'm engaged, you see, and I thought things had gone far enough."

"I understand."

"I don't wear a ring, because my fiancé hasn't been home yet to buy me one, that's all. He's in Canada in a job. We were friends before he left, and he proposed by post. You naturally wouldn't expect him to send a ring all that way. We're being married in spring."

"I hope you'll be very happy, Miss Quine."

"There's no reason why we shouldn't. He's Manx. Name of Mylchreest. But that doesn't answer your questions. Any more, Mr. Littlejohn?"

"How did you and Pamela Fallows get together?"

"She fell for Levis, it seems. They met somewhere and she was completely smitten. Husband, children went completely by the board. She *had* to have him. She was very ingenious about it and paid a lot for the experience. She must have found out that I was working on the bungalow at Bradda and one day she called here and asked about coming in with me. I was busy at the time and guessing she might have heard I was getting married soon, I thought she might have the idea of taking over later. She paid me five hundred for a share. The money was welcome and she was well qualified and smart at the job. But all she wanted at the time was to get to Bradda and Levis. She had, as I say, a way with her. She'd soon captivated Cedric, though she didn't reckon with his light and fickle fancy. Before long it was on the rocks and Pamela found herself left in the lurch."

"Who was Levis's new love?"

"I don't know. It was said she was a girl from the other side of the Island. I heard she was a good-looking, young one. Then Levis disappeared. After that, there was no doing any good with Pam. You'd have thought she was really in love with him, in spite of his being such a bounder."

"Or that she knew something about his disappearance?"

Dora Quine's eyes opened wide.

"You're not suggesting that she ...?"

"No. But she might have known or suspected something about what had gone on."

"Everybody thought at first that Levis had left the Island and gone abroad."

"Had he talked about it, then?"

"Oh, yes. He was going on the Continent. He'd told his housekeeper and she soon spread it around."

Littlejohn rose and put his empty cup on the desk under the window. There was a boarding-house over the way and from the second floor a woman was shaking an eiderdown. A man and his wife and two children were ringing the bell at the front door, their suitcases in a line on the doorstep. *Mrs. Mulloy. Sea View. Apartments.* A card in the window, *Vacancies.* Littlejohn casually wondered where they saw the sea from. ... Below, in the street, a thin stream of passengers from the boat which must just have docked, was winding its way uphill.

"Where were you on the afternoon of August 21st, Miss Quine?"

He turned and said it suddenly. Dora Quine looked quite taken aback. Her smile faded and her eyes grew angry.

"You're not suggesting that I had anything to do with Levis's death, are you?"

"No. That would presuppose you were a woman scorned, if you'll forgive my putting it that way. You weren't, and never had been in love with Levis, so revenge doesn't enter into it. Did you ever go with him to his cottage, or caravan, or whatever he called it, at Gob y Deigan, Miss Quine?"

A change had come over Dora Quine. Much of her self-confidence and good humour had gone. She was worried about how much Littlejohn already knew!

"This isn't fair, Inspector. I've already told you, I'm going to be married. It's not right to suggest that…"

"You did go down to Gob y Deigan, though?"

"Yes. He said he wanted me to see the spot. He'd a sort of summer house, a wooden place there, and thought of erecting a brick one. I went. He tried getting fresh and I told him I was going home. And I did…in his car…and he'd to walk part way and take a bus the rest."

"What kind of a car was it?"

"A Bentley. He didn't do things by halves."

"Have you seen it since he died?"

"What a funny question."

"Not very funny. It's completely disappeared. He must have gone to Gob y Deigan in it and met his death there, but the car was never found. What happened to it?"

"Don't ask me. I didn't take it."

"Do you think Pamela Fallows capable of murdering Levis?"

"No."

"Why?"

"She's too fastidious, and all the time I've known her I've never seen her violent or even in a temper. She is normally as cold as ice. I wonder how Levis found her? I never knew her anything but frigid and just a bit scornful of any show of emotion. She's certainly not a killer."

"So her husband says, too."

"You've even asked Leonard! She doesn't deserve a man like Fallows. She treats him like a dog."

"Perhaps after Levis she'll change her mind and be a good wife in the future. Meanwhile, you haven't told me where you were the day Levis died."

She grew flustered again.

"I don't know. It's so long since."

"Please think again. It might be most useful."

"I can't see in what way."

"Have the local police questioned you at all, Miss Quine?"

"Several times. Inspector Perrick has thoroughly grilled me, I can tell you."

"And he didn't ask where you were on August 21st?"

"Yes. Inspector, you're a fearful nuisance with your questions. You've caught me out because I told Mr. Perrick I was here in the office alone and I guess I should have told you the same when you asked."

"You weren't here?"

"Look here, Inspector, you don't suspect me ...?"

"No. Why should I?"

"I thought you might still think I loved Cedric. Well I didn't. I never loved him. He'd a sort of fascination ... like a snake, but I got out of the toils in time. I swear I didn't do it."

"All the same, why keep trying to put me off the track of where you were at the time I mentioned?"

"If you aren't the official police, you can keep it dark if I tell you. You won't let it get out, unless it's a matter of life and death?"

"I'll see. I shall use my own discretion, you know."

"I hope you don't think I'm mean and a sneak when I tell you, but I was at Gob y Deigan."

"Ah! Now we're learning things. Go on."

"I'd nothing to do with the crime, though. That morning I was down at Peel, at Pam's place. She has an office there where she does some of our work. Leonard was on his rounds and suddenly the telephone bell rang for her. She closed the door as she went out to take it, but I crept up, gently opened it again, and listened. It sounds all so mean here, in cold blood, but then it was frightfully exciting. You see, I knew Cedric was leaving the Island and I wondered if he was wanting to see Pam again before he went. It was Cedric on the 'phone!"

"And he wanted to meet Mrs. Fallows?"

"I heard her say she couldn't and she didn't want.? Then he said something else and she called him a beast. Finally, she said something like 'If you bring them with you, I'll be there at four, but I shall just collect them and go...' I hurried back and she came in the room again. She looked angry and excited, more passionate than I'd ever seen her. I left just after noon, lunched, and went down to Gob y Deigan in good time."

"May I ask why, Miss Quine?"

"I couldn't help myself. I know it sounds dreadful spying on my partner, but I thought it was all starting over again and that perhaps Levis was running away with Pamela... taking her with him on the Continent. You see, as I said before, Dr. Fallows is older than Pam and a bit stodgy, but he's so decent... well... I had to make sure he wasn't going to be fooled again. Say what you like about it, Inspector, but that's it."

"I'm not particularly interested in your motives, just now, Miss Quine. That's your own business. But I'm keen to know what you saw at Gob y Deigan. Why didn't you tell Inspector Perrick what you're telling me?"

"It didn't seem of any importance. I didn't see the crime or anything. All I saw was Levis, strolling on the

GEORGE BELLAIRS

little beach there, waiting. Inspector Perrick is so severe
and domineering, I was afraid to say much, lest he took
me off to prison or something. So I simply put him off by
saying I was here."

Her eyes grew wide and appealing and Littlejohn smiled
as he thought of her giving Perrick such a look in similar
circumstances, only with a different tale.

"What did you see, if you didn't see the crime?"

"I saw Levis, as I said, waiting. He'd his coat over his arm
because of the hot weather and kept looking up the path
from the glen as though he expected somebody. Then just
as I'd settled to wait and see Pam arrive, I saw a man crossing the field to the edge of the cliffs. I was at the top of the
glen, hidden by gorse bushes from where I expected Pam
would come, but the man who was approaching would see
me if I didn't move. The result was, I'd to creep round the
other side of the bush where I couldn't see a thing, except
Pam just passing."

"Let's get this straight. Who was the other man you saw?"

"A short stocky man, like a fisherman, who came from
the farm near Gob y Deigan. ..."

"Ned Crowe."

"I don't know his name."

"The man approached you, and to avoid being seen, you
moved round the bush."

"Yes."

"Which cut off your view of the beach and Levis, but
gave you still a sight of the glen and Pam Fallows when she
arrived?"

"Yes."

"Did she arrive long after Crowe?"

"Five minutes."

"Did you see Crowe return?"

"No. He must have gone down the cliffs. He wasn't about when I left and he hadn't gone back the way he came."

"So you saw neither him nor Levis again?"

"No. Only Pam. She went down the glen. I daren't move because I didn't want to meet her or the man or Levis coming back. I just stayed put. Then Pam came running back, stumbling and scrambling to the road. She was as white as a sheet and I've never seen her in such a state of panic. I thought Levis had been trying something on...assaulted her, or something. It was only when I heard he'd been killed that it all came back."

"Why didn't you tell the police?"

"What was there to tell?"

"You were apparently the last to see Levis before he was killed. Either the man from the farm or some other intruder murdered him, and Pam Fallows found his body on the shore when she arrived."

"Who says she did?"

"She told me. I've questioned her."

"I didn't dare tell the police. I don't know why I'm telling *you*. I don't want my part as spy on my own friend to be made public. I hope you're going to keep your word, Mr. Littlejohn, and not spill the beans unless it's absolutely necessary."

"I'm watching this case and if anybody is likely to suffer through your silence I shall have to tell Perrick. I'll have to think about it and if I decide the facts of your case are vital, I shall ask you to go to the police and make a clean breast of it."

"Thank you so much, Mr. Littlejohn. I'm very grateful."

"Can you think of anyone else who might have had it in for Levis?"

"I can't. He's gallivanted with a lot of women over on holiday, I do know that, and got a bad name on the Island, but I can't think of anybody who might wish to kill him."

"Not even Dr. Fallows?"

"Len? Whatever makes you think that? Len's too detached and above that sort of thing."

"But he still loves his wife."

"No doubt about that, but Len's not a killer. Besides, he's a doctor."

Littlejohn wondered what that had to do with it and remembered the passion with which Fallows had defended his wife and threatened her accusers.

"Well, thank you for telling me a straight tale, Miss Quine. It's been a great help. I'll let you know if I want you to to repeat it to Inspector Perrick."

"Uh! I hope you don't. You're much easier to talk to than Mr. Perrick. He's as hard as nails and hangs on like a terrier. I know he's a first-rate detective, but he might be a bit more human. He's just a machine."

"I find him very helpful and I like him."

"He's suffered a lot, I know. He was going to marry a WREN girl he met here during the war and she went back to London to buy her trousseau and was killed in a raid. They say they didn't even find the body. He's never looked at a woman since; just lived for his job."

"And you say he isn't human! He must find comfort in his work and he's a wise man. I wish I had him at Scotland Yard. We need men like him."

The girl known as Carrie now returned, rather nervously, for her walk had taken an hour instead of a quarter. She had met a bank clerk on the promenade, and love's young dream had made time seem short. The youth was now suffering a much less hearty welcome from his manager. ...

"Thanks again, Miss Quine, and good-bye."

"Good-bye, Inspector. I hope you don't think I've been disloyal to Pam talking as I have done. Pam rather made a fool of me with Cedric Levis, and I see no reason why I should try to shield her in anything connected with him."

She almost whispered the last part to prevent Carrie's overhearing, but she needn't have worried. Carrie was still in a happy daze.

Littlejohn paused on the mat.

"A fool? I thought you didn't care, Miss Quine."

"I didn't, but she was so mad to get Cedric to herself, she didn't mind making me small when we were all together. I used to see the builder's men eyeing us, looking at me almost pityingly, and then muttering out of the corners of their mouths about us. It wasn't nice. Pam might have been a bit more discreet. That's all I meant."

In the car below, the Archdeacon was asleep. His gentle snores mingled with those of Meg on the back seat. The dog awoke first and her joyful noises roused the parson.

"Well? Had a good interview, Littlejohn?"

"A puzzling one. Dora Quine didn't want Levis herself because she's getting married next spring. But she was annoyed that Levis should suddenly switch his interest from her to Pamela Fallows, all the same. Her pride was hurt, I guess. That made her rather more talkative to me than the police. I mean the official ones."

"And did you get any useful information from her?"

"Yes. She, too, was at Gob y Deigan on the fatal afternoon that Levis was murdered there."

"Another!"

"That's right. Only she didn't see much. She overheard Mrs. Fallows making a reluctant appointment with Levis for four o'clock ... presumably to get the letters she told us of ... and Miss Quine followed it up by appearing there herself. She says she wanted to be sure Pam and Levis weren't going to take up their affair where they'd left off and she was anxious that Dr. Fallows shouldn't be wronged again. All of which may be quite true, or it may have been a little morbid but perfectly human and feminine curiosity; or again, jealousy prompting Miss Quine."

"But she's engaged!"

"Her fiancé's in Canada and they've got engaged by post. I'm not for a moment suggesting she's giving him a double deal or being in any way disloyal to him, but she admits that Levis was fascinating. So is Dora Quine. Given, say, two more inches, she would be extremely beautiful. Her small stature is a bit out of proportion to her development. ..."

"Really, Littlejohn!"

"*Yes, sir!* Levis must have found her very attractive, but she also had a conscience and she repulsed his unseemly advances, as they used to say in the old melodramas. Or was it dastardly suggestions? However, she was flattered and felt Pamela Fallows had made a bit of a fool of her when she stole Levis away. But the main point is this: before Pamela arrived on the scene to meet Levis, Ned Crowe had, according to Dora Quine, arrived and, apparently gone down to the beach. That's not what Crowe told Dr. Fallows. He told Fallows he arrived and found Levis dead and Pamela bending over him."

"Which means that Dora saw Levis alive just as Ned Crowe arrived, and he was dead shortly after Pamela got there. Crowe saw it all, the murder included, or else ..."

"Yes. Or else, Crowe killed Levis. And the motive stares us in the face. Margat was going away with Levis and Crowe killed him to prevent it."

"And Crowe is in hospital and likely to talk at any time and throw the blame on Mrs. Fallows!"

CHAPTER FOURTEEN
A JUMP AHEAD

I t was late afternoon when Littlejohn and the Archdeacon arrived back at Grenaby. From the distance, the place looked dead or asleep. All the doors shut and not a soul about. Then, as they crossed the bridge, it was as if everybody had been awaiting their return. Women came out and waved to them as they passed the cottages, Joe Henn emerged from his summer-house, locally known as *the 'ut*, and gesticulated to indicate that he wanted a talk with them, and Meg awoke from a deep sleep on the back seat, began to bark joyfully, and roused an answering chorus of other dogs. The wanderers were home!

Mrs. Littlejohn was out at tea with a neighbouring farmer's wife and Mrs. Keggin, the housekeeper, received them rather bitterly.

"You didn't say you were stayin' out for lunch and I made it and it spoiled? And that man's been again. He left this."

She handed Littlejohn a note written on a sheet of a pocket-book. It was from Perrick.

Dear Chief Inspector,
    I called and sorry I missed you. Ned Crowe is better, but unable to speak or remember much. I tried

to get something out of him but no use. A constable at his bedside, just in case, but the doctor won't allow visitors. Crowe seems to have turned religious and keeps asking for his Bible. I will get it for him from Cursing Stones. On my way to see Dr. Fallows. Will call on my way back.

S.P.

"When did he call, Mrs. Keggin?"

"He's not been gone half an hour. He waited a bit an' kept askin' where you'd gone. I didn't know, so couldn't tell him. Then he wrote the note and went off."

The Archdeacon looked bothered.

"I think I ought to go and see Ned Crowe, in spite of what Perrick says. The note says he's asking for his Bible. He must be seeking spiritual comfort or suffering remorse for something. There ought to be someone there to help him. I'll get Looney to drive me down whilst you wait here for Perrick's return, Littlejohn."

And he was at the telephone hiring Teddy Looney's old car before they could stop him.

Before they had finished a hasty tea, the rattletrap shook its way up the drive and bore off the parson to Noble's Hospital in Douglas. Littlejohn was left to wait alone with the dog until Perrick returned. He paced the floor restlessly, something quite unusual for him. Picking up ornaments, putting them down again; taking out books from the shelves and replacing them after scarcely reading the titles; examining the pictures on the walls with half-seeing eyes. He was quite at sea in the case!

Had Fallows cooked up an alibi for himself and persuaded the people at *Eairy Cushlan* to say he'd been there all day? The idea was preposterous and yet...Littlejohn shook himself. To doubt the integrity of a decent old man like Billy-Bill-Illiam and his nice daughter was almost a sin.

Could it have been Johnny Corteen, after all? With the clannish ways of fisherfolk against landsmen, had Johnny got support from his friends in Peel and was his alibi a fake?

Or Pamela Fallows? Had she murdered Levis at the moment when Dora Quine and Ned Crowe weren't looking? Did Fallows himself know the truth?

Or Ned Crowe?

Or...?

A thought struck Littlejohn, a fantastic idea, and he hastily thrust it aside, like someone who hides a shameful thing. The room seemed to grow cold, a vague fear filled him, although he was a brave man. The dog was looking up at him with a fond, possessive look, and he felt glad she was there and grateful for her company and her love. But he could not put from his mind the figure which haunted it. A figure with its back to him, crouched over the oars of Ned Crowe's little boat, straining out to sea, with a grisly cargo of death on the other seat.

The gate clicked and he saw Perrick's face smiling at him as he walked jauntily up the path. Littlejohn felt thankful for the Manx Inspector's company and, before he could ring the bell, hastened to the door and greeted his colleague on the mat.

"Hullo, Perrick. I didn't hear you arrive."

"I left the car just down the road. Thought I'd be stretching my legs a bit. I've been crouched in it all day."

An indescribable feeling of relief filled the Inspector as Perrick joined him. He couldn't understand it. It was as if danger had been around and had, with the arrival of law and order, fled away.

Mrs. Keggin ran to the hall.

"I didn' hear the bell...."

She, too, looked queer and eyed Littlejohn curiously.

"Go inside, Perrick. Glad to see you and sorry we weren't in when you called. Could you do with some tea?"

"I wouldn't say no, sir. I've had a gruelling day with few results. I feel whacked."

"I'm the same. I just can't see any way through this case."

Perrick's worried brow cleared.

"That's a comfort. I'd hate for you to spot some clue, or find a solution, without me having kept abreast. Not that I've had your experience, sir, but I'd like to show you that I'm worthy of my job."

"Of course. I'll see about some tea."

Mrs. Keggin was busy already, brewing, and cutting up soda buns. She eyed Littlejohn with a kind of relieved affection.

"I'm that glad you're all right, sir."

"What do you mean, Maggie?"

She passed her old hand across her brow.

"I felt danger for ye, sir."

"Danger? Whatever for?"

"I don't really know. But ye see, I've got the Sight, sir. What they call the Second Sight. It runs in the family. It's known all over that we have it in our family.... The Kaighens, of Michael, sir. Ask anybody. I was a Kaighen before I married Keggin. Not much change, Kaighen to Keggin."

"Now don't try to put me off. What was it, Maggie? What did you see?"

"It wasn't what I see, sir. It was what I *felt*. Us that have the Sight knows things that's comin'. I *felt* for you, master, *felt* the danger and I couldn' do nothin' about it. It's gone now. But take care. I'm sure there's danger for you."

Littlejohn took up the tray she had prepared and stood for a moment.

"Don't worry, Maggie. I can take care of myself. I've been in danger before. I'll be all right."

In the brief minute, as he carried the tray from the kitchen to where Perrick was modestly sitting by the fire, Littlejohn felt baffled, not by the case, this time, but by what Maggie Keggin had said. By what she called the Sight, she had sensed danger for him and, at the same time, he had felt it, too!

"Any luck to-day, sir?"

Perrick stirred his tea and took an appreciative gulp of it.

"No, Perrick. Every idea seems to lead to a dead end. What about you?"

Perrick chewed his soda-cake meditatively.

"I've told Dr. Fallows he'd better not leave the Island. I'm not satisfied about him."

"Why?"

"I called to see him and he told me, or as good as told me, to do my damnedest. Just like he did when I called there with you. Unless he talks, and talks quickly, he's going to find himself in queer street. He won't even tell me where he was when Levis was killed."

"I know where he was."

Perrick held himself absolutely still and looked Littlejohn in the face. He was thoroughly taken aback.

"You *know*, sir? Then you're a jump ahead of me, at last. I thought we were keeping abreast. *What* do you know?"

Littlejohn took the poker and stirred the fire into a blaze.

"I was going to tell you. As for getting a jump ahead, I really ought not to be jumping at all. My work on this case really ended when Johnny Corteen was in the clear, because that's what the parson asked me to look into. By the way, *is* Johnny in the clear? Had he an alibi for the afternoon of August 21st, as well as the night?"

Perrick looked impatient.

"Of course he had. He was boozing most of the day with his pals, celebrating his return. There was one or another of them with him from morning till night. What about Fallows?"

"He was up at *Eairy Cushlan* from just before noon till eight in the evening...."

"What! Why didn't he say so, then, instead of making a fool of me?"

"I rather think he was trying to take the spotlight off his wife. You know Pam Fallows was a discarded mistress of Levis. It might be that her husband thought *she* murdered him. Ned Crowe had told the doctor she was down at *Cursing Stones* on the day... the very afternoon Levis was killed."

The empty cup rattled in Perrick's saucer and Littlejohn, glancing at the Inspector, saw that he was trembling with anger.

"Everybody seems to be pulling my leg, Chief Inspector! How did you come to know all this?"

Littlejohn told Perrick of the note on the doctor's visiting-pad; of *Eairy Cushlan*; of the testimony of Billy-Bill-Illiam; of the evidence of Fallows and his wife....

"And what about Mrs. Fallows?"

Perrick seemed to hold his breath, waiting for the last link in the chain.

"You'd better have another word with Dora Quine, who was also at Gob y Deigan on the fatal afternoon."

"To hear people talk, the scene of the crime must have been like a football match! Everybody there when it happened, but nobody looking! Who the hell *did* do it?"

"I haven't the faintest notion, Perrick. It looks as if Ned Crowe might have an idea. In fact, he might have done it himself. Has it occurred to you that he has no alibi? And that he'd every motive in the world for killing Levis?"

"Motive? Why should Crowe kill Levis?"

"Did you know his daughter?"

There was a pause; a long silence. The clock ticked solemnly and the dog snored on the hearth. That was all.

"Well! I'll be damned! Of course, I knew his daughter. Margat, was she called? I hadn't thought of that! How did you come across all this information?"

"The neighbouring farm to *Cursing Stones*, the Kellys'. . . . We took tea there one day and Margat was mentioned. She's left the Island. She was Levis's latest light of love. He threw Pamela Fallows over for her. And when he was murdered, he was on his way to join her on the mainland, and together they were going to San Remo."

Perrick's face was a study. Littlejohn felt a bit sorry for him. He was like the apprentice who had tried to teach a master-hand how to do the job, and had found himself lacking in the end.

"You make me feel an amateur, sir. A step ahead of me all the time! You think Ned Crowe might have killed Levis, then? I wouldn't blame any father doing the same to protect his daughter. And no wonder he's turned religious and asked for his Bible. . . ."

"Did you get it for him?"

"No, sir. Mrs. Kelly had been before me. She called at Noble's this morning and the sister said Crowe had been asking for his Bible. Mrs. Kelly couldn't see him, but she went back to *Cursing Stones* and got in the house with a key Ned Crowe once gave her. When he was out, she used to feed his hens and even do a bit of milking for him. She took it back to Noble's and probably gave it to him. Her husband saw me leaving *Cursing Stones* and said she'd just gone back with it to Douglas on the bus. She's a meddling fool!"

"Whatever for? It seems a charitable action…"

"It'll get Crowe all upset. He'll get worked up religiously now. So far, he's refused to answer any questions and the doctor says it'll be days before we can press him, because of his head. He gets confused. He'll be more confused after reading the Book of Job! I wish people wouldn't interfere. I'd have taken the Bible with me when I went to see him, and I'd have got in a question or two by asking him why he wanted… well… why he wanted the consolation of religion, if you see what I mean, sir."

"Yes, I do."

"How do you think it'll all end, sir? There's no clue, not a trace of one. Mrs. Fallows might have done it out of revenge, or Ned Crowe to save his daughter, but if they don't confess, how can we hope to bring home the crime to them?"

This was a different Perrick from the buoyant Inspector who had first met Littlejohn, ready to arrest Johnny Corteen and secure a conviction right away!

"The only thing to do, Perrick, is to keep plugging away patiently. You have your suspects, your ideas of what went on. Keep at them till sooner or later just that little bit of information, just that little straw in the wind indicates the right trail. Then follow it. You can't think of putting the case in the unsolved files yet, you know."

Perrick sighed.

"I guess you're right, sir. It's a bit discouraging to find all the paths lead into the sea, as they say over here; all the trails peter out. We're not beaten yet. Or rather, *I'm* not. You'll be leaving us soon, I expect. We can't keep you here for good, although I'd like it. But if the Chief is to ask for

Scotland Yard to help, I'll have to confess to him that I'm beat. I wouldn't like that just yet."

"No. You take my advice and plod along patiently. You'll hit the right trail before you've done. I'll be here a few days more and if I can help, let me know."

"You'll be in the same boat as I am now. We know the suspects, but we can't pin anything on them. By the way, where's the Archdeacon? I haven't seen him around."

"When we got your message about Ned Crowe turning religious, the parson went off to Noble's just to see if he could do anything for Ned, spiritually."

Perrick jumped to his feet in anger.

"Jumping Jehoshaphat! First the scene of the crime's like a football match, and now it's Noble's Hospital! Why the hell can't they leave Ned Crowe alone? Parson Kinrade'll be there reading and praying with Crowe and upset him that much that he'll not be fit to tell me a thing…"

"On the contrary, he might get something from Ned that neither of *us* could get. The parson's got a way with him you and I haven't got. People tell him what's in their hearts, whereas with the police they just get stubborn and shut up. If you care to wait, the Archdeacon won't be long, I'm sure."

"All right, then. I only hope he hasn't upset Crowe, that's all. Are you holding the fort alone, then?"

"Yes. The dog and I. Mrs. Keggin's gone to the farm for the milk and my wife's out to tea. They'll be back soon."

"There are one or two things I'd like to discuss with you then, before they come back. …."

Perrick rose and stood with his back to the fire. He looked ready to expound some long theory or other, but the dog interrupted him by raising her head and barking gruffly at first, and then with added vigour.

"What's wrong with the dog?"

"There must be somebody coming. She's sounding the alarm."

Perrick strode to the window.

"Yes. It's that gasbag Henn from the village. What does *he* want?"

Joe Henn, the parson's neighbour, was making his way up the path. He wore old clothes and no collar. Just a neck-tie round his scraggy throat, and a bright brass stud shining in the neckband of his shirt. An old cloth cap on his head. On the way, he kept pausing to look at this and that in the garden. Littlejohn met him at the door.

"Hullo, Mr. Henn."

"*Kynnas-tha-shu,* as we say in Manx. That means, how d'ye do. ..."

Mr. Henn had come from Lancashire long ago, but pretended to those who didn't know it, that he was a native.

"You on your own, Inspector?"

"No, Mr. Henn. Inspector Perrick's here with me. Come in, won't you?"

"Not if you're busy. It'll do another time. *Traa dy lioor,* plenty of time, as we say in Manx. If Inspector Perrick's with you, it's all right. You're safe. But I think I ought to tell you, there's been prowlers round here that's up to no good. Ask Perrick. He'll know. There's not much here the police don't know."

"Come in, then. We'll talk to Perrick."

"No. I'm not fond of the police myself. That is, exceptin' present company. I've had one or two quarrels with 'em. You remember how last time you was over here, they trampled all over my garden huntin' for clues without so much as a by-your-leave, and they even let one of the criminals drive a car over my garden and park it in the 'ut I built. But when intruders come pinchin' the fruit in my garden, me gooseberries

and raspberries, me apples and me pears...even me daf-
fodil bulbs...there's no police about. Never there when
they're wanted. I went to Douglas and gave 'em a piece of
me mind, and now them and me's not so friendly. I'll come
another time, thank you. But just you ask Perrick about the
prowlers round this place."

Joe Henn turned and slowly made off the way he'd come.

"I'll be seein' you, Inspector. I'll call again. You must
come across and see me garden, too, and the 'ut I built. ... So
long, then."

"So long, Mr. Henn."

Littlejohn scratched his head. Joe Henn was getting
more and more eccentric! Usually you couldn't get rid of
him; now he was anxious to be off!

Prowlers! Littlejohn remembered the reputation
Grenaby had for strange goings-on. Ghostly prowlers, in fact.
There were at least half a dozen regular haunters accred-
ited to the village. Jimmy Squarefoot, a sort of man with a
pig's head, the *Purr Mooar*, as the natives called him. And
a satyr, the *phynnodderree*, who haunted the bushes. To say
nothing of the water-horse, the *cabbyl-ushtey*, who appeared
in the river now and then; the *buggane*, or evil one; and the
night-man, the *dhooiney-oie*, who called to foretell disaster.
Prowlers, indeed! The place was alive with them!

"What's *he* after?"

Perrick stood in the doorway of the dining-room watching Littlejohn intently.

"Henn says there are prowlers around, and *you* know all
about it. What's he mean?"

"Oh that! Henn's got a bee in his bonnet. The lads keep
coming and ravaging his garden and he thinks we ought to
have a constable perpetually there. An all-the-year-round
watch. He never eats the fruit he grows. He can't do. There's

too much of it. It does no harm to have some of it pinched, although it's immoral for a policeman to give vent to such sentiments. ... Half of it rots away. The kids might as well take it. Is that all he wanted?"

"That seemed to be all. He was embarrassed when he heard you were here."

"I'm not surprised. I was the one who interviewed him when he came to complain in Douglas. We'd a right ding-dong row."

The dog bounded from the house, along the path, and to the gate. Mrs. Littlejohn was returning with Maggie Keggin, whom she'd picked up on her way home. Littlejohn was glad to see her. She brought a cheerful spirit to the depressed atmosphere of crime and criminals and unsolved cases that had been haunting him. ...

Far away the rattle and whine of Teddy Looney's car, coming nearer every minute, judging from the growing noise.

Evening, the *little everin'* of the Manx, was approaching. The sun was sinking over the high hills of the interior, and the quietness which falls before dark was settling over the village. The odd noises seemed intensified. The clanking of a milk churn somewhere, the distant siren of a ship at sea, the rattle of someone's buckets as they fed the calves, the lowing of cattle turning out of the cowsheds after milking. ... Then the crash and thud of Looney's rattletrap at the gate.

"Hullo, Perrick?"

The Archdeacon appeared, his cheeks pink and his white hair and whiskers a bit dishevelled from his wild ride.

"Hullo, sir. Did you see Ned Crowe?"

"Only for a minute, Perrick. There's a constable there with him. I don't know why you're doing that. It hardly seems fair."

Perrick looked ready for a hasty reply and then controlled himself.

"You see, sir, Crowe might have important evidence about the murder and we can't be sure when he'll talk. Our officer stays with him just in case he gets lucid and says something that matters. We can't help it, and our man's quiet and doesn't interfere."

"I see. Crowe still seems very dazed. He keeps asking God to forgive him, in a sort of delirium. He's evidently got something on his mind. I read him a passage or two from the Bible, which his good neighbour, Mrs. Kelly, brought for him, and then we had a little prayer and he settled. There's obviously something upsetting his conscience. I quite understand your anxiety to get a statement from him, though I fear he won't be fit for it for some time."

Perrick nodded his head gravely.

"Someone is going to have to answer for Ned Crowe's accident in due time. But that will all come out when Crowe can talk lucidly."

"Won't you come in for a meal with us, Perrick? You're very welcome."

"No, thank you, Archdeacon. It's very kind of you, but I've still got work to do. Shall I see you to-morrow, Chief Inspector? You know I'll be grateful for all the help you can give."

"Of course. I'll ring you up if I have any ideas, and you do the same if you need me."

"Thank you, sir. Well … good evening to you all …"

Watching him on his way to the gate, Littlejohn thought Perrick's step less jaunty than when he'd arrived. He felt somehow that he'd deflated Perrick and robbed him of some of his self-confidence. The Manx Inspector was putting up a gallant fight, but was gaining no ground.

"What's the matter, Tom?"

His wife took his arm and looked questioningly at his serious face.

"I'm afraid Perrick's getting a bit out of his depth. So am I, for that matter. I can't make head or tail of this case. It eludes me. The murderer was either very lucky or very clever. It's either a perfect crime or a fluke."

"You'll feel better after a good night's rest. ..."

But Littlejohn didn't get his rest that night.

CHAPTER FIFTEEN
THE VALENTINE

It was late when Cromwell rang up Littlejohn to say he had found Margat Crowe at her aunt's house in East Croydon.

"She'd got a job in a local shop and I found her there behind the counter. She absolutely refuses to come back to the Island. ..."

"Why, old man?"

"I had a long talk with her. In fact, I took her out to lunch. After all you'd told me about her running away and going to meet the murdered man and take a trip with him to San Remo, I was able to lead the conversation. I told her Levis was dead. She knew already, of course. It had been in the mainland papers. She said she had booked in at an hotel in Bayswater and he was to pick her up there. When he didn't arrive, she didn't know what to do. She hadn't much money and she naturally thought that Levis had left her in the lurch."

"So she went to her aunt's?"

"Yes. After three days, she went to East Croydon. It seems she's a great favourite with her aunt there. She didn't tell the old lady anything about Levis. Just said she'd had a row with her father and had come to London to get a job. Her aunt took her in. She was too ashamed to go back or even write to her father for the time being. Even now, I can't persuade her to come back to the Isle of Man with me."

"What is she doing?"

"She is in a large stores at present, learning her way about. From what I can gather, they're going to train her to be a mannequin.... She's just the type, you know. A real beauty."

"So I believe. Well, you'd better tell her that her father has met with a serious road accident, is very ill in hospital in Douglas, and is asking for her."

"Is he really very bad?"

"Bad enough. He'll pull through, but you'd better not tell her till you get on the way home. Bring her by 'plane as soon as you can. She ought to have been here long ago. She'll probably turn out a vital witness in this murder case."

"Very good, sir. I'll get her along as soon as I can. Anything else?"

"Only that we'll both be very glad to see you, old man. Also, don't say you're a policeman when you get here. Just a friend of the Archdeacon over for a few days' holiday...."

"I've already told the girl."

"Tell her to keep quiet about it, then... especially on the Island. It won't seem right for me to bring over another man from Scotland Yard when I'm not officially on the case. Come straight to Grenaby when you get to the airport, and bring the girl with you. If I can't meet you myself, I'll send somebody else."

"Right, sir. Good night...."

"Good night, old chap. See you to-morrow."

After supper, they drew round the warm log fire in the parson's study and discussed the only topic in their thoughts.

"They seem a bit baffled by Ned Crowe at the hospital, Littlejohn. I asked the sister about him. He pretends he can't remember anything of what happened in connection with his accident...."

"That, of course, might be quite right, sir. In such cases, the victims often forget events just before they lost consciousness. That is so, isn't it, Letty? You're a first-aider."

"Yes. Quite right. They do."

But the parson shook his head.

"That's not all. He also says he doesn't remember Gob y Deigan on the day of the murder. If what Fallows and Dora Quine say is right, Ned Crowe was there all the time. Now he pretends to have lost his memory about it. And yet, when he asked for his Bible, he told them where to find it at the farm. It just doesn't tally."

"He doesn't *want* to remember; that's it, sir."

"Which looks very suspicious. At present, there's no evidence that Crowe didn't murder Levis himself, Littlejohn. I'm sorry to say it, but that's the only conclusion I can reach."

"The motive was a very strong one. Margat was so obviously going off with Levis. I confess I wouldn't blame Ned Crowe for trying to stop it. He'd every right to protect his daughter."

The parson knocked out his pipe.

"I think I'll go to bed. The way this case runs round and round in circles makes my head ache. Dr. Fallows, Pam Fallows, Ned Crowe...or even Dora Quine. Dora might have been fonder of Levis than she makes out, and have killed him in a fit of jealous rage when she heard he was going away with another woman."

"Margat Crowe should be home to-morrow. When she arrives here, we'll ask her for fuller details of Levis and his affairs, if she knows them. He might have confided in her."

"Could it be, Littlejohn, that Margat had another lover who killed Levis out of jealousy, or to protect Margat?"

"Quite easily. Ned Crowe might have seen him do it and be keeping quiet to save him. In such a case, we've a lot of work to do. We'll have to comb the Island for the missing lover. Anyhow, Margat might be able to throw some light on that to-morrow. We'll sleep on it, shall we?"

"If we can. This case has taken complete possession of me, Littlejohn. I lie awake thinking of it, trying to see the way out, and arriving nowhere."

Maggie Keggin closed the kitchen door, called goodnight to them, and they could hear her mounting the stairs.

"By the way, parson, is Maggie gifted with second sight?"

The Archdeacon sat down again.

"The Sight, they call it over here. Yes. Now don't ask me the metaphysics of it. It's a peculiar phenomenon found among Gaelic peoples. The Highlands of Scotland, for instance, too. It runs in families. Maggie is one of the Kaighens of Michael, a family famous for generations as having 'queer things' running in it. I can't explain it and I'd be tempted to pooh-pooh the whole idea, if Maggie hadn't a time or two told me beforehand things that were going to happen, which eventually have come about. But why do you ask?"

"Just a remark she made this afternoon. She told me about the Sight and said I was in danger.... Or rather, that I'd been in danger and it had passed off."

Mrs. Littlejohn stirred uneasily.

"No need to be afraid, Letty. I'm always in danger. It's my job...."

"All the same, Littlejohn, let it be a warning to you not to take your safety lightly. I often think, myself, how easy it would be for a criminal, as the detective draws nearer to him in establishing guilt, to kill the detective. I wonder why it isn't done more frequently. After all, the police can't be on their guard against violence *all* the time."

"It doesn't often happen, sir, so be easy in your mind. It was strange, however, that after Maggie spoke to me, Joe Henn called to warn me against prowlers. He's done that when I've been here before, though. He believes, of course, that there are a lot of ghostly intruders around Grenaby, doesn't he?"

"Yes. But what in particular did he mean?"

"He didn't say. Perrick was with me at the time, and that seemed to comfort Joe. He thought I was being well looked after, no doubt. He left easy in his mind."

The parson rose again.

"It's rather late to be discussing the supernatural just now. We'll be imagining things. At any rate, you'll have the dog in your room. She'll give the alarm in case of prowlers or intruders. ...."

As a rule, Littlejohn soon got to sleep. He had the capacity for putting aside the cares of the day as soon as he got in bed and this night was no exception. The creaking of the old house settling down after the day, the call of owls, the rush of the water under Grenaby Bridge, and the rustle of the leaves of tall trees overhanging the parsonage did not disturb him. Nor did the snores of Meg, curled up on the mat at his bedside.

Littlejohn didn't seem to have been asleep long when the dog barked. Two or three short wuffs, a protest against noises in the night, that was all. Not the angry alarmed barking against intruders.

"The telephone's ringing," said Mrs. Littlejohn, who always awoke quicker than her husband. Littlejohn hurried into his dressing-gown and ran downstairs.

It was Cromwell again.

"Sorry to disturb you, sir, but I thought I'd better ring and tell you that Margat Crowe has gone. After I spoke to you, I thought I'd go to Croydon right away, tell her, and arrange to pick her up and take her to Northolt first thing to-morrow. When I got there, her aunt said there was a 'phone call for her just after she arrived home from the shop. She didn't know who it was, but it upset Margat. She packed her bag and left right away. She said something about her father being ill and she had to leave at once. Her aunt pointed out that she couldn't travel tonight, but she wouldn't listen. Said she'd let her aunt know all about it later. Then she went off and her aunt couldn't stop her."

"Have you tried the airport bookings? Has she booked for the 'plane in the morning?"

"I tried the B.E.A., but nobody in that name had booked."

"Did you see the booking list?"

"Yes. But I couldn't do much. You see, she might have booked in another name."

"She might have gone back to her old hotel. ..."

"I tried it. She wasn't there. At the same time, I checked that she was there the day Levis was killed. That gives her an alibi. Thought I might as well kill two birds with one stone."

"I'm very grateful, old man. You seem to think of every-thing. All right. You know her. Better be down at Northolt first thing, just in case she's taken panic and is hurrying home. You didn't get a chance to tell her about her father, did you?"

"No."

"In that case, someone else might have forestalled you. We might be worrying about nothing. Perhaps you'll find her on the 'plane to-morrow."

"Yes, but why has she left her aunt's to-night? You'd have thought she'd have slept there and gone off in the morning."

"See what you can find out. I'll ring you again tomorrow or, if it's anything vital, you ring me first. Goodbye, old chap, and thanks again."

Littlejohn replaced the receiver and then took it up again.

"Exchange?"

A sleepy man's voice replied after a pause.

"Yes."

"Were you on duty when the call from London came to Grenaby about eight o'clock this evening?"

"Yes, sir."

"Was there a call to the mainland, to East Croydon, shortly after that call?"

A pause.

"Sorry, sir, I can't answer questions of that sort. It's against the rules."

"This is the police...."

"I beg your pardon, sir?"

"Police. I'm a police officer staying at Grenaby parsonage."

Another pause.

"I'm sorry, sir, but I can't answer you. How am I to know you're police? Anybody might say that. You see what I mean? It's as much as my job's worth."

"I'll come along to the exchange then. It'll probably take me half an hour. You'll let me in, won't you?"

"Certainly, sir. If you can prove you're police, I'll be glad to do all I can."

Littlejohn hastily dressed and got out the car. He found his wife beside him dressed and ready, too.

"I'm coming with you, Tom. All this second sight business and Joe Henn's anxiety make me anxious, too. Two of us will be better than one."

They struck the main road at Colby and Littlejohn took the inland route through Ballasalla, and then past Mount Murray. It was one o'clock and they passed only a solitary car travelling south in the opposite direction from themselves. At Richmond Hill, the lights of Douglas, shining over a calm sea, appeared. Littlejohn forked right through Kewaigue and it was near Kewaigue day-school that he saw another larger car moving at high speed along the old Castletown road which converged with that along which he was travelling. Judging from his own pace, he should meet the crossroads well ahead of the other lonely car....

But just at the corner, the strange vehicle suddenly increased speed and made straight for Littlejohn as he rounded the bend. Luckily, Littlejohn was climbing and as he raised his toe from the accelerator, the gradient helped him as well. Even then, he had to take the footpath, run parallel to the other vehicle, and mount the hedge. Before he could stop to investigate, the large car had righted itself, swept into the main road, and vanished, with all lights extinguished, in the direction of Douglas.

"Are you all right, Letty?"

He put his hand on his wife's arm. She was trembling.

"Yes, I'm all right. Are you? That was deliberately done, Tom. I wish this was over and we were going back home.... It's not safe."

"Don't worry. It soon will be, now. Whoever's guilty is getting rattled, and that means he or she is going to make a slip. That was a big car. Put out his lights as he approached us. Pity. I didn't even see the make."

"It looked like a big taxi to me. Let's get on, Tom, and get back to Grenaby. I'm scared...."

They ran into Douglas and to the Post Office for the telephone exchange. The man on duty was expecting Littlejohn. The Chief Inspector showed him his warrant-card.

"Scotland Yard, eh?"

The operator was a middle-aged man, dressed in flannels with an open-necked shirt. He looked to have been asleep. There wasn't much doing at that time of night.

"Are your lines tapped at all?"

"What do you mean, sir?"

"Does anyone listen in to the calls … the police?"

"Since the murder they have done to certain ones."

"To the mainland, you mean?"

"Yes. Some of the insular exchanges are automatic, but we report any special ones we can, especially to and from the mainland."

"What happens?"

"We report anything special to the police and then, if they want to listen-in, we can switch it over to the police-station, where they can record it if they want."

"My calls to and from Scotland Yard, for example; were those reported or listened to?"

"They were reported along with the rest, sir, but nobody listened-in."

"You just telephone the list to the police?"

"Yes. About every half-hour, if there are any."

"And my incoming call from Scotland Yard to-night, how long after did you report it?"

"Nearly right away."

"I see. And was it followed by another call from this side to Croydon? An East Croydon exchange number?"

"No. There's been nothing out to-night for that."

"Are you sure?"

"Yes. Quite sure."

"In case you've forgotten, let me see your list, please."

The man was up in arms at once. He took a pad from the switch-desk and slipped it in a drawer.

"I'm not allowed. It's against the rules. You've no right to ask."

"Why have I no right?"

"You're not the Island police. You're not on the job and it's not right of you to insist."

"Who told you I'm not on the job?"

"Everybody knows."

"Do they? Very well. Thanks for your help. I won't trouble you any further."

"No offence, sir. But it's as much as my job's worth to break the regulations."

"I don't blame you at all. Have the police been to see you to-night?

"Yes. They generally call to see things are all right. Things get a bit quiet, sir, at this time of night."

Littlejohn turned suddenly on the man.

"Who are you reporting calls to besides the police?"

The operator recoiled.

"Nobody… I tell you, nobody. I won't keep being quizzed like this. It isn't fair. I've my job to do and it's against the rules for me to be interrupted. …."

The buzzer on the switch was going and the man hurried to answer it.

Littlejohn waited.

"Put me through to the police-station, please," he said when the man was free again.

"Very good, sir."

Littlejohn spoke to the officer on duty at the police-station and reported the event at Kewaigue.

"I can't even describe the car, but if any of your men saw it on the road or in Douglas just around one o'clock, you might let me know. You'll look into it, won't you?"

"Of course, sir. I'm sorry it's happened. Was it deliberate?"

"No doubt about it."

"Phew! We'll do our best."

"Let Inspector Perrick know when he comes in, will you?"

"Yes, sir. He's only been gone ten minutes. Shall I ring him up at home and tell him?"

"No. Don't trouble him now, officer. It's late. ..."

Littlejohn was sitting at the switchboard with his instrument plugged in to the police-station. In his younger days he'd done a training spell on telephones at Scotland Yard. Before him were the trunk switches to the mainland. He removed the plug from the local switch and thrust it in the Liverpool one.

"Liverpool. ... Liverpool. ..."

The man on duty hurried to Littlejohn's side.

"What are you doing?"

"Just a minute. ..."

"But it's against..."

"I know. Now please be quiet. Liverpool? Did you book a call to East Croydon from here about eight to eight-thirty? This is the police."

"Just a minute..."

The man at his side didn't know what to do. He looked to be pondering whether or not to use force.

"Yes. ... East Croydon 03452. ... 8.32. ..."

"Thank you very much."

He turned to the agitated operator at his side.

"That's all I wanted to know. Your work is confidential, I agree, and you have to be careful about inquiries. I shall say no more about this and neither will you; not to a soul. You understand?"

"Yes, sir."

"Very well. My visit here is to be forgotten. Understand that, too?"

"Yes, sir."

"Good night, then, and thank you."

All the way home, Littlejohn was silent. He couldn't make head or tail of things. Probably because he didn't know the local background. Perhaps the telephone operator was a relative or good friend of some party to the crime. Fallows, Dora Quine, or the unknown lover of Margat Crowe. Certainly it wasn't Ned Crowe, now. Ned was in Noble's and would never have thought of the car incident at Kewaigue, or been clever enough to find out what went on between Littlejohn and Scotland Yard over the telephone. Or again, the local police might have ordered the man at the switch to remain mum.

Margat Crowe's unknown lover. He'd be the likely man to get in touch with her and warn her not to let the police get hold of her and question her, because then, ten to one, his name would come out.

They dropped down the hill to Grenaby. It was always the same. The peace of the place got you and you forgot the world outside and its crimes and troubles.

The vicar was up and fully dressed, standing at the door with the dog waiting for them.

"Come in, come in. There's a cup of tea for you and a bite of something. You'll need it after your night ride. Have you found out anything?"

"As much as ever.... A dead-end again. We're up against someone very clever, someone who tried to smash us up in a collision on the way."

The Archdeacon threw up his hands in horror.

"Maggie Keggin's Sight seems to be right. I beg you be careful, Littlejohn."

"I will be, sir. Now I know what we're up against, I'll take care."

They ate a hasty snack and drank some tea, and Mrs. Littlejohn left Littlejohn and the Archdeacon together. The old man was obviously eager to say something else to Littlejohn.

"There's just one thing I want to ask you, Littlejohn. It's probably a stupid business, but I must get it off my mind."

"Fire away, sir."

"I went to the hospital and saw Ned Crowe, as you know. And I told you I read a chapter of the Psalms and had a little prayer with him. I used his Bible; the one kind Mrs. Kelly brought for him from *Cursing Stones*... his own Bible. It's a very old one. In fact, it must have been his mother's and her father's before her, for I remember looking at it with curiosity.

Jamys Kelly is my name,
Peel-town is my station.
The Isle of Man's my dwelling-place,
And Christ is my salvation.

That's what is inscribed in it. There were also a lot of little cards marking favourite chapters and book-marks commemorating dead and gone Kellys and Crowes."

"Yes?"

"Now this is what I'm getting at. One of those bookmarks fell out as I was reading. I went on reading and picked the card up when I'd finished. I must have held it in my hand as I was praying, for when I got up after you were called out, I found it in my coat pocket. I must have slipped it in unconsciously in my preoccupation. When I came upon it, I looked at it and the writing seemed familiar. I can't think where I've seen it. Does it strike any chord with you, Littlejohn?"

The anxious-faced old man handed over the card. It was a simple, cheap greeting card. *To My Valentine*, with a lovers' knot under the title, and then a verse.

The sky above is blue, love,
The Bird is on the dhrine,
My heart beats true for you, love,
My flower, my Valentine.

"Dhrine means thorn-bush, Littlejohn, but read on...."

Margat, Neen beg villish my chree.
Pat. 1938.

"Margat, little, sweet girl of my heart. She must have been about twelve then."

"Well?"

"May I see the note that was waiting for us when we got in to-day?"

"You mean...?"

"Yes."

Littlejohn took the paper from his pocket and placed it beside the card. Together they examined the writing and looked in amazement at each other.

"It's the *Pat* that started me thinking, Littlejohn. You see, it's a diminutive of Patrick, isn't it? Well in Manx, the garbled version of Patrick is Perrick!"

Chapter Sixteen
The Return of Margat
Crowe

"I've got to think things out, parson. I can't let it rest there and I shan't sleep till I've settled things in my own mind. I think I'll take a long walk."

Outside, the moon was shining and it was almost as clear as day. A rare night for a long tramp if only you could enjoy it.

"I'll come with you, Littlejohn. Let me get my boots on and then …"

"It's past two, parson, and you ought to be in bed. It'll knock you up."

"I couldn't sleep, either. And it won't knock me up; I'm used to watching by the sick, even at my age. If you'll have me, I'll come. It may do you good to have someone to talk to when you feel like it."

"I'll be very grateful if you will. …"

The trees round Grenaby stood etched in the moonlight as they set out. There was hardly a sound, except the river rushing under the bridge and the cries of owls. From the village, they took a minor path which brought them out at Ballamodha on the long straight road from

Upper Foxdale to Ballasalla and Castletown. All around spread the little farms, sleeping in the night, and behind and to the left of them, the massive hills stood silhouetted against the clear sky.

"I can't believe it, parson, but it makes very many things clear. The obstruction of the police, for example. I thought the men at Ramsey were friends of mine, but when I went to ask their help, they were as tight as oysters. Perrick must have told them... ordered them... to say nothing about the case to me, because I wasn't officially on it. And then there was the way Perrick was always on my heels, quizzing if I'd found anything he didn't know. He was quite angry when he found I was what he called 'a step ahead of him'. He was scared about what I'd find next."

Their pipes kept going out and they halted now and then to light them. The Archdeacon strode out at Littlejohn's side like a young man. The Inspector kept shortening his stride out of respect for his companion's aged legs. Then the old man got ahead of him. They ought to have been enjoying the beauty of the night; instead of which...

"I can't understand it, Littlejohn. Perrick comes of an old and well-liked family and is known all over the Island for his industry and integrity. I never thought for a minute he was in love with Margat Crowe."

"What else could it be? He must have killed Levis to prevent his taking her away and treating her like he'd treated all his other women. I can't say I blame Perrick. Levis had it coming to him and it may have happened during a fight. I wish I'd never got mixed up in this case. Now I've got to see it through. I'll have to speak to the Chief Constable to-morrow."

"Has it occurred to you that Maggie Keggin's Sight, as she calls it, somehow scented danger for you when you were

THE CURSING STONES MURDER

alone with Perrick? And the anxiety of Joe Henn about prowlers, as he called them. Might you not have been in real danger for your life when you were alone to-day."

Littlejohn halted in his stride and faced the Archdeacon.

"That's what worries me, sir. The attempt to wreck my car and, presumably, kill me on the way to Douglas to-night. It's not like Perrick at all. I've worked with the man for a week, know him and his ways intimately, admire his manner and his modesty, like him as a man.... It's not right, sir. I'd almost as soon think my old colleague, Cromwell, would try to kill me. If Perrick did it, I shall feel like resigning from the service, taking my pension, and keeping hens. I'd feel my knowledge of human nature had failed me...."

"Oh, come, come, Littlejohn. Perrick must be in love and men in love are completely changed, for good or evil. He must have gone demented to think of Margat and Levis. What did he call her in his Valentine? 'My flower....' He must have sought every way to save her and failing, gone mad and killed."

"It's not that, parson. I'm not a Sherlock Holmes, an intellectual detective, who sits in an armchair and solves his cases. Neither am I a scientific one, hunting for clues, fingerprints, cracking alibis. I've always depended on my simple knowledge of human nature. I've tried to get background, the feel of cases, to soak myself in the environment of crimes and those who commit them. I've grown to depend on the solution coming almost instinctively, or subconsciously, after I've got to know all the parties and their homes and their circumstances in a case. Now.... If Perrick has done this, I shall lose confidence in myself. I shall lose, so to speak, the password which has opened so many doors. Better pack up when that happens...."

"Could it be that Perrick is shielding Ned Crowe, the father of the girl he's in love with?"

"I hope to God he is.... Anyone but Perrick. That's how I feel and it does me no credit."

They were standing at the top of Ballamodha, looking to the east. The long white road, the "straight", shone in the moonlight as far as they could see, and beyond it, the "fish tail", the spreading peninsula which holds on one side the wide Castletown Bay and on the other, the quiet hamlet of Derbyhaven. At one point, St. Michael's Isle was plainly visible and, at the other, the lighthouse of Langness flashed across the water and then over the land rhythmically. And farther than that, the moonlit sea and the horizon along which the light of to-morrow was faintly showing.

Another day! Both men wondered how it would end.

"What are you going to do now, Littlejohn?"

"The first thing is, to get hold of Margat Crowe. We can't ask Perrick face to face how things stand between them. We've got to ask Margat. If she was ready to run away with Levis, she can't love Perrick much, and therefore she's the weaker vessel of the pair. Perrick must be very strong in his love to do as he has done. We must find Margat...."

"And meanwhile?"

"Meanwhile, we must be patient. If Perrick doesn't suspect what we know, he'll not make a move. You see, parson, *Pat* on the Valentine might be anybody. If we assume that it's Perrick, and it isn't, we'll look very foolish indeed if we start a hare with the Chief Constable. The more I think of it, the more I think patience and silence are the best. Meanwhile, we'll work away and try to find out more facts. This walk and your company have cleared my mind and perspective."

The vicar lit his pipe again.

"I'm relieved to hear you say so, Inspector. I thought earlier that you'd lost heart. Work's the best thing to restore you. Now what about Margat? How do we get her?"

"It will be difficult. I can't telephone Scotland Yard without the local police knowing. The telephone exchange report all unusual calls to the police. If I telephone Cromwell, Perrick will get to know."

"What of it? He can't stop her coming once the police on the other side find her."

"If I ring up Cromwell about Margat, Perrick will warn her to lie low. I believe he knew where she was staying in London. After all, what I can discover about her whereabouts, he can. ... Even more so, because he's presumably a friend of the family. To-night even, after I telephoned Cromwell to find Margat and bring her over, Perrick got on the 'phone to her, and she had gone when Cromwell called for her at Croydon. You see, the telephone exchange had warned the police and Perrick knew and took steps. *He must not let us get hold of Margat.* Otherwise, his love affair with her would come into the open and we would connect him at once with Levis."

"You want to get a message out quickly and without the police knowing?"

"Yes, sir. I wonder if we could send a letter to Scotland Yard by first 'plane to-morrow, like you did to me when you wanted me to come over. ..."

"Too much time wasted. I know a better way. By wireless."

"I must be slipping; I never thought of it. What do we do, sir? Where's the radio station?"

"On the *Manx Shearwater*. We'll go to Peel and wake up Tom Cashen, get him to send a message to Port Patrick on the mainland, who, in turn, will telephone Scotland Yard right away."

"Parson, you're a genius!"

"It won't go through official channels then. There's always the risk if we use the official radio, that Perrick will get to know sooner or later. It's very sad, by the way, to think as a result of the little Valentine, Perrick has suddenly become the villain of the piece. I hope it proves to be untrue."

"So do I. Now, we'd better cut through the fields to the vicarage and drive off to Peel without any delay."

The path they took led them out by the bridge at Grenaby and Mrs. Littlejohn was waiting for them at the door of the parsonage. Clad in her dressing-gown, she'd kept looking out every five minutes. She was pale as she greeted her husband.

"I'm glad to see you both back. Whatever's the matter, Tom? You weren't white when you went out, you were *grey*. Has anything happened?"

"I'll tell you later, Letty. Could we have a cup of tea? And then we've got to get along to Peel."

"Shall I come, too?"

"If you don't mind, I'd like you to hold the fort in case there are any calls from the Yard."

"All right. There's some tea ready. We kept the kettle on the boil."

Maggie Keggin, fully dressed, brought in the tea things.

"You'll take care, sir. The danger's not over yet. The Sight keeps botherin' me, off an' on. ..."

"We'll look after it, and thank you, Maggie. Now that we have an idea where the danger lies, we can look out for it."

"I'll take the dog," said Littlejohn as they rose to go. He didn't say that Meg and he occupied a world of their own in their relationship, and when hard pressed, he got a kind of spiritual refreshment from it. The dog leapt in the back seat, settled, and was asleep before they started on their way.

Once in Peel, the main thing was to avoid the police. Any encounter with a bobby on patrol would call for explanations, and even if they didn't divulge the purpose of their visit, it would certainly be reported to Perrick that they'd been there in the small hours, and his quick brain would jump to conclusions. The parson therefore directed Littlejohn to where Tom Cashen lived in Castle Street, known locally as "the Big Street", and himself stayed in the car, parked in a cul-de-sac outside the town.

Littlejohn almost tiptoed into Peel, choosing all the dark alleys, pausing to listen for the footfall of the patrolling constables, encountering nothing but a few prowling cats wailing dismally. The little city was asleep under the moon, the light of which hardly penetrated the narrow streets. In the distance, the soft splash of the waves on the shore like the breathing of someone asleep. Nothing more.

Cashen's cottage was a low one and Littlejohn, with the help of a walking-stick the parson had lent him, was able to reach the upstairs window and gently tap on it. After three attempts, a woman's head appeared. Her hair was in curling-pins and she looked scared.

"What is it at this time o' night? It's come to something when people's..."

"Let me speak to him, missus."

Tom Cashen's tousled head took the place of his wife's.

"Why, Inspector! What's bringin' ye out at this early hour o' the mornin'?"

"Can you come down and let me in?"

"Sure...."

The head was withdrawn. Littlejohn listened again. All was quiet. The door opened after a rattle of bars and a chain, and Cashen in his shirt and trousers let him in.

Littlejohn told Tom that not a soul must know of this night's work. That was enough. Tom Cashen said little at the best of times. He could be relied on.

"I don't want to disturb anybody, least of all the police. I'd hate to run into a constable on patrol at this hour, Tom. The Island police would be thinking we're a mad lot at Scotland Yard."

Cashen looked hard at Littlejohn. He scented a mystery, but was ready to fall in without questions. He laughed.

"Aw, nawthen happens in Peel at this time o' night, master. Lek as not, the police'll be by the fire in the police-station. What's to bring 'em sleechin' out in a peaceable li'l place lek Peel. They've tried the shop-doors long ago, an' afther that they'll have shut up shop for the night, unless someborry calls 'em out on a case."

He pulled on his blue jersey and put on his coat and cap. He was right. They reached the *Shearwater* without meeting a soul.

On about wave-length 135, they picked up Port Patrick on the neat little transmitter in the wheelhouse, and then Littlejohn dictated his message. The receiving station promised to pass it on to Scotland Yard at once, and call him back.

Tom Cashen produced a bottle of rum and glasses from his locker, boiled water on a primus, and mixed some grog. They drank it and took a turn on deck.

The sea was like glass, and silver in the moonlight. They could see far out and, along the coast, it was bright enough to make out the rocks and caves north of Peel, Gog y Deigan and Lynague, and beyond, the turn of coast to the Ayre, with

Jurby church standing out clearly, high above the shoreline. There were a number of boats tied up in the harbour, but all except one were in darkness. The crews were either at home or sleeping ashore in the town. The solitary lighted ship was the *Robert Surcouf*, still in dock for repairs. There was a light on deck, and now and then, the man on watch coughed or cleared his throat.

"Peaceful, isn't it, sir? Better tek your fill of it, because it won't last long. The weather'll break any time now."

"Is the glass falling, then?"

"Aw, yiss. If you care to look in the wheelhouse, you'll see it's goin' down fast. An' to-day's September 21st. That's what we call here *Oie'l Vian*, Matthew's Eve. I believe in the year 1787, the whole of the herrin' fleet was destroyed in Douglas Bay on *Oie'l Vian*. Navar since then do the boats from Peel go out to the herrin's on *Oie'l Vian*. More modern, they're called the equinoctial gales, I believe. They're not here to a day or so, exac', lek, but they come. It won't be so quiet here to-morrow night, I can tell ye, master."

"So soon?"

"The old fishermen at The Corner there don't need the weatherglass to tell the weather, an' they've all been surprised the day's held out so good. Some of 'em h'ard the Howlaa moanin' in the dusk this everin, and that's a sure sign of gales. ... Another glass of grog, sir?"

"The Howlaa?"

"Aw, that's the sperrit that wails on the shore before storms. A sure sign. They say nowadays it's the noise of the wind changin', but the old ones still say it's a sperrit."

He took the glasses, descended to the fo'c'sle, and brought them up refilled.

"The Frenchy there's runnin' it fine. ..."

He pointed to the *Robert Surcouf*.

"The smith finished the propeller-shaft to-night and everyborry advised the skipper to up anchor an' off if he wanted to make home port before the storms break. But he's a difficult fellah, lek. He won't take advice, and said he'd not sail till to-morrow. An' the smith had been tellin' him that the repair would only see him across in calm weather, and he'd need a complete new part when he got home. Didn't make any difference. The Frenchy said he'd go his own way. Well. ... He'll rue it if he tries to cross the channel in the *Oie'l Vian* storms. ... Shall we try Port Patrick again, sir?"

The mainland station had moved fast. They'd sent the message to Scotland Yard at once; then they'd stood-by for a reply for Littlejohn. A Mr. Cromwell had been roused from his bed and had taken charge at the other end. He sent his best wishes to Chief Inspector Littlejohn and told him to listen for results before the eight o'clock news the following morning.

Littlejohn thanked Tom Cashen for all his help.

"Aw, it's nawthen, Mr. Littlejohn. Don't forget the trip we're going to have together before you go."

"What about the Howlaa, Tom?"

"He won't last long and maybe there'll be a quiet day between times. We'll see."

Littlejohn joined the Archdeacon again, and as they drove home, the Inspector gave his companion a full account of his meeting with Tom Cashen and what they had done together.

"Do you think you'll sleep now, Littlejohn?"

It was past four when they arrived back at the vicarage and Littlejohn, putting aside all his worries and fears when he got in bed, fell asleep right away. Maggie Keggin wakened them at a quarter to eight in the morning. Archdeacon Kinrade was already fully dressed and awaiting them, bright-eyed, in the dining-room, where they joined him in their dressing-gowns. The weather forecast was being read; it bore out all that Tom Cashen had said. Gale warnings in all parts, high winds, some rain; the gales gradually increasing as the day went on. Then:

"Here is an S.O.S. announcement. Will Miss Margat Crowe, late of Cursing Stones Farm, Peel, Isle of Man, now believed to be in London, get in touch with New Scotland Yard, telephone number Whitehall 1212, at once, in connection with her father, Edwin Crowe, who is lying seriously injured at Noble's Hospital, Douglas, Isle of Man. I will repeat that…"

"Good old Cromwell," said Littlejohn and hurried upstairs to shave. He repeated it much more fervently an hour later, when the telephone bell rang.

It was Tom Cashen from Peel to say he was coming down to Grenaby right away. That meant that, in accordance with arrangements between them and Port Patrick the night before, Cromwell had telephoned further news to be transmitted to the *Shearwater* on a private wave-length. Half an hour later, Tom followed his message. His brother, a farmer, had brought him along in his land-rover. All the doors opened in the village and the occupants turned out to greet him in great curiosity.

M.C. telephoned at 8.0, just after broadcast. Receptionist at an Hotel in Bloomsbury, where M.C. staying, took down and gave it to her. I went and picked up M.C. right away. Just after my arrival, there was a call for M.C. from Douglas. Told operator to say M.C. out. Did not try to trace call pending your

instruction. Leaving Northolt about noon—arrive
I.O.M. about 2.0. Will you please meet me?

Tom Cashen was drinking a cup of coffee with the
parson.

"Will you do me another favour, Tom?"

"Anything, sir."

"A final message to Sergeant Cromwell, Scotland Yard,
via Port Patrick."

"A pleasure, sir."

Airport and landing-stage likely to be watched by
police. Ask Assist. Commissioner to arrange private
'plane and landing at Jurby R.A.F. airfield: Will meet
you about 2.0.

Littlejohn.

Littlejohn now thought it best to get away from
Grenaby, lest Perrick should arrive and cause embarrassment. True, the local Inspector might be busy at the airport or Douglas quay, but Littlejohn didn't care to risk it.
He therefore took his wife off to Ramsey for lunch, and
then they left for Jurby.

The Officer in Command at Jurby had heard from
London. The plane was already on the way and due in twenty
minutes. Littlejohn could hardly wait, and felt more excited
than for a long time as it appeared over the airport and
finally taxied to rest. A bowler hat appeared in the doorway
and turned as the wearer helped out his companion.

Cromwell scanned the airfield and waved with frenzied joy as he spotted his friends. He shook their hands as
though they'd been parted for years.

"And this is Miss Crowe."

Margat Crowe was all Littlejohn had expected from descriptions of her. Dark, taller than average, and delicately beautiful, but pale with worry and anxious about her father. She was nervous and troubled in many ways and showed great relief when Littlejohn told her Ned Crowe was out of danger and that she would soon be able to see him. For lack of somewhere better to call for a cup of tea on the way to Grenaby, Littlejohn halted at the *Claddagh Hotel.* Greenhalgh was sober and welcomed them.

"Good afternoon, Miss Crowe. Welcome back."

Littlejohn took a turn alone with Margat in the garden, the last roses of which were blooming and the leaves of which were gathered in heaps for burning.

"I want a word or two with you as soon as possible, Miss Crowe. There have, as you know, been strange happenings here since you went away. You can help me sort out some of them, I think."

She smiled, an open, almost childish smile.

"What do you want to know?"

"First, you were going to San Remo with Levis?"

She paused and flushed unhappily.

"Yes. We were to be married in London and going there for a honeymoon."

"You went on ahead and waited, and he never came. What did you think?"

"The worst. I knew his reputation. In fact, he was quite candid about it when he asked me to marry him. When he didn't turn up, I thought he'd changed his mind. I waited a day or two, then I went to my aunt's at Croydon, got a job and waited for news. You see, I hadn't much money. I asked the hotel I'd left to forward anything. There was nothing. Then I read in the paper he was dead. ..."

"Meanwhile, you didn't think of returning home?"

"I had a terrible quarrel with father. He wouldn't hear of my even associating with Cedric. So I said I'd go. When it turned out wrong, I was too proud to come back. I'm sorry, now. Poor dad must have suffered terribly."

"And why did you leave your aunt's home so suddenly the other day?"

"I didn't know father was ill. A friend of ours in the police over here, telephoned to say that the newspaper men were after me for a statement about Cedric's relations with me, that they would trace me to auntie's, and I'd better lie low for the present in a London hotel. He gave me an address, and I moved out in panic. I didn't tell auntie where I was going, but promised to keep in touch with her. I was afraid, and wanted to hide."

"Who was your friend in the police, Miss Crowe?"

"Inspector Perrick...."

She smiled and showed not the least embarrassment.

"Forgive a very personal question, but is Inspector Perrick by any chance in love with you?"

Her eyes opened wide.

"Why, no."

"Did he ever send you a Valentine?"

She paused and thought. She seemed amused.

"Oh, I remember. Mr. Perrick used to be the constable at Michael when I was at school. He used to see me safely home quite often. He once sent me a home-made Valentine because I'd told him I didn't know what a Valentine was. How did you know that?"

"We found it in your father's Bible."

"He used to keep little keepsakes of me as a child in it. Where did you get the Bible?"

"We sent it to him in hospital. He wanted it. The Valentine fell out."

"There's never been anything between Inspector Perrick and me. His nickname was Pat in the village in those days; short for Perrick. I know there's a silly idea that a woman always knows if a man's in love with her, but I'm quite sure Inspector Perrick never felt that way about me."

"Let's go and get our tea, then."

Cromwell and the Archdeacon were getting on like a house on fire. The sergeant was telling the old man about his latest and best hobby; a boys' club in the East End. ...

Greenhalgh was hovering round the table obsequiously, seeing that everything was right. When Littlejohn entered, he made cryptic signs that he wanted a word with him in private. Littlejohn excused himself from the party and followed the landlord into the little cubbyhole of an office under the stairs.

"Oh, Inspector, I just wanted a word with you. Is this Levis affair finished? Because I don't like the police keep hanging round here. Not you; I don't mean that. You're a friend of mine and you're always welcome. I mean that fellow Perrick. He's been twice quizzin' me, and I've got fed up with it."

"Inspector Perrick? What did he want?"

"A day or so after you first called, in walks Perrick and says he knew, of course, you'd been to see me, and would I just go over the interview again for the official record. I told him what we'd said. He didn't seem pleased. The day after, he was here again. Was I sure that was all? Of course I was sure, I said, and I asked him what he was driving at. I'm not fond of Mister Nosey Perrick. I think he was responsible for the raid, though he didn't join in."

"Raid?"

Littlejohn smiled.

"Not exactly *raid;* inspection. What about a drink?"

"I'm just going to have some tea, thanks. Go on with your tale, Mr. Greenhalgh."

The landlord drew close. He reeked of whisky as though soaked to the very marrow in it.

"Well, it's like this. The Sunday before the … the inspection, Perrick called here, all on his lonesome, to have dinner. He cast his eyes round at the drinks to some tune, and I'm sure he made a note to send the Ramsey squad the next Sunday. The place was full and we gave him a good time. In fact, he'd such a good time, it was a dirty trick of him to tip off the police on us."

"What sort of a good time?"

"You know how stern and starchy he is. There wasn't a free table, so we asked him if he'd share one. He jibbed a bit, but then said he would. There was a lady at the table, *a neglected lady*, if you get what I mean. After the fish, the ice thawed and they got on together as if they'd been friends all their lives. It ended by him taking her home in his car. Friends had dropped her here and were calling back for her. You should have seen their faces when they found she'd gone."

"Who was the lady?"

Greenhalgh closed one eye.

"You'd never guess. She'd come here to make a scene. I'm sure of that. For some time previous, she'd been coming here with a man, and he'd let her down for somebody else. She must have expected him being here, you see, and was wantin' to see who'd put her nose out or else kick up a scene with him. He was the chap who was murdered, Levis. And the woman was Mrs. Fallows.… Last time Perrick was here, he tried to pass it off lightly. It might have been something and nothing in the way of a bit of gallantry, so to speak, but what I objected to was him going and turnin' loose the

Ramsey police on us the week after. I've a score to settle with Mr. Perrick. …"

Littlejohn didn't tell Greenhalgh how fully he had paid accounts! He was quiet all the way back to Grenaby. They called with Margat Crowe at *Cursing Stones*, where she lit a fire and then made arrangements to stay with the Kellys until her own home was in ship-shape. Littlejohn promised to take her down to see her father as soon as they'd dropped the rest of the party at the vicarage.

At Grenaby, Maggie Keggin met them at the door.

"That man's here again," she said ominously. "He insisted on waitin' this time. He's in the dinin'-room."

But Perrick had followed her to the door.

"No; here I am. Hullo, Chief Inspector. …"

His eyes turned to Margat Crowe.

"*Kynnas-tha-shu*, Margat. So they've found you at last! And this, I presume, is Sergeant Cromwell. Glad to meet you, Cromwell. I just called to take Margat to her father. He's fit to be seen now."

CHAPTER SEVENTEEN
THE RETICENCE OF NED CROWE

Littlejohn went with Perrick and Margat Crowe to Douglas. On the way they chatted amiably about all kinds of things, including Margat's stay in London. Relations between Perrick and Littlejohn seemed just as they'd always been from the beginning, friendly and cordial.

"I understand your anxiety to get Miss Crowe over here to see her father," Perrick had told Littlejohn in the moment they spent alone before leaving Grenaby. "But why did you send out the B.B.C. call without mentioning it to me? I could have helped."

"The Archdeacon had seen Crowe the night before and the old man was asking for Margat."

"How did you get the message over?"

Littlejohn cocked one ear. So....But Perrick went on quite openly:

"I know it wasn't telephoned over. You see, since this case began, we've tapped all the lines to the mainland and there was no outward call either to Scotland Yard or the B.B.C."

"It went by radio. Our friend Tom Cashen was good enough to send it on the set of the *Shearwater*. I didn't want the telephone operators cutting-in and interfering...."

There was a pause and, for the first time in their association, the air grew tense.

Littlejohn changed the subject.

"A much more serious thing happened last night, Perrick. I took my wife to Douglas and on the way, a large car tore at us and tried to smash us up...."

Perrick changed countenance; his healthy colour grew dead white.

"Where, was this, sir?"

"At Kewaigue."

"You didn't report it."

"I did. To the man on night duty, with a description of the car, such as it was. You were off duty, of course."

"I heard nothing of it."

"I intended to see you about it. However..."

They drove on in silence.

Ned Crowe was in a single ward at Noble's. There was a policeman sitting by his bedside; a nice comfortable type of constable, reading a novel by Ethel M. Dell from the hospital library. He had his false teeth in a handkerchief on his knee. They were new and hurt him. He tore himself away from his book, with abashed and furtive gestures replaced his dentures, and left the party with the patient.

Ned Crowe with his head shaved and his pale face, looked a shadow of the formidable drunken sailor Littlejohn had first met in the *Captain Quilliam*. Margat rushed to him, put her arms round him, kissed him, and wept.

"Margat, *my chree... me villish....*You've come back. I knew you'd come back home to your ould daa...."

The old man was mixing his tears with his daughter's. He looked better already. He turned his face to Perrick.

"Thank you, Master Perrick. You promised to bring her back, and you did. Bless you!"

Littlejohn didn't say a word. He didn't even glance in Perrick's direction.

"You'll stop with your dad, now, Margat *veg*?"

"I'll never run away again."

"You'll be able to get the house tidy and nice for me...."

"The kettle'll be on the hob ready for you when you come in at the door. You'll soon be home now...."

"Margat.... *Graih villish*."

They let them take their fill of homely talk and endearments. Never once did Perrick show the least emotion about Margat or Ned. He just stood there quietly, letting them have it out.

"Do you feel fit yet, Ned, to tell us what happened the night of the accident?"

Margat sat on the chair beside the bed and Ned Crowe looked hard at Perrick.

"Not a thing, Mister Perrick. Not a thing. The docther said it might tek months for me to be rememberin'."

"I see. You don't call anything to mind?"

"I just seemed to be walkin' along the road and then I don't remember anythin' else. I wasn' dhrunk...."

Littlejohn spoke for the first time.

"What time was it?"

Perrick jerked his head in the Inspector's direction and gave him a keen look.

"Eight o'clock. The clock in Peel-town had just sthruck."

"I thought you couldn't remember anything?"

Perrick was on it like a shot.

"I don't, Mr. Perrick. But in me mind I still seem to hear the Peel clock chimin', lek."

"Very well."

"Do you remember anything about the day you saw Mr. Levis dead on the shore at Gob y Deigan, Mr. Crowe?"

Littlejohn took it up again.

Ned Crowe looked hard at him.

"You're the man I ordhered off my farm. When was it? Who are you ...?"

"A friend of mine," said Perrick, and Littlejohn was sorry that their ways were slowly drifting apart. He still admired the Manxman.

"I don't remember a thing. Maybe when I'm home at me farm an' see the place again, it'll all come back."

"Who did you see on the shore beside the body?"

Ned Crowe began to show signs of distress.

"I can't remember. I tell ye, I don't recollect. It makes my head ache when I try to think."

He grew excited, pressed the bell above his bed, and a nurse appeared.

"They're botherin' me, nurse. The doctor said I wasn't to be bothered. Don't let them keep on at me."

"All right, Mr. Crowe. They won't say anything more. They're going now."

"Margat isn't goin', yet?"

"No. She'll stay and have tea with you."

"That's right, *me villish.* ..."

Outside, Littlejohn and Perrick parted. They had come in Perrick's car and Mrs. Littlejohn had promised to follow to Douglas with Cromwell to pick him up, and take Margat Crowe to her lodgings at Ballacurry on the way back.

"Sure I can't take you back, sir?"

"No, thanks, Perrick. I'll just take a walk around. I've never had a moment to relax since I got here. It'll be nice to have a change."

"Right, sir. If Crowe says anything, I'll let you know."

The Inspector tried to put the whole thing from his mind and enjoy the stroll. He went down to the quay, across

the swing bridge, and along the steep road to Douglas Head.
When he reached the top, he could hardly stand. The gale
was rising and the sea below was churned into heavy white-
topped rollers. A small coaster making for harbour was taking it right in the teeth; every wave washed her from stem to
stern. Out at sea, vessels of all kinds were running for shelter in Douglas Bay. The storm cone was dangling from the
harbour-master's office at the pier-head. The sea pounded
the rocks below the Head with a noise like thunder.

On the way back, Littlejohn passed a telephone-box
overlooking the old quay. He entered and rang up the parsonage. Letty was just ready to leave.

"Do you mind taking Cromwell down to Peel, get him
to run round to all the garages he can find, and see if they
hired out a car last night after midnight. Don't worry about
me, Letty. I'm just going for a breath of air along the promenade. I'll be at the *Fort Anne Hotel* at five. That do?"

"Mr. Henn's been here wanting to see you. He had
something on his mind, he said, and he thought he ought
to tell you…"

"Did he tell you what it was?"

"He told Cromwell and Cromwell told me and the
parson…"

Suddenly Littlejohn stiffened.

"Don't tell me now. Wait till we meet."

He remembered that now even the telephone
wasn't safe.

"Take care of yourself, Tom."

He walked down to the promenade. The footpath on
the sea side was out of bounds; the sea was washing over
in great waves and filling the gutters with foam and water.
Littlejohn had to hold his hat. The wind tore along the
length of the gardens and the long level curve of the bay.

Every wave and every gust of wind seemed mightier than the last. Finally, quite exhausted with battling against the elements, Littlejohn turned in at *Fort Anne Hotel* and ordered himself some tea. The rest of those in the place were gathered round the window watching the heavy seas, talking about the storm, and wondering when the boat from Liverpool would arrive.

"It was just such another night when the *Ellan Vannin* was lost," said an old man. "I remember it well. An' she'd battled all the way over again' it, and just at the Mersey Bar it was too much for her, and she went down with all aboard. ... Fifty years since, nearly, that was."

Silence. Nobody commented. An event still remembered with grief and softly spoken of on the Island. Grief so deep that it seemed indecent to speak of it in public.

Outside, more boats seeking shelter between the two great headlands and, in the distance, others running for safety to Ramsey Bay.

"A dirty north-wester. They'll cop it in Peel to-night."

The man who said it looked happy to be indoors and swallowed a toasted muffin almost whole with satisfaction.

Littlejohn thought of the *Robert Surcouf,* still tied up in Peel harbour. The stupidity of the skipper had caused them to miss the weather. They might be here now for another week.

Cromwell and Letty arrived at *Fort Anne,* at last.

"I went round Peel garages, sir. None of them had a taxi out, but one of them which runs a little hire-and-drive business, lets out a big pre-war Austin sometimes. It's used all hours, so they keep it in a lock-up, at the side of the main garage. It was out last night, after they closed at ten."

"Who hired it?"

"Dr. Fallows has a key of the lock-up. If his wife has their own car out and he's called out, he can get at the hired one."

Littlejohn sighed. Over and over again, round and round, like a man on a treadmill. Every time it came back to Fallows, the man who had a perfect alibi for the day Levis was murdered! Could he be trying to kill everyone who might bring suspicion to bear on his wife?

"Mr. Henn was a bit agitated about you, too, sir."

"Joe! He told me as much the other day. He thought I was in danger, but was relieved to find Perrick guarding me when he called at the vicarage. What's troubling Mr. Henn?"

"Just this, sir. On the day he called to warn you, he said he was up a tree in his garden, looking round it on a ladder because he's thinking of pollarding it later. Looking down at the vicarage, he saw a woman carrying a rifle, peeping in at the windows over the hedge. He thought she was out rabbiting or something. Then he found she was watching the house as if she might be ready to take a pot at someone. Perrick came up, saw her, and went and spoke to her. They both seemed angry and he sent her off. She went away looking very grim."

"Who was she?"

"Perrick, Henn said he recognized; but he'd never seen the woman before."

"Let's drive to Noble's and pick up Margat Crowe."

They didn't go in the ward again to disturb Ned Crowe, but picked up Margat and took her straight to Kellys', Ballacurry, where she was to stay until her father's return home. Margat said little on the way. She was relieved to find her father so much better, but, it seemed, he had confided nothing to her about happenings at *Cursing Stones* on the fatal afternoon of Cedric Levis's murder.

Mrs. Kelly, on the other hand, was very talkative when they arrived at Ballacurry. She was full of Ned Crowe's accident and of the wickedness of motorists who knock down pedestrians and leave them to perish on the road.

The newcomers sat round the large blazing kitchen fire and drank tea. Mr. Kelly was in his rocking-chair, a legacy from his grandmother, in which he spent a lot of his scanty spare time, rocking to and fro in a kind of silent ecstasy.

"Did you see anything going on at *Cursing Stones* Farm on the night Ned Crowe met his accident, Mrs. Kelly?"

She turned to Littlejohn with a gesture of regret.

"I was out at the Chapel that night, Mr. Littlejohn. It was Mothers' Meetin', and I remember they told me the news when I got home...."

Mr. Kelly stopped his rocking and pondered a minute.

"I saw Ned Crowe leavin' the farm that night. I'd been in the yard shuttin' up the hens and I see him lockin' his door and a bit afther I heerd him walkin' down the road. Between seven an' half-past, it would about be. Mother had been gone to the meetin' around half an hour."

He paused and thought again and then seemed to decide to hold his peace.

"Did anything else happen after that, Mr. Kelly? Was there anybody else around the place?"

The rocking ceased again.

"Somethin' an' nawthen'....Jus' a woman sittin' there in a car...in the bit where the road widens round the corner, lek. She sat there a while and then druv off."

Everyone stiffened except Charlie Kelly, who relaxed in his chair, started rocking again, and puffed his pipe contentedly. He seemed to think he had had his say.

"But you never told me o' that!"

Mrs. Kelly was up in arms.

"Tell us exactly what went on, Mr. Kelly," said Littlejohn.

"Aw. . . . Afther I heeard Ned passin', I looked up the road an' I see the lights o' the car, parked there, lek. I thought perhaps it was someborry from the town doin' a bit o' courtin'. When I got inside, I fills me pipe for a li'l smook, an' then it comes over me, there's been a lot o' robbin' of hen-roosts goin' on, so afther I'd lit me pipe, lek, I went an' had a little sleech round to see what was happenin'.'"

"Do get on with your tale, dad. You an' your li'l smook. We don' want to hear about your smookin'."

"I was comin' to it, missus. It's my field comes down to the road by the corner there, so I walks along the hedge and looks over. It was a woman in the car. Not one as looked like hen-stealin'. So with that, I come indoors agen an' finished me smook. As I shut the door, I hears her tek off in the Peel direction."

"You're sure it was a woman, Mr. Kelly?"

Charlie Kelly chuckled in his innocence.

"Not likely a man would be wearin' a green hat with a feather in it, unless it was one of the li'l people, the fairies, lek, drivin' a fairy car."

A woman! So it looked as if Fallows had been at it again. Taking the blame for his good-for-nothing wife.

There was nobody but the maid at the Fallows's home as Littlejohn and his wife and Cromwell drove back to Grenaby.

"May I leave a note, please?"

"Come in, then," said the girl. "The office'll be the best place for writin'."

She led Littlejohn to a room he'd not seen before. It was the office in which Pamela Fallows and Dora Quine had been working on the first day he called.

A large airy room, with a wide fireplace holding an anthracite stove, two desks, a case of books, and the odds and ends of an architect's job. At one end, a broad window occupied almost the whole wall.

The maid handed Littlejohn a writing-pad and showed him a number of pencils lying in a tray on the desk. Littlejohn glanced quickly round the room. Over the fireplace hung a framed diploma in architecture and beneath it, a small silver shield, mounted on an oak surround. Littlejohn scibbled his note, saying he had called and would return the following morning. On his way out, he glanced at the silver shield.

Awarded to Pamela Fallows for the
bestrifle-shooting at the 1948 contests.
Hopley Ladies' Rifle Club.

He paused and screwed up the paper in his hand.

"I don't think I'll leave a note after all," he said to the surprised maid, and hurried out.

CHAPTER EIGHTEEN
THE TRAP IS SPRUNG

"The whole thing is fantastic, but there seems no other explanation…"

It was seven o'clock when the party got back to Grenaby and, much to Maggie Keggin's dismay, they didn't want any food. Luckily, she had prepared cold chicken and salad.

"It won't spoil. That's why I did it. Cookin' for anybody in this queer house nowadays is a thankless work, an' no mistake. Shall I make it into sandwiches, then, and give ye coffee wi' it?"

"That'll be fine, Maggie. So sorry to be a nuisance…"

"Aw, if makin' a few sandwiches is the worst o' this night's misfortunes, I shan't be worryin'. But it won't be. Listen to that wind.… The *Gaalyn Oie'l Mian*.…An' I've heard the gallopin' horses, too, and when one of the Kaighens of Michael hears *them*, there's goin' to be loss of life at sea. Mark my words…"

The Archdeacon, eager to be hearing the news, shooed his housekeeper away.

"Awright, awright. But don' say I didn't warn ye…"

"What is it, Littlejohn?"

Letty had taken the dog down the road. She never made a point of intervening in her husband's cases, but she had a good idea of what was coming.

"Fantastic…"

The Chief Inspector sat down wearily in a chair.

"The whole thing's fantastic! It's Perrick. As far as I can see, he's aiding and abetting the doctor and Mrs. Fallows in getting away with the murder of Levis. And the reason he seems to be doing it, is that he's fallen for Mrs. Fallows…"

"No! Not Sid Perrick. Surely there's some other reason."

"What other? Look at the facts. Cedric Levis vanishes just as he's about to run away with Margat Crowe. He and Pamela Fallows have been having an affair. He throws Pam over for Margat."

"That's feasible so far. Go on."

"Levis is killed, and his weighted body dumped out at sea. There it would have remained and never been seen or heard of again, had not Tom Cashen gone and fortuitously fished it up whilst scallop-dredging. Even then, it remained unidentified. It was likely to remain so, because the surgeon who examined it and the Inspector on the case, were both concerned in the crime."

The parson looked up quickly.

"But that presupposes the husband and the lover har-moniously co-operated. Surely that wasn't the case."

"The husband might not have known the policeman was the lover. They weren't deliberately working together. Each might have thought the other a bit dimwitted in not perceiving the obvious. For example, all the time, I've been struck myself by Perrick's slowness in not arresting Fallows. The doctor confessed to knocking down Crowe and is still at large. Why? Because Perrick has turned a blind eye and delayed action. That is because he either knows Pam Fallows knocked down Crowe…"

"Wait, Littlejohn. If the doctor confessed to it…?"

"He confessed to it just as he confessed to the murder he thought his wife had committed. Charlie Kelly saw a woman waiting for Crowe to set out for Peel on the night he met with his accident. She followed Crowe a little time after he left. It must have been Pam Fallows, not the doctor; but Dr. Fallows when we discovered damage on his car pointing to the accident, again took the blame. And there is another thing which has puzzled me, which now becomes plain. Both Quiggin, who saw the accident, and Ned Crowe spoke of it happening at *eight.* Yet Perrick, the clever observant Inspector, said over and over again, eight-fifteen ... eight-fifteen. ... Why? I think he was trying to give Pam Fallows an alibi. She must have been somewhere at, say eight-fifteen and, had we pressed it, could have produced witnesses. Instead, Dr. Fallows ruined it all by saying *he* did it. And Perrick didn't arrest him, because he knew it wasn't so. Whatever he was prepared to do for Pam Fallows, he was too decent to saddle her husband with the blame."

There was a pause as Maggie Keggin brought in the sandwiches. Her face was grim as she laid the cloth, set the table, and poured out the coffee.

"Mrs. Littlejohn's takin' her food with me in the kitchen. She's havin' a *proper* meal; not bird-food. ..."

And as she reached the door she addressed the Archdeacon.

"Did you hear *that* ...?"

"That? What?"

"There's a tree fell by the bridge. But you wouldn't be hearin' the likes. The Kaighen horses are out. There'll be deaths at sea this night. Listen to the gale ..."

The house shook with the gusts, even in that sheltered valley, and they could hear the trees outside groaning in the wind.

"It looks as if she'll be right...."

The parson shook his head.

"I hope our little ships, to say nothing of the big ones, are in safe shelter to-night; but it's a forlorn hope, I fear..."

Another blast of the gale hit the old house like a battering-ram, but the sturdy walls resisted it like a rock.

Cromwell had been sitting thoughtfully, munching his sandwich.

"It must have given the doctor quite a turn when you produced the alibi he didn't want," he said quietly.

"Perrick's mistake was in trying to show his assiduousness and also trail a red-herring, by arresting Johnny Corteen. Perrick must have intended releasing Johnny in due time, because he obviously couldn't let him hang for a crime he'd not done. But the arrest of Johnny brought *me* over. Otherwise, probably the case would have gone into unsolved files. It must have shaken Perrick when the Archdeacon produced me in the role of amateur on the case. He couldn't keep away from me, asking how I was getting along, wanting to know what I'd discovered. He even had my telephone calls to the mainland tapped and reported."

"But it surely wasn't he who tried to smash you up in the car at Kewaigue, Littlejohn?"

"No. The large car was one the Fallowses hire at Peel now and then. Perrick must have confided in Pam Fallows just how far I was getting on the case. He must have told her over the telephone when I went to Douglas about the telephone calls and she set out in the hired car intent on murder. As it has slowly been revealed that I was getting on her trail, she's become rattled almost to madness. She was round here with a rifle, according to Joe Henn, the other evening and was presumably thinking of taking a pot-shot at me. Perrick arrived and found her and put the idea out of her head."

"But why was Perrick so anxious to keep Margat Crowe away? What good did that do?"

"Another red-herring. Whilst Margat remained silent, we were bound to think the murder was something to do with her running off with Levis. Now we've found her, we know there was no jealous rival in the background, and that Perrick wasn't in love with her. Perhaps she'll soon be able to make her father talk and tell us what he saw that afternoon."

"What's to say Ned Crowe didn't kill Levis to save Margat from him?"

"Nothing. But why all this fuss and bother by Perrick and Fallows? Neither of them would be likely to take the blame for a man like Crowe. I admit that if the Fallows couple and Perrick can clear themselves of their strange behaviour, we might have to turn to Ned Crowe, even now. He and Dora Quine are the last of the suspects."

"Dora Quine?"

"Oh, she was fond enough of Levis and resented Pam Fallows taking him from her. She told me she was engaged, and tried to make out that she put up a great fight for her virtue against Levis. But if he'd asked *her* to go to San Remo, instead of Margat, she wouldn't have been able to pack a bag quickly enough. In fact, there's just as much reason for suspecting her as Pamela Fallows, *if* the doctor and Perrick hadn't drawn us off her trail."

"What do we do now?"

"Do you know where Hopley is, Cromwell?"

"Yes. Buckinghamshire. We once had a jewel robbery there. You remember, sir? The Ridgway case. ..."

"Yes. I wonder if they know Pam Fallows there and what they can tell us about her."

"Why? What's Hopley to do with it, Littlejohn?"

"She used to be a member of Hopley Rifle Club. When I called earlier this evening, I was looking round for the rifle Joe Henn mentioned. Instead, I found a trophy she'd won at Hopley. May I use your 'phone, parson?"

"It's likely to be tapped, isn't it?"

"That doesn't matter now, sir. In fact, it's all to the good. I hope to set a trap for Perrick that way later."

It took about five minutes to get Hopley. Littlejohn was lucky. Later that night half the lines were down.

"Hullo. ... Hopley Police here ..."

"Chief Inspector Littlejohn, of Scotland Yard."

"Eh? Isn't that the Isle of Man?"

"I'm on a case here. ..."

"How d'y do, sir! This is Sergeant Mallory. Remember me on the Ridgway case, sir?"

"Yes. How are you? Look Mallory. Do you happen to remember anybody in Hopley called Fallows, Pamela Fallows, married a Dr. Fallows? They live here now."

"Fallows? Can't say I do, off-hand, like. Who was she?"

"Won the championship for ladies' rifle-shooting in 1948."

"Oh. ... Yes, I remember. I'm a member of the men's section, sir. But that was Pamela Hartnell. Now, I remember! She *was* married when she won the shield. I'd forgot her married name. Yes, she was a native of here. I knew the whole family. Pamela, Irene, and their father and mother. Nice lot they were, too."

"What about the rest of the family?"

"All dead, sir. The old lady died last year, the father durin' the war, and Miss Irene was killed in the bombing ... a WREN she was. ..."

Littlejohn paused. A WREN. Where had he heard that before?

"Are you there, sir?"

"Yes. A WREN, you say? Was she killed on duty?"

"On leave, sir. In London. It broke her dad's heart and he wasn't long in following her. She was just goin' to be married, too. To a policeman, of all people."

"A policeman? Where from?"

"A sort of security officer drafted from the force. Now I come to think of it, sir, I think he was from the Isle of Man. Lucky I know so much about the Hartnells, sir. You see, old Mr. Hartnell died in his seat one night at the pictures and there was an inquest. I was in charge of it. I was a constable then and the old lady told me quite a lot.... Are you there, sir?"

"Yes, Mallory, I'm here. Thank you so much. You've told me all I wanted to know. Good night...."

"Well, Littlejohn, did you have any luck?"

The Archdeacon's face was bright and eager.

"More than enough, sir. Had Pamela Fallows's sister, Irene, lived, instead of being blown to bits by a bomb in the war, Sid Perrick would have been Pamela's brother-in-law. He was going to marry Irene."

"Good God!" said Cromwell. "You mean for the sake of his old girl, Perrick had taken the Fallowses under his wing, and even risked his career and going to gaol?"

"That's about it. I never believed Perrick was a criminal. Now, I think more of him than ever. It only makes what we've got to do harder. We obviously can't let this go on any longer. We've got to get to the bottom of it and find the culprit. I've got to spring the trap now and bring Perrick out into the open. I'll have to telephone again."

This time he left the door into the hall open so that his friends could hear what was going on.

"Give me Whitehall 1212. Scotland Yard, please. The Assistant Commissioner...."

"Lucky if he's in at this hour. At any rate, there'll be somebody to deal with it."

Cromwell explained it to the Archdeacon *sotto voce*, which Littlejohn could hear all the way in the hall and above the nagging of the gale.

"Yes. ... Hullo Harvey, Littlejohn here. I thought he'd be at home by now, but there's something requires immediate attention. Could you get the Chief Constable of the Isle of Man, and if you have any trouble on the line, use the radio. It's blowing a hellish gale here, and the lines might be down later. I want the Chief Constable to be advised to call in Scotland Yard at once on the Levis murder case. Yes, Levis. And for me to be authorized to take over. I'm afraid one of the local police officers is involved in it, so you see why I think they ought to have an independent man on it. ... Right. I'll wait till I hear from the Chief. My address is The Vicarage, Grenaby... Grenaby 4149. ... Thanks, Harvey. ... Good-bye. ..."

"I'm afraid that will come as a shock to Perrick when the call is reported to him. He'll have to move now. So will we. If the gale keeps up, there isn't likely to be much flying. That will take care of the airport. As for the boat, ... if the Chief Constable hasn't moved before nine in the morning, I'll have to go down myself. Pity you don't know Perrick, Cromwell. You could have gone. It'll tie me up a bit. ... Still ..."

"What about me? I could watch the boat, Littlejohn."

"It's good of you Archdeacon, but ..."

"I'll take no buts. I can sit in Looney's car with Cromwell, just by the gates to the pier. If Perrick shows up, well ... Cromwell can arrest him. Or I can let you know he's aboard. You can arrange for him to be stopped at Liverpool, then. Oh, how distasteful all this is! Perrick, of all people."

"I don't think he'll bolt. He might pack off Pam Fallows or the doctor, but he's not the kind to run himself. He'll stay and face the music. I'm sure of that."

"What do we do now? Just sit and wait?"

"No, sir. I'm off to see Fallows again, now. I've got to try and get a proper tale out of him. If I break this case before Perrick can act, we might save Perrick's face, at least."

"But that's the very thing you've been complaining about Perrick doing, Littlejohn. He's protecting Fallows and his wife. Are you going to do the same for *him?*"

"Not quite. Perrick's motive is good, even if he is seeing a bit cockeyed in it because of his love for the ghost of the girl he's always loved. He'll have to leave the force in any case. I don't like the idea of a fine chap like Perrick going in disgrace, however. Whatever I do, I'll have to depend on you two supporting me."

"Not a doubt of it, Littlejohn."

"I don't need to tell you what I think, sir. ..."

As Littlejohn and Cromwell emerged from the shelter of Grenaby to the higher ground at Ballagilbert and Corlea, the wind seemed to take hold of the car and try to fling it in the air. It was as much as Littlejohn could do to keep it on the road and then, as they joined the main highway at South Barrule plantation and left the shelter of the trees, it was like battling against a wall of solid air.

"It's a wonder the wind doesn't pick up the whole Island and carry it off. I've never seen it so rough," said Cromwell. He looked at the speedometer which registered 20 with the engine going flat-out. They could see nothing, near or distant, but the funnels of road lighted by the headlamps. Then they passed a lighted house or two and could imagine the inhabitants hugging themselves round the fire against the thunder of the elements outside. It was like being in a whirlpool of frenzied air. They passed through Foxdale and under the slopes of Slieau Whaullian, a sudden jolt and they were over the level-crossing at St. John's, and then they struck the main Peel road. It was like entering a wind-tunnel, in the teeth of the blast.

The red light glowed over the porch of Dr. Fallows's house. Littlejohn rang the bell and then beat upon the knocker. It was about half-past ten and the occupants could hardly be in bed. At length the maid let him in.

"Is the doctor here?"

"Yes. He's in the surgery."

"At this hour?"

For a minute Littlejohn grew cold at the thought of Fallows, probably warned by Perrick of new developments, and loose among the poisons of his profession. He flung open the door of the consulting-room without more ado.

At first, he thought his fears were right. The light was on, illuminating the now familiar bare room, with the eye-testing charts on the wall, the weighing-machine in the corner, the instrument cabinets, the poison cupboard, the dispensary partitioned off from the main room, the books in the case, and the examination couch with the white pillow and dark blanket.... Even the stethoscope, twisting across the desk.

Fallows was sitting at the desk, or rather sprawled across it. His arms were outstretched and his head was between them. Before Littlejohn could reach him, he slowly raised himself. The sight of him gave Littlejohn a shock.

He was without his glasses and his eyes were dark-ringed and bloodshot. At first, Fallows didn't seem to recognize Littlejohn. He looked at him with lustreless eyes, his mouth open, his shoulders sagging.

"What do you want?"

Fallows fumbled on his desk and found his spectacles. Slowly he put them on, first one hook, then the other, over his ears. He jerked back his head and looked through the lenses.

"It's you, is it?"

He didn't seem curious about the visit, nor did he appear angry. Just stunned. Then he spoke again.

"She's gone."

"Where is she? Where's she gone?"

"Gone. ... Perrick's taken her. I'll never see her again. ..."

"Has he arrested your wife?"

"Arrested? No. Just taken her ..."

Littlejohn crossed to the cabinet where he knew the whisky was kept, poured out a stiff glass, and handed it to Fallows.

"Drink this and pull yourself together, doctor."

Fallows looked at the glass, then at Littlejohn, took the whisky, tipped the whole of it down his throat, sat up, and didn't look any better. In fact, tears began to stream down his cheeks.

"I knew it would end like this. I was bound to lose her, sooner or later. If not one way; another. Now she's gone. Just 'good-bye an' thanks, Len'; then off into the bloody howlin gale. Just that. ..."

"What do you mean? Has your wife bolted?"

It was hopeless. Fallows seemed in a stupor. And at a time like this when every minute counted!

"Look here, Fallows. ..."

Littlejohn didn't get any further. Outside, above the crash of the gale, rose a mightier noise. It was like the thud of a high explosive bomb hitting the ground and flying to pieces in showers of debris and wreckage.

There was a momentary silence, and then it was broken by Fallows who threw back his head, opened his mouth, and emitted a despairing high-pitched wail.

"Oh, God.... Dear God.... I've got to go. Pam ... Pam...."

Littlejohn shook him by the shoulders.

"Pull yourself together, man. What's the matter with you?"

But Fallows was out of the room, struggling into his raincoat with wild arms, his body writhing in haste.

"Did you hear that? It's the maroon for the life-boat. It's the *Robert Surcouf* in distress, and Pam's aboard her.... Pam ... Pam ... Pam...."

Fallows rushed out of the house, into the night, and was lost. Above the shriek of the gale they could hear him calling his wife's name until it faded on the wind.

CHAPTER NINETEEN
THE DEPARTURE OF THE *ROBERT SURCOUF*

The gale at Peel was so violent that on the quays and open promenade you couldn't keep on your feet. Those who had to stir out of doors clung to the walls and cut through the narrow streets for safety. The wind seemed to be blowing in all directions; wherever you sought shelter from it, it followed you. Nobody about; not even a dog or a stray cat.

The street lamps swung and shuddered, casting uncertain pools of light beneath them, floodlighting the heavy rain falling almost horizontally, reflected back by the wet pavements. In various parts of the town, the crash of falling slates and chimneys, tearing woodwork, and the rattle of anything loose.

Above the thunder of the gale, the boom of the waves breaking in huge masses over the seafront. Even the water in the shelter of the harbour was tormented by gusts which whipped and tore at it, making the ships there bump one another and strain at their ropes. The only things undisturbed and constant in the scene of confusion were the illuminated dial of the church clock and the harbour lights steadily shining at the pier and breakwater.

The harbour was packed with small craft of all kinds which had run for shelter as the gale grew in intensity. They were moored side by side to bollards, their furnaces damped down for a few days' stay. The only boat showing any signs of activity was the *Robert Surcouf,* tied up at the end of the West Quay, smoke gently emerging from her funnel until the wind caught it and scattered it all over the place.

The man on watch on the French trawler was smoking in the skipper's cabin, a cubby-hole, untidy, with a bunk with a dirty counterpane. The whole place smelled of pitch. In the fo'c'sle, the galley-boy, his fair hair cut very short, was sitting alone, picking out a new tune on his accordion. He wasn't allowed to drink with the rest at the *Captain Quilliam,* and it was too rough to roam the streets and follow the girls about, as was his habit. He looked older than his years; a tall, slightly-built lad, with tired, dark-ringed eyes, who hadn't wanted to go to sea and who got homesick and wept a lot when he was alone.

A single electric lamp illuminated the deck of the *Robert Surcouf* and threw a faint light on the adjoining quayside. The noise of the gale drowned the footsteps of a solitary figure in a cap and raincoat and made him appear suddenly like a trick of magic, on the swaying ship. He did not pause, but went down the iron ladder to the crew's quarters. The boy with the accordion suddenly looked up and found himself face to face with Inspector Perrick. He flung his accordion on his bunk, took his feet from the iron stove, and rose deferentially. At first there was dead silence.

"Speak English?"

The boy shook his head.

"Captain Camus? *Le capitaine?*"

The galley-boy shook his head, said something in Breton, and pointed in the direction of the town.

Perrick took a letter from his pocket.

"Captain Camus. ..."

He indicated the letter and pointed in the direction of the *Captain Quilliam*. The boy understood, took sea-boots, an oilskin and a sou'-wester from a number hanging on hooks from the bulkheads, and indicated that he was ready.

"Hein!"

The man on watch had arrived; a fresh-looking, heavy youth with a sea-cap twisted over one ear. When he saw Perrick he nodded. The galley-boy spoke to him in Breton and the newcomer dismissed him with a flick of the fingers.

The ship heaved up and down, like something struggling to breathe. Perrick looked round and then spoke to the man:

"Speak English?"

"Captain's cabin?" he said slowly and loudly, as though, by shouting, he could make the sailor understand. *"Chambre... cabine du capitaine...?"*

The man grinned, jerked his thumb upwards, and started to climb the ladder again. Perrick followed, making his unsteady way after his guide. In his mind's eye he could see it all going on. A handful of men cowering in the tortured hold of the vessel, tossed and beaten about by the storm. The bow of the ship heaving its way hour after hour, making little progress, and the wretches huddled below wondering if every pitch or roll would be the last.... He shuddered.

They were back in the cabin. Perrick contemplated it with distaste; the shabby fittings, the soiled floor, the untidy bed and the dirty counterpane. The smell of pitch caught him by the throat. Beyond, through another door, the small wheelhouse with the binnacle light glowing over the compass. There were grubby charts, a jersey, sea-boots, and a crumpled, filthy shirt on the floor in one corner. Perrick regarded it all with dismay....

The man on watch was standing there smiling. He couldn't exchange an intelligible word with the visitor, whom he knew by sight and thought was conducting a search for contraband.

Suddenly Perrick was seized with frenzy, angrily took the sea-boots and the litter from the floor, and flung them with a disgusted gesture into the wheel-house. Then he straightened the bed, beat it into shape, turned the counterpane cleanest side up and laid it across the berth. The sailor's eyes opened wide.

"Good night...."

With that, Perrick turned, crossed the deck, climbed to the quay and disappeared into the dark and rain. The sailor looked round the cabin, shrugged his shoulders, took his mess-tin from the top of the stove, and resumed his supper....

The taverns on the waterfront were all busy. The men from the boats sheltering in the harbour had filled them. Even a large pub under listless management and normally flyblown and forlorn, was full up and some of the sailors had indulged in the luxury of a change and booked seedy bedrooms for the night. The windows of the inns cast pools of light on the wet quayside.

The *Captain Quilliam* was packed to the doors; both rooms were full and the bar was crowded. The landlord and Rhoda had their hands full serving drinks, and a fisherman who was sweet on Rhoda had pulled off his jacket and was helping to pump the beer behind the counter. The crew of the *Robert Surcouf* were sulkily playing cards at a table in one corner. They thought Camus, the skipper, had done them a bad turn not sailing for home whilst the going was good. Now they might be here for another week.

There was a confused babel of voices above which, now and then, there would be a shout in Breton to show that the Frenchmen maintained their independence. They had grown a bit hostile towards the natives, as though the Peel men were responsible for their present plight.

Captain Camus was standing at the counter drinking steadily with his first-mate. He was a thick-set, plump man, short, and with enormous shoulders. No neck, and his hair clipped so close that he looked entirely bald. He wore a sea cap and a reefer coat. He was half-drunk already and the landlord himself was now serving him because Camus kept making passes at Rhoda, solemnly taking her by the arm, and trying to pull her across the counter so that he could kiss her. The landlord didn't want any trouble....

The mate was half seas over, as well. Another huge man, but whereas Camus was short and stocky, Donadieu, the mate, was tall with it. His bulging steel-blue eyes were glassy, and he took his drinks in one gulp and then asked for more. Now and then he shifted a quid of tobacco from his left cheek to the right and back again. The crew of the *Robert Surcouf* cast black looks at them....

"Listen!"

At intervals, one or another in the pub would call out. There would follow a dead silence. Men's heads would jerk and they would strain to hear what was going on outside. Every crash or roar of the gale might have been the signal of a ship in distress. Those in the crew of the lifeboat, scattered about the rooms of the *Captain Quilliam*, were going easy on their drinks. They might need steady heads and hands before the night was out.

Now and then, the door would open and someone would come in or go out, admitting a blast of wind which swept through the place. It was like that when the galley-boy entered.

At first he was blinded by the bright light and screwed up his eyes. Everybody knew him and he was loudly greeted.

"Come for a drink, Jean?"

"Lost your girl friend?"

"Why didn't you bring your accordion and give us a tune...?"

The lad was bewildered.

"Capitaine Camus.... Capitaine Camus...."

He said it over and over again.

When they led the boy to the counter, Camus eyed him and then seized him roughly by the shoulder and spoke in Breton to him. The boy handed him the note.

Camus screwed up his eyes, and breathing hard, slowly read the message. Then without a word he fumbled in his pocket, took out a greasy wallet, threw a dirty note on the counter, ploughed his way to the door, opened it after a struggle, and vanished into the dark. In a minute or two he was back.

"Donadieu!"

Camus had put on his oilskins as he went out and now he stood there, the rain dripping from him and forming pools on the floor of the bar.

"Donadieu!"

The shout could be heard all over the building.

The mate casually drank off the last of his rum, wobbled to where the skipper was standing, ruddy and glaring, and held a whispered Breton conversation with him. He seemed to be arguing and Camus grew angry and ripped out orders at him. Donadieu shrugged his shoulders and slowly moved to where the crew of the *Robert Surcouf* were sitting... seven of them... trying to make out what it was all about.

There was more conversation and the men grew sulky, then truculent and argumentative.

Donadieu bent and seized two of them by the collars. With a mighty heave he lifted them from their seats, held them suspended in mid-air for a minute, and asked them another question in *patois*. Then the whole crew rose and followed him to the door.

"You're not puttin' to sea on a night like this, are you, Frenchy?"

The man who addressed him was a tall, flashy fellow, the representative of a mainland company exploring a project for making bone-meal from herrings. He eyed the mate brazenly.

For answer, Donadieu raised his hand, spread out the fingers, placed them over the nose of the fishmeal financier, and thrust him across the room. Then, remembering something, he fumbled in his pocket, took out a handful of silver, thrust it at the landlord without counting it, and went unsteadily to the door. There he turned, eyed the resentful and silent company defiantly, and made off.

Pandemonium immediately broke out all over the house. The idea of the *Robert Surcouf*, or any other vessel for that matter, putting out to sea on such a night seemed madness.

Fishermen and landsmen alike shouted at one another about the signs and forecasts of the weather, the danger of the passage, the unseaworthiness of the Breton boat.

The blacksmith's voice was heard above all.

"The repair won't hold out. The first big sea and she's a gonner. I told Camus to pick a decent day. Now he's committing suicide...."

"There's somethin' dirty afoot. I never liked that Frenchy...."

"Can't we stop him?"

The fish-manure prospector, now recovered, was loud in his denunciations.

"Let him go to the bottom of the sea, if he wants to. It's his funeral. If he gets in trouble, I'd see to it, if I was a lifeboatman, that he didn't get me out on a night like this. It's plain murder...."

Tom Cashen only smiled. He knew it meant a stand-by for him and his men all night. The *Robert Surcouf* would be lucky if she reached St. George's Channel in one piece....

Men were hurrying off for their oilskins and sea-boots. The wiser ones were all for going to the French boat and trying to persuade the skipper to wait until the weather improved. Others filled their talk with the *Howlaa*, the gales of *Oie'l Vian*, the dangers of the Manx coast and currents, and the folly of a foreigner taking upon himself the navigation of local waters in defiance of local lore.

News had spread round Peel that the skipper of the *Robert Surcouf* was putting out to sea in the teeth of the gale. Outside, the weather had not abated. Great waves pounded the promenade and the quays and beyond the breakwater they could hear the inferno of tortured waters boiling in the darkness. Knots of men in oilskins gathered in the side-streets leading to the harbour. Others more venturesome, congregated on the quay, struggling to keep on their feet, tottering about in the wind, silent, because it was impossible to be heard for the noise of the elements.

Nobody could see what was going on at the West Quay. It was pitch black and impossible to hear a sound. The first indication of any activity was the switching on of the *Robert Surcouf's* deck and navigation lights. Then there was a glow from her funnel as the draught of her boiler was increased.

The party of Peel men who had battled round to the moorings of the French ship to try to talk sense to the skipper arrived just as Camus rang off on the engine-room telegraph. The *Robert Surcouf* was already lying loose in the harbour and, as they ran alongside, the engine began to beat. Camus must have been keeping up steam for some reason. Now, the ship began to pitch and roll, her masthead light describing wild arcs in the night. The shouts of the men on the quay were lost in the howling of the gale. ...

From any part of the waterfront where they could obtain a safe foothold, the men of Peel watched with bated breath and straining eyes the wild course of the *Robert Surcouf,* indicated by the frantic pattern of her lights. She took what seemed to be hours to pass the breakwater and then, like a match extinguished by the wind, her lights vanished. Someone or other said he saw a glimmer of her, still near the coast, but finally even the imaginative ones ceased to talk and fled to the pubs again. There they waited; nobody bothered about licensing hours that night.

All along the sea-front men stood on watch. The experts, like Tom Cashen, calculated from their knowledge of the ship, the elements, the strength of the gale, the local currents, and their ideas of the seamanship of Camus, exactly where the *Robert Surcouf* ought to be at given times.

News was telephoned to the lifeboat stations at Port Erin and Port St. Mary to stand-by. The crew of the Peel lifeboat was mustered.

"They ought to let 'em damn' well drown," said the expert in fishmeal, who had now a black eye.

At half-past eleven, Tom Cashen said to his companion:

"They should be somewhere about the *Mooir ny Fuill* by now. ..."

And as if to confirm his surmise, what looked like a ball of fire flew into the air over the sea and burst into stars. Two more rockets followed.

The signal maroon at the lifeboat post exploded and, weather or no weather, a crowd of men ran, fighting the wind, to the boathouse on the West Quay under the break-water. As the Peel lifeboat was launched, her sister ships at Port St. Mary and Port Erin took to the water.

And at the same time, Leonard Fallows was running for dear life down the road from his house to the harbour.

Once outside again and with the car started, Littlejohn and Cromwell met the full force of the gale which howled and roared round the car and made it shiver in every joint. Guided by the flickering street lamps, Littlejohn battled his way to the town, through the narrow streets, and to the waterfront. There he was met by a solid wall of wind which almost pulled-up the car and reduced the journey to a quivering crawl. They parked in the marketplace and hurried as best they could to the *Captain Quilliam*. They saw nothing of Fallows on the way.

The landlord of the pub was busy preparing for whatever might happen in the way of casualties. Hot tea, stimulants, blankets.... Two doctors were in the bar, standing-by....

"They're launching the lifeboat, sir. Camus, the damn' fool captain of the *Robert Surcouf*, the French boat that put in for repairs, has put out to sea and he's in trouble already. There's rockets gone up...."

Littlejohn and Cromwell ran all the way to the lifeboat station. They were too late, as she was already well on her way.

"Are you Inspector Littlejohn, sir?"

A man in oilskins addressed Cromwell.

"No. *This* is my chief."

The man handed a note to Littlejohn.

"Inspector Perrick asked me to give you this. He's gone out with the lifeboat. It seems there was some funny work abroad the French ship and he took the place of one of the men as has a broken arm...."

Littlejohn, leaning his back on the wind, was able to read the letter under the powerful lights of the launching station. It was written in pencilled scrawl, and damp, on a sheet from the familiar note-book.

Expect you here any time. Have gone with the life-boat. Will see you when we get back and explain everything. And just in case I don't get back, I'm sorry.... Good luck, sir.

S. P.

That was all.

It wasn't the wind that gave Littlejohn a catch in the throat as he tore the note in small pieces and scattered them.

Men were still running about on the breakwater, like so many ants scuttering in the dark. Here and there, the less excitable ones—those who had been through it so many times before—stood in knots in sheltered spots.

Littlejohn found Dr. Fallows standing by himself clinging to the huge figurehead of a ship at the doors of the lifeboat-house. Fallows was as still as the figurehead itself. He did not move when Littlejohn took him by the arm.

"You'd better get inside, doctor. You're all in."

"I'll wait here...."

He was staring in the direction of the stretch of water between the breakwater and the shore, as though expecting at any minute the lifeboat would return.

"They'll be hours yet."

"I'll wait till they get in."

"Your wife was aboard the *Robert Surcouf*?"

"Yes."

He didn't argue or show the least spirit or anxiety. First things first; all Fallows wanted was to see her back.

"I'll never see her again...."

Far out at sea another rocket rose and burst into stars.

On the breakwater, facing the spot where the distress signals had risen, stood the priest who usually looked after the Breton sailors when they came to Peel. He was reciting the Last Offices for the dying....

CHAPTER TWENTY
MOOIR NY FUILL

The *Mooir ny Fuill*, the Sea of Blood, had taken its toll again. But it wasn't as bad as everybody had expected.

Dawn was breaking before news came through from Port Erin that the local and the Peel lifeboats had put in there. The one from Port St. Mary had got home, too. There were survivors on all three. Old seamen at Peel said before the news arrived that the ship had gone down and dead men with it. They swore that the first light of dawn was dazzling, the living light, the *soilshey-bio* which accompanied such tragedies.

The gale had not abated in the night. The promenade at Peel was awash. Great seas driven by the wind split at the breakwater, which at a distance in the early light seemed like a mighty circular saw cutting wood and casting a spray of sawdust high in the air and along each side. Waves crashed and slapped on the quays and you couldn't keep your feet unless you clung to the walls. The boats tied up in the harbour beat themselves against the stone sides and against one another. You forgot you were on dry land and seemed to be struggling in an inferno of boiling water.

Nobody but the very young and the very old slept in Peel that night. The pubs on the seafront were open till dawn and relays of men came and went, drying themselves a bit, warming themselves before the fires, taking refreshment, drinking coffee generously laced with rum, thawing out their stiff oilskins.... The old ones told the young ones about past disasters.

"I'd a' been aboard her myself if it hadn' been for a premonition...."

A long tale of lost ships and the warnings and supernatural signs which had resulted in the teller surviving to give a full account.

At five o'clock the telephone rang from Port Erin. The three lifeboats were back....

The news seemed to spread all over the place without anybody telling it.

From the far end of the breakwater, men began to run back to town, gathering up their comrades on the way. It was like a small army on the march when it reached the *Captain Quilliam;* the young men trying to run in the teeth of the weather; the older ones moving at a steady pace which covered the ground just as quickly.

The police had telephoned a list of names to the landlord and he stood behind the counter reading them out. Whenever a fresh batch of newcomers entered, he read them all again. For the most part, it was double-Dutch; Breton names which the landlord couldn't pronounce. Two lives had been lost on the *Robert Surcouf;* the skipper and a passenger. Camus had refused to leave his ship and gone down with her.

"A passenger...?"

The word was passed from mouth to mouth.

"Who was it? We didn't know nawthen about no passenger?"

The landlord couldn't help. The name wasn't given by the police.

Four of the Frenchmen had been rushed to hospital in Douglas; three with broken ribs and another with suspected fracture of the skull. The audience nodded. Little emotion; just relief that men had been saved. The *Robert Surcouf* crew had been a queer lot. Full of the joy of life for a day or two; then morose, sulky, even quarrelsome, as though a sort of curse or evil eye had descended on their ship. They'd taken their moods from the skipper and he had been like a man with a load on his conscience for many days.

"What about the lifeboats?"

"They're all right.... One casualty...."

The landlord said it as though he hoped it would be contradicted; that somebody would suddenly declare it had been a mistake and all the crews had returned safely.

There was dead silence.

"It was Sid Perrick...."

"Aw...."

Just that...." Aw".... The Manx interjection into which, according to inflexion, is poured joy, hope, relief, sorrow or grief.

"He was drowned.... It seems that lad, Jean ... the one with the melodion, you know, got hysterics and as they was takin' him in the lifeboat, had a sort of fit and fell in the water. They thought they'd lost him.... Then Perrick dived after him, brought him in, shoved him over the side of the boat...."

The men hung on the landlord's words, one after another removing caps, sou'-westers and berets, hanging their heads as though already at Perrick's graveside.

"...Just then a wave broke over the boat.... They saw Perrick for a minute.... Then he was gone...."

"Aw...."

Littlejohn and Cromwell, crushed against the wall of the bar, heard it all. They had turned over Fallows to one of his medical colleagues, who'd given him a sedative and taken him to his own home in the town for food and rest.

Littlejohn bit hard on the stem of his pipe. It didn't seem like the same place without Perrick around. Even now, you somehow expected the crowd to part, and the sturdy, bustling form of the man in the raincoat to force its way through, smiling and efficient, ready to take over. ...

"Tom Cashen and the crew are on their way home by bus. They'll have to go back and bring the boat. Somethin's wrong with the engine and it'll take an hour or two to get her seaworthy again."

Outside, the rain had ceased and the wind was abating. A few adventurous spirits were out, inspecting the night's wreckage, and news from other parts was circulating fast.

A wreck off Maughold Head; ships in distress in the Channel and the Ramsey and Douglas lifeboats out all night; and Castletown promenade wrecked again and all the houses along it flooded. ... To crown all, the Steam Packet boat from Liverpool, fifteen hours on the way instead of four. The daylight revealed, too, a large Irish cargo-boat, which had crept in Peel for shelter in the dark. Tied up beside the crowd of soiled and weather-beaten fishing-vessels and coasters, she looked mawkish and out of her element, like a stately, self-conscious hen, mothering a lot of unruly ducklings.

The Peel lifeboatmen were in before nine. They were due in Port Erin again to bring back the boat at noon, but after the night's inferno they felt like a meal at home, a sight of their families, talk with friends, a look at the home town. ...

"It was at the *Mooir ny Fuill* we let up with 'em," the skipper reported to the police. They'd asked him to call at the police-station where Littlejohn and Cromwell were having breakfast.

"…Funny enough, the screw had held and the engines was awright; it was the steerin' gone…she wouldn' answer her helm. Roun' and roun' in circles, lek…an' shippin' wather fast. Camus was in the wheelhouse, swearin' in French like all hell, an' he'd barricaded himself in and wouldn' come out. We tuck off the crew. All three lifeboats was there, but it wasn' easy."

"What about the passenger?"

The skipper grew silent.

"None of us'll forget that for many a long day. We didn' know there was a woman aboard. We knew how many crew and worked accordin'. We couldn' hear one another speak, lek, in the noise and tuck off the men one by one, havin' got a rope across. Then the mate, Donny-dew, appears with someborry across his shouldhers. We turns the searchlight on him and we see he's carryin' what looks like a woman. … An' of a sudden she starts to struggle. He puts her on her feet an' tries to tell her to mount his back, and he'll tek her with him across the rope. Instead, she looks round, wild lek, loses her hold of him, and a wave breaks over her and she's gone. She didn' seem to want to be rescued. …"

Tom Cashen beat the table with his fists, a burst of emotion quite out of keeping with his calm temperament.

"It was Mrs. Dr. Fallows. … What she was doin' aboard the Frenchy, I don' know. Who put her aboard and what was she doin' there on a night lek las' night? Bad enough the mad French skipper takin' out his ship and crew and not only riskin' them but emperillin' my men as well. What was Mrs. Fallows doin' aboard? Had she been kidnapped or someth'n'?"

"No, Tom. It'll all come out in time. It was to do with the murder of Levis. ..."

"She did it?"

"I believe so."

Littlejohn paused.

"Yes. She must have been trying to get out of the country to avoid arrest. That's why Perrick went out with you. *He was going to bring her back.*"

Cromwell's head slowly rose from his plate. He turned to Littlejohn with admiration in his eyes. Perrick had messed-up Littlejohn's case, but the Chief Inspector was going to let him finish with honour. Last night's events had washed clean the slate.

"Aw, Perrick. A brave man. One of the best. As long as the men in that lifeboat lasts, they'll talk of what he did las' night. An' all the young Frenchy's botherin' about now, is that his blasted accordion went down with the ship. ..."

CHAPTER TWENTY-ONE
THE SILENCE IS BROKEN

They had barely finished breakfast when the telephone rang from Noble's Hospital to say that Archdeacon Kinrade was there and wanting to speak with Littlejohn.

At midnight, the telephone wires at Grenaby were blown down and as Littlejohn had taken the car away, the vicar and Mrs. Littlejohn had waited without news all night. Then, about eight o'clock, a police car had arrived from Douglas to say that Ned Crowe had been asking for the parson and would he come right away?

Archdeacon Kinrade had found Ned Crowe in a state of high excitement and anxiety. The casualties from the *Robert Surcouf* had been brought in and had given a full account of the disaster to some of the nurses who could speak French. It had travelled from ward to ward, and Ned Crowe had heard of the deaths of Perrick and the mysterious woman passenger, Pamela Fallows. He had thereupon begun to shout for Archdeacon Kinrade and nothing would pacify him but a promise to bring the parson right away.

"You're not going to die, man. Hold your peace," they'd told Crowe, but he wouldn't rest until they did as he demanded.

When the Archdeacon arrived Ned Crowe began to pour out a long tale.

"I've had it on me conscience all this time, pazon, and maybe if I'd told it before, last night's shipwreck an' loss of life would have been pervented. I can't bear it on me mind a minyute longer...."

And what he told the Archdeacon sent the good man scurrying to the nearest telephone.

"You'd better tell that to my friend, the Chief Inspector...."

"Will that mean I's be sent to jail, pazon?"

"Now don't be silly, Ned...."

Ned Crowe looked a lot better when Littlejohn arrived in his ward. Relieving himself of his tale to the vicar had done more than any amount of medicine, and now he was anxious to make his peace with the police and go home to Margat and his farm.

"I din' do it deliberate, sir. What Mr. Perrick told me skeered me, lek.... When everybody kep' askin' me things and he kep' advisin' me to keep quiet till he said it was right, I got bewuldered.... I tuck to the dhrink... an' then I met with me accident. If I hadn' been so keen on the dhrink, it would never have happened...."

"Tell it in your own way, Mr. Crowe, and take your time."

They gave Ned a drink of orange-juice to encourage him. Cromwell took down his statement in a mixture of shorthand and scribble which he had invented himself.

"I wanted to say, an' I've already told Mr. Kinrade, I saw Mr. Levis get himself killed that afternoon at Gob y Deigan. If someborry else hadn' done it, I might have done it meself...."

Ned Crowe raised himself in his bed and thumped the counterpane for emphasis.

"My gel, Margat, had met Levis somewhere and was all excited-up on account of him. He used to take her out in his car and gave her ideas quite above her, lek. I was bothered about it and I asked people about Levis. They said he was a bad 'un and his ways with women wouldn' bear thinkin' of. That was enough for me. I told Margat she hadn' to see him again. ...."

"But she did."

"Aw, yes, she did. I went the wrong way about it. A man shouldn' tell women they're not to do things, nor yet that the man they fancy's all wrong. That makes 'em want the fellah all the more. Instead of doin' it open, after that, Margat starts seein' Levis underhand, an' one day she tells me he wants to marry her an' she's agreed."

The very thought of it depressed Ned Crowe and they had to give him more orange-juice to pull him together.

"I said I'd never agree and rather than that, I'd lock her in her room till she came to her senses. You see, sirs, it was said that Levis had a wife over in England. In any case, I wasn't havin' my gel wed to a fellah like that ... a man as has lived sinfully with more women than he could count. ... An' for the first time, Margat turned on me ... turned on her father, and said she wouldn' obey me. She packed a bag an' went off to London without sayin' why or where. She left behin' her a paper with trains and the lek, train an' boat times to get to foreign parts, and it came to me that she was runnin' away with Levis. My pride tuck it so hard, that I thought she could go her own sinful way, an' I got dhrunk off some rum in the house. ...."

Crowe looked anxiously around. "Margat's all right, isn' she?" As though he couldn't believe she was home again and his nightmare over.

"Yes, Ned. She's at the Kellys', safe and sound."

"Thank God! The nex' day, as I was still wonderin' what to do, I looks up from some job or other in the farmyard, an' there I see Levis walkin' down the glen to Gob y Deigan. So he's not gone off with my gel, I thinks, and I makes afther him with murdher in my heart. I crossed the field to the edge of the cliffs, and I looks down, lek, to see where he is. There's another woman there with him. I seen her around Peel… a docthor's wife called Fallows, an' people had told me Levis was once knockin' about with 'er, like he'd been with my Margat.…"

Through the glass panels of the door, they could see an orderly and a nurse wheeling a trolley on which a patient was lying on his way to an operating session. Crowe followed it with his eyes alive with enthusiasm, a member of a small community of the sick and interested in every detail of what went on.

"They done grand for me here, pazon. I couldn' have wished for better treatment if I'd been the Governor himself.…"

"Go on with your tale, Ned."

"I lied down on me all-fours an' watched what was goin' on between Levis an' the woman. She seemed to be pleadin' for some thin' and Levis jes' laughing, lek. All of a sudden, Levis grabs her and starts kissin' her, and her strugglin' to get away. The more she struggles, the more excited an' lustful he seems to get, till in the end, it looks as if he's goin' to have his way with her. She goes quiet an' stops strugglin', and gives-in.… She even sits down on the stones, pantin' after the rough handlin' she's had, and Levis sits by her and teks a hold of her and his hands go all over her.…"

Crowe's eyes bulged as he saw events again in imagination.

"Then, of a sudden, she ups with a rock she's picked up, and hits him hard on the head. He tries to defend himself, and that rouses her proper. She hits him over an' over agen, till he's lied there dead.... Or that's how it seemed to me. Then the woman ups and runs as fast as she can hare it, up the glen an' away in the car she's come in. I didn' know what to do. I couldn' think of the body lyin' there untended for me to see every time I crossed my land. ..."

Crowe was getting tired and faltering in his speech.

"Tell us briefly what happened next, Mr. Crowe...."

"I'd alwis been friendly, lek, with Sid Perrick. He was once policeman at Michael, an' was rare and good to Margat when she went to school there. He'd bring her home at times when the roads was busy with charabancs and the lek. I can see her now, sittin' on his bicycle an' Sid Perrick pushin' her along.... Well, I went to the telephone, an' I asked Sid Perrick to come right away an' see me. He come an' tuck it rare an' bad when I'd told him my tale. I never see a man so upset. It might have been his own brother got killed.

"'With your Margat consarned and run away from you because of Levis,' he tells me, 'it might look black for you, Ned, if the body was found on your land. There's only your word for it that someborry else did it, an' the best thing is to keep quiet till I've cleared things up. No matter who asks you, you're not to tell a thing about Levis, Margat or Mrs. Fallows unless I say so.' That's what Sid Perrick said. Then we go down to the shore, hide the body in one of the Lynague Caves, an' afther dusk we fill up the trousers with stones, tie them at the bottom, an' row out far to sea and drop it. An' there it would be to this day an' noborry the wiser, but for Tom Cashen findin' it when afther his tanrogans. It was lek the will of God seekin' out wrongdoin'. It hit me so bad that I tuck to the dhrink to forget it all...."

"There was Levis's car. What happened to it?"

"Mr. Perrick took it; I think he hid it in the old Foxdale mine workin's."

"And that's all, Ned?"

"Should there be some more? I'd have thought it was quite enough for one man, pazon!"

"What did you think when Johnny Corteen was arrested for the crime you knew he'd not committed, Mr. Crowe?"

"I told Mr. Perrick I couldn' be silent if another was to suffer. He said to hold my peace, lek, an' no harm would come to Johnny. An' it didn', did it? If no harm came to anyborry, I wasn' goin' to see anyborry suffer for the likes o' Levis. A right bad lot. An' Mrs. Fallows only, in a manner o' speakin', defendin' herself against him. Though it might 'ave been said I killed him because of Margat. I still think Sid Perrick was right about that...."

The gale blew itself out in the course of the day. Littlejohn, Cromwell and Archdeacon Kinrade were in Peel when, late in the afternoon, the lifeboat arrived home. There was a considerable crowd in the *Captain Quilliam* later on. The Breton sailors had been brought to Peel, and without Captain Camus were a lot more sociable. In spite of the fact that they'd lost most of their gear on the *Robert Surcouf*, they insisted on standing rounds of drinks for the men who had saved their lives. Only the mate, Donadieu, remained morose. He kept thinking of his lost share of the £500 which had induced Captain Camus to take aboard the woman passenger and put to sea in a gale. Half a million francs! And Camus had insisted on going down with his ship and the money next to his skin! Donadieu was so helplessly drunk at closing-time, that his men hadn't the nerve to take him to a lodging-house for the night. They bedded him down in the hold of the *Ernest Renan*, from Tréguier, which had tied-up for shelter in the harbour and was taking the crew back to St. Malo as soon as the casualties could travel. ...

Littlejohn and Cromwell had parked the Archdeacon with the car during their visit to the *Captain Quilliam.*

"Dr. Lennox spotted me here," said the vicar, when they returned. "He says he'd like to see you at his home, Littlejohn, before we go back. Fallows is staying with him. His place is on the Patrick Road. ..."

Dr. Lennox, another general practitioner in Peel, and his wife had befriended Fallows. Littlejohn found him with them.

"You'll find him quite himself. I've given him a few shots of sedative, but he's able to talk about things and seems anxious to see you, Chief Inspector. Don't push him too hard. ..."

"I won't trouble him at all, if you say so, doctor. But perhaps he wants to get it off his mind. I don't suppose the future is very clear for him just at present?"

"Strangely enough, it is. ... He is comforting himself a little by thinking of it. To tell the truth, he's eaten out his heart here in general practice. The man's a born teacher and research specialist. He only left it for his wife's sake, and hid himself. Only last week he had an offer of a job in one of the great mainland teaching hospitals. He was thinking it over and now, I'm sure he'll go. ... You'll find him in the next room. ..."

You had to hand it to Fallows. He could take it. Littlejohn had expected to find him broken and confused by events. Instead, either from pride or restraint, he was calm and self-possessed. The domestic turmoil and emotional chaos of years was suddenly over, the blows of his unseen opponents had ceased, and he was already regaining moral strength and poise.

"I'm terribly sorry about all this, Dr. Fallows. ..."

Fallows hung his head a moment and then offered his hand to the Chief Inspector.

"You were always most kind to me. ... In fact, in spite of the duty you had to do, you treated me almost like a friend, Inspector. I shall never forget it. ..."

The doctor gathered himself together.

"There are one or two things I ought to tell you ..."

"Another time will do, if you like."

"No. Better get it over. There's very little. You know, of course, who killed Levis. You've known all along, but you hadn't enough proof. All my efforts to trail red-herrings were useless. I know that."

"That's right, doctor. But ..."

"I have tried to seal off my emotions for the present. I dare not face them ... but you know I was utterly devoted to my wife. She had been a weakly child and was spoiled in her early days. Then, the war made mincemeat of established codes. ... I ... I ... I was so much older than she was and of a different world. She married me on the rebound. A flying officer. ... He was killed. ... I was content to take her on those terms. ... I must share the blame. ... I. ..."

He was getting a bit off the rails.

"How did the murder occur, sir?"

Fallows paused and pulled himself together.

"Levis was a perfect bounder. He wouldn't leave my wife alone. I admit I perhaps neglected her a bit. There was an affair. I found out, and didn't know what to do about it. Fate took a hand, however. Pamela broke it off with Levis. She told me all about it, and she said she'd do what I wanted ... leave me or let me divorce her. I couldn't bear either. I asked her to stay. I am sure she broke it off with Levis out of a sense of duty ... wanting to do the right thing by me and the children … feeling she'd been weak and gone off the rails a bit and trying to make amends. I shall always think that and cherish it. …"

He was breaking down again. It seemed a bit callous of Littlejohn, but there was nothing else for it.

"The murder, sir. …"

"Eh? Oh, yes. Levis still loved her. She told me all this before she … before she … left … Levis was mad about her. He tried the tactics of flaunting other women, but he pestered Pam to return to him. She told me so. And then he telephoned to say he was leaving the Island, going to get married and leave for good. He had some of her letters. Would she meet him at their old rendezvous and say goodbye, and he'd give them to her? She ought to have known him better. It was a trick. She ought to have told me. But she said she didn't want me to see the letters. …"

The doctor told his tale colourlessly. He might have been relating the story of a third party … some patient or other … instead of his own dreadful unhappiness.

"She begged him to post them. He wouldn't. She agreed to meet him to get them back. When she got there, Levis started to make love to her all over again. She said he was violent … like a madman, begging, imploring her to come back, threatening to kill himself. … And then, he tried to force her … they had a struggle and Pamela hit him with a rock. It killed him."

"I've heard the full account from Ned Crowe, sir. It tallies with your own. …"

"Yes; but who would believe it? A woman whom all the Island knows has been Levis's … Levis's … I mean …"

"I understand."

"You see what I mean. … If she'd gone to the police, and said she'd killed Levis … Well …"

"They wouldn't have believed she was defending herself against the man who had been her lover. Instead, they'd have said she'd killed him because he'd thrown her over."

"Exactly. She came home like one in a dream. She roamed about the house. I heard her screaming in her sleep, walking her bedroom, weeping. Finally, one night I heard her go down to the surgery and I followed. She was just taking a whole palmful of sleeping-pills, when I caught her. I took her by the throat and stopped her from swallowing until I'd scooped them all out of her mouth. Dreadful...."

Fallows put his head in his hands and shuddered.

"Have you had enough, doctor? It can wait."

"No, no, no. It's nearly over. It can't wait. I've got to tell you. She confessed what she'd done. But that was after three days and no news of the murder had come through. We couldn't understand it. She said the struggle occurred above the tideline and she left the body where it fell. It couldn't have been washed to sea.... Next day, at dawn, I went there. No body. I thought she'd imagined it. Then...."

Fallows gulped and seemed to hesitate to live it all over again.

"Then, one afternoon, the police rang up. A scallop dredger had found a body on the beds. I knew without being told. I went and met the boat, calmly did my work in the mortuary, removed the one means of identification, a sleeve-link, made a report, and went quietly home convinced it was all over....

"You know the rest, Chief Inspector. A week or so later, Perrick called. He was quite calm, as usual. He asked to see Pam and me together. 'You know of course, whose the body was that Tom Cashen found on the beds?' he said. 'It was Levis. And I know who committed the crime. It was you, Pam....' He called her Pam. I'll tell you why in a minute...."

"I know, sir. Had Irene Hartnell lived, Perrick would have been your brother-in-law. ...."

For a second, the doctor's eyes glowed with admiration at Littlejohn.

"You know, Inspector, you did make a thorough job of it. And in spite of all of us being against you and drawing our red-herrings across the trail."

"I can't understand one thing, though, doctor. Why wasn't it known that Perrick had close associations with you? Surely the whole Island would know the connection."

"No. Pam wasn't very kind to Perrick. She didn't want Irene to marry him. She thought it *infra dig*... a policeman. She and Irene quarrelled about it. I liked Perrick. We got on well together. But he never came to visit us socially. ... Pam held it against him that if Irene hadn't been in London shopping to marry Perrick, she'd never have been killed. Rather stupid, you think, but women think differently from us. I shall never forget all I owe to Perrick. A fine man and a fine officer. ...."

"Why did he do so much for your wife, then, if she treated him so badly?"

"It was like him. I got in trouble in my London job. I'm a bit hot-tempered. I hit a colleague. He was unconscious. I had to resign. ...."

Littlejohn knew all about it. He made no comment.

"As far as I was concerned, I couldn't expect any other post like the one I was leaving. Perrick, who always seemed to take a kindly interest in us, came to see me. He mentioned the Isle of Man. He was devoted to his native land. The picture he drew of it, combined with the fact that it was remote and out of the way of gossip, made up my mind. I'd start again here. There was a practice going in Peel. I wish to God I'd never seen the place."

"You can't say that, doctor. It might have happened else-where … all this, I mean … and no Sid Perrick to put things right."

"That is true. One of the last things Perrick said to me was that Irene had once told him how impulsive and unstable Pam was. She'd said how since they'd been kids, Irene had always protected Pam, got her out of scrapes, looked after her. 'When we're married, there'll be two of us to do it,' she'd told Sid. Then she got killed. Perrick never seemed to have loved any other girl. Her death just turned him into a kind of automaton, his whole life in his work and nothing else. I sometimes think he got us over here so that he could keep an eye on Pam. Just as Irene would have done. Perrick did it all for Irene. That's all there is to it."

"And when he called about the murder?"

"He said they were holding somebody on suspicion; but he would be released. Until the affair blew over, he would protect Pam all he could, and provided nobody else looked like taking the blame, Pam would be safe. Then, one night, he called to say you had come over. I've never known him scared before. He was a brave man. But your arrival gave him a bad turn. He tried to stand between you and Pam, but you got closer and closer. And as you got nearer to the truth, my poor wife seemed to lose her head. She said one night she'd kill you for your interference. That but for you, it would all blow over. …"

Littlejohn didn't mention the rifle and the car escapades. Fallows had quite enough to bear without them.

"… Perrick got to know from you all that was going on in the case. He carried off all Levis's papers from the house at Bradda and destroyed all that referred to my wife. He said he even had to obstruct you now and then. He didn't like that. It was distasteful to me, too. I got desperate about it and told you I'd committed the crime. But even then, it turned out wrong. You presented me with an unwanted alibi."

"And the accident to Ned Crowe?"

"Perrick said Crowe had seen Pam actually kill Levis, but that he'd persuaded him to keep quiet, because they might have said Crowe himself had killed Levis because of Margat, whom Levis said he was going to marry. But Crowe had a conscience and took to drink. One day he stopped Pam in the street in Peel. He was half drunk then. He told her he knew all about her and would see that nobody else suffered for her sin. She was afraid, and went one night to see Crowe. He turned her away rudely. She waited a bit in the car outside. Crowe came out, she followed, intending to make another appeal. Then, she said, she stopped him outside Peel and he was more than rude. He called her some vile Biblical names. She said it all went black, she let Crowe get ahead, and then ran him down. I knew she was out in the car. I took the blame."

"Did she ever go out in any other car than your own?"

Fallows looked puzzled for a minute.

"Oh, yes. Sometimes when I needed the car and she wanted to go out, we'd borrow a hire-and-drive car in Peel for one or the other. A couple of nights ago, Perrick rang up after midnight. Something had happened and he wanted to see her. I was out on a case. She took the hired car to Douglas...."

That was it! Littlejohn said no more.

"Then, last night, Perrick called to say it was all up. You knew who'd done the murder and also that *he* was implicated. It seems he had the telephone lines tapped and overheard you telling Scotland Yard. He'd arranged a passage to France for Pam in a boat tied-up in Peel. He had some hold over the skipper. Smuggling, or something. I said I wouldn't allow it. The night was the worst I ever remember. It was that, or an arrest, Perrick said. He'd stay and face the music, but Pam was to go and I could join her one day. ... Perrick had fixed it all, and took Pam away. She never made it. I must be callous, Chief Inspector, because I feel relieved. Poor Pam. ... It's over and done with for her. All the mix-up, the torture, the hunting, is done with. It's over, and she's gone. ..."

Fallows could bear no more. He shook with sobs and beat the arms of the chair with his fists.

Littlejohn called in Dr. Lennox and left him to deal with his friend.

The wind had eased and in the sheltered valley of Grenaby, it was quite calm. People were about, gathering the broken branches and boughs after the gale, the birds were singing, and the vicarage cat, which always ran away before rough weather, was home again, calmly snoozing by the fire, disturbing Meg by her unwanted presence on the rug. In spite of the disasters of the previous night, the atmosphere of the old house seemed happier for being cleared of the turmoil and tension of unsolved crimes. Mrs. Littlejohn and Maggie Keggin were in the kitchen preparing lobsters for evening, the parson settled in his study to polish up his forgotten sermon for the coming Sunday, and Littlejohn took Cromwell for a walk to Ronague. ...

First thing next morning, Littlejohn gave the Chief Constable a full account of the Levis crime and its solution. Ned Crowe's testimony, the collaboration of Littlejohn and Perrick, the flight of Mrs. Fallows, the loss of the *Robert Surcouf*. Dr. Fallows didn't enter into it, and a few days later left for the mainland and his own people.

Sid Perrick's body was washed ashore at Dalby. There was a smile on his face and he looked a bit strange in his oilskins instead of his raincoat. He was buried in the soil of the Island he loved and his heroism on the night of the St. Matthew's Gale was mentioned at the service and in police records.

The body of Pamela Fallows was never recovered, nor was that of Captain Camus, who went down with his ship and his five hundred pounds.

A few days later, Littlejohn and Tom Cashen made a day of it at the tanrogan beds. Cromwell was persuaded to go with them. The sea was choppy and Cromwell, a poor sailor at the best of times, never saw a scallop afterwards without a queasy feeling inside.

DEATH TREADS SOFTLY

GEORGE BELLAIRS

CHAPTER ONE
THE HARBOURMASTER OF
CASTLETOWN

Saturday November 6th. The *King Orry*, Liverpool to Douglas, Isle of Man, ploughed her way through seas the colour of lead under heavy skies. There was a slight swell; otherwise the crossing was easy.

Twenty-four hours of endless rain! The downpour had started at noon the previous day, when Littlejohn had first met Finlo Crennell, his travelling companion, and it was still at it. Now, they were eating their lunch in the dining saloon. No pleasure on deck. A meal helped to pass the time away.

Chief Inspector Littlejohn looked up from his plate at the man opposite. Before midday yesterday, he'd never set eyes on him. Another of those strangers who suddenly drifted into his life and then, after a few hours or maybe days, vanished in the crowd and were never seen again.

The man seemed to sense the Chief Inspector's scrutiny, met his gaze, and smiled broadly. Twenty-four hours of the smile that wouldn't come off! They'd even occupied the same room in the Liverpool hotel the night before and Crennell had smiled in his sleep....

A little, robust, powerful man with a rolling gait, who'd once been at sea and then had settled down as harbourmaster of the small port of Castletown, until he'd retired a year ago. Now, he wore a ready-made dark-grey suit which fitted where it touched him and looked as if he'd slept in it for a week. A soft collar and a red tie round his bull neck, and a cloth cap on which he was now sitting because he hadn't known what to do with it when he entered the room.

Finlo Crennell, aged 66, born Ballabeg, Arbory, Isle of Man. Height: 5 feet, 8½ inches. Eyes blue. Bald. Portly....

That was how the description had run and the accompanying photograph, an enlarged section of a crowd at some yacht races, had shown a round, smooth face, a sharp little nose, and a head shaped like an orange.

Missing since October 28th.

Superintendent Jenks had sent for Littlejohn and he had found him in his office with Finlo Crennell sitting beside him eating ham sandwiches and drinking tea from the canteen.

"I wonder if *you* can do any good with this chap, Littlejohn...."

And Crennell had looked up very happily, munching his bread and ham, and had given the Inspector his now famous perpetual smile.

"He was found wandering about Limehouse last night. He'd been robbed of his pocket-book, if he ever had one, he wore a torn and dirty suit of sailor clothes, and a cap with a Dublin maker's name. No means of identification at all...."

The unknown man looked at the new badly fitting suit they'd given him and smiled with pleasure at it.

"He's lost his memory. There's a nasty mark on the top of his head and the surgeon says its recent, but not too recent. He doesn't know who he is and he doesn't remember a thing, and he seems damned pleased about it, too. ..."

The man nodded at them and gave them the smile that wouldn't come off.

"It's getting on my nerves, Littlejohn. We've been at him, on and off, for hours. The missing persons files haven't helped us. We've combed them. Seems to have come off some ship or other. All we know is, that when he says any-thing ... and it's small talk, saying he's hungry and such like ... he speaks with a kind of brogue that nobody seems to recognize. It isn't Irish, Scotch or Welsh. And now, here's where you might help. Is it Manx? You've been in the Isle of Man a lot. See what you can do. Him and his smile and his lost memory. He's getting me down."

Littlejohn looked the man over. The orange-shaped head, totally bald except for a thin thatch of fine grey down. The innocent blue eyes. And, of course, the smile.

"How are you getting along?"

"Aw, middlin'."

Littlejohn smiled back.

"*Cannas-Tha-Shu*?" he said.

The blue eyes met Littlejohn's and the smile broadened.

"*Braoo, Braoo*," replied the stranger.

"What's he say?"

Jenks eyed Littlejohn with suspicion and the Chief Inspector didn't tell him that he'd just uttered the only words of Manx he knew.

"I asked him how he was, and he says he's fine. He's Manx all right."

"We'd better get in touch with Douglas, then."

And that had started it. Finlo Crennell had, on the 28th of October, left his usual pub, the *Jolly Deemster*, in Castletown, at closing time and had apparently walked into the harbour. Two men passing by had heard the splash and a shout and had raised the alarm. There had, more or less, been an all-night search and when they hadn't found Crennell, the local police had assumed his body had been carried out on the ebb tide.

"And now he turns up in Limehouse. The tide can't have ebbed all that way. How did he get there?"

"He must have been picked up and brought to London by some ship or other."

"We're making inquiries, Littlejohn. Meanwhile we'd better get him home. He doesn't know who he is, or where he is, and it isn't safe to let him loose. What about taking him yourself? Get him identified, and then leave him in safe hands...."

"More roast beef, sir?"

The polite steward, with nobody else to look after, bent solicitously over the man without a memory. Again the smile. Crennell must have been starved on his strange travels; since Scotland Yard had picked him up, he hadn't stopped eating, except when smiling in his sleep!

Finlo Crennell ate his meal with robust relish and obvious pleasure. Now and then he would look up at Littlejohn and give him a smile of utmost confidence, like a child who trusts a grown-up to do the right thing.

Littlejohn left his companion still eating and took a stroll on deck to stretch his legs and to smoke his pipe. As they neared the Isle of Man, the rain slackened and gradually changed into drizzle, then a sea mist. The boat checked speed and blew a blast on her siren. From ahead in the fog, the foghorn of Douglas Head lighthouse bleated. Suddenly, they could see the pierhead at Douglas and the *King Orry* glided into the harbour.

The fog wasn't as thick over the land. Visibility reached half-way along the broad sweep of Douglas promenade. In the season, you could hardly toss a coin between the thick mass of holidaymakers; now, there wasn't a soul in sight, except on the quayside, where a compact mass of vehicles, porters and sightseers was waiting for the arrival of the boat.

If Finlo Crennell had left the Isle of Man without dignity, he was certainly arriving back to a fuss. An ambulance, two police cars, a taxi, and an ancient touring-car with leaking cushions and an old hood. When they saw that the harbourmaster wasn't coming off the boat on a stretcher, they sent the ambulance away.

As Littlejohn and his charge descended the gangway, the official reception party met them. People started to wave to Crennell and he smiled back, as usual, and looked puzzled. Otherwise, he didn't recognize anybody.

From the old touring car emerged the shovel hat, the fine head, the white froth of beard and the gaitered legs of the Rev. Caesar Kinrade, Archdeacon of Man. Littlejohn hastened to him and they met with a warm handclasp.

"I got your message, Littlejohn. You'll be staying with us the night, at least."

From the taxi descended the elderly woman who kept house for Finlo Crennell at Castletown. A small, motherly, peasant type, dressed in black from head to foot and carrying an umbrella and an imitation crocodile skin handbag. When she saw Crennell, she began to weep.

"Whatever have they be doin' to ye, Finlo? We all thought you was dead and we'd never see you again...."

She eyed him up and down and then got annoyed.

"Who's dressed ye up like that?"

She pointed to the natty, ready-made suit which Scotland Yard had provided. She wasn't used to seeing him in anything but his navy blue reefer suit with brass buttons and his jaunty peaked cap.

"I'll get your other suit out an' air it. That one's a disgrace; and who gave you that cap?"

Finlo Crennell kept up his eternal smile, as though thoroughly delighted with it all. It was obvious he didn't recognize anybody, but was quite suited with things as they were.

"He's lost his memory, Mrs. Cottier. …"

One of the policemen tried to explain.

"What have they been doin' to ye, Finlo? He'll get it back, won't he? He'll be all right?"

"We'd better be getting along. It'll be dark soon."

The procession started. Two police cars, Mrs. Cottier in state in her taxi, for which Crennell's friends at home had passed round the hat, and Littlejohn, Archdeacon Kinrade and Crennell bringing up the rear in Teddy Looney's old rattletrap with its canvas hood and side-curtains opaque with age.

Round the quayside, past the Nunnery, and to the Castletown road. Here and there the fog thickened. At Mount Murray it was clear; heavy again at Santon. Through Ballasalla and past the airport, where all the planes were grounded for the day. Then, Castletown.

Littlejohn sat back and enjoyed the ride. It was always the same. As soon as he set foot on Manx soil, the atmosphere got in his blood, as though he breathed in with the very air itself, some sedative essence which soothed his nerves and slowed him up. *Traa di Liooar.* … Plenty of time for everything.

"Castletown," said Littlejohn to the harbourmaster, and he watched his face for any recognition.

Finlo Crennell kept smiling, but there seemed a bit of anxiety, a puzzled suggestion in his face now.

"Castletown."

He almost whispered it, savouring it, and then he sighed as though somehow it comforted him.

Early dusk was falling when they reached the town and the mist didn't improve matters. Over the swing bridge, under the shadow of the great castle and into the small square with its lining of trees and fine old houses. The police cars stopped.

"We'll leave you here for the time being, sir. Maybe we'll see you later this evening. Mr. Crennell will be tired and it's not much use botherin' him in his present condition. He'll want his tea."

The homely police sergeant put his head in the touring car and arranged it all. Then he and his mates drove away.

The taxi led the way and Looney's car followed. Round by the side of the church and along a narrow street of small houses with backs facing the sea across Castletown Bay, Queen Street. At a house in the middle of a row, the taxi drew up and Mrs. Cottier got out heavily. She waited at the front door until the rest joined her.

A small cottage, two up and two down, to which Crennell had retired from the large official harbourmaster's house on the quay. Bright brass knocker and letter-box and a fire with the light of flames visible through the window. A few neighbours came to their doors to greet the returned man, but he smiled at them and said nothing. Then, he made for the door of his own house and tried the knob. He waited until his housekeeper unlocked the door. She turned a delighted look on the parson.

"He knows his own house, you see, Mr. Kinrade. He'll soon be all right again, won't he?"

They entered the living-room and Mrs. Cottier removed her hat and coat, took Crennell's cap, and left to dispose of them. Crennell, meanwhile, sat in his chair. Then he rose again, opened a drawer in the sideboard, took out a pipe and tobacco and started to fill-up. Mrs. Cottier entering noticed it all.

"You see, he knows where he keeps his pipe and tobacco. He'll soon be himself again."

Finlo Crennell took no heed of the comments. He was still like someone who'd been hypnotized and just told to keep smiling.

A cosy room, not overcrowded with furniture; sideboard, two old-fashioned, leather-covered easy chairs, a few small chairs and a corner cupboard. An open, old style grate with three bars holding in the large red mass of coals. Crennell seemed to have settled-in as he did before his adventures.

"Is there anything more we can do, Mrs. Cottier?"

Archdeacon Kinrade seemed anxious to be off and to get his visitor to himself. It was a bit awkward trying to talk to a man who didn't know a thing and whose only replies were nods and smiles.

"We'll be all right, Mr. Kinrade. Now we've got him home again, we'll soon have 'im all right. The doctor's due to call an' see him any time now. Then we'll know just what to do for the best."

The clock on the wall struck five. A small wooden affair with a flashing pendulum and weights and chains. Its steady ticking formed a background for the other noises in the room.

"You're sure you'll be all right?"

"Yes, pazon. I've only to knock on the wall and the neighbours'll come in. And as soon as it gets round the town that he's home, there'll be everybody callin' in to see 'im. The police said they'd come to put another sight on him after tea. Will you take a cup o' tea, the both of ye?"

"No, thanks. We'll be getting along."

Littlejohn strolled over to where Finlo Crennell was contentedly puffing his pipe. He put his hand on the ex-harbourmaster's shoulder.

"You all right now, Mr. Crennell?"

For answer he got again the smile that wouldn't come off.

Even as Littlejohn and the vicar left the house, a large man stood on the doorstep. A nautical type, with blue serge clothes and a cloth cap.

"Has himself got back? I thought I'd be puttin' a sight on him. Everin', Mr. Kinrade. Nice to see ye."

They set off in Teddy Looney's car for Grenaby in the last of the daylight. The mist was still thick in parts and hung over the bridge by the cross-roads just near the vicarage. The river was in full spate, driving its way under the bridge and through the narrows which had once held the mill-race.

The strange and penetrating peace of Grenaby took hold of Littlejohn again. He'd been away twelve months and done a lot in the meanwhile. Now, the intervening time didn't seem to count. It was as if he'd never left the place.

The car pulled-up at the door of the parsonage and Looney stopped his engine. They climbed out into absolute silence. A thick blanket of white mist; a few square yards of clearness, and then, beyond, a world completely muffled to sound and sight. From far away, the fog-horn at Langness roared and then left a silence deeper than ever.

There was a shaft of light coming from the fanlight over the vicarage door. They felt their way to it.

"Come in for a cup of tea, Looney. Go right through to the kitchen. Maggie Keggin will see to you."

They took off their outdoor things and went in the parson's study. The same as ever. The place Littlejohn had used for his headquarters a time or two. The old, well-polished mahogany, the books lining the walls, the bright fire and the shaded lamp, with the Hoggatt picture of the Little Fields of Man above the mantelpiece, the focus, as it were, of the room.

"Let me have a look at you. …"

The parson put his hands on Littlejohn's shoulders and looked straight into the Inspector's eyes with his own penetrating blue ones.

"How long will you be here with us?"

"Just to-morrow, sir. I'd better see that Crennell is properly settled and then I'll go back by the Monday morning boat. I'll be able to hear your sermon."

"This Crennell business is a bit of a mystery, Littlejohn. The police seem to have the idea he fell in the water after a drink too many and was picked up by an outgoing boat. There was a Dutch timber boat going out at the time. Could they have taken and dropped him off in London? Or, was it a bit more sinister? Was he shanghaied, or something?"

Littlejohn smiled.

Since the parson had been associated with him in two earlier crimes on the Isle of Man, he was always on the look-out for more mysteries, more cases to solve.

"It seems simple enough, sir. Our people at the Yard are trying to contact the boat you mention and probably it'll all be cleared-up when they do. Crennell, in falling in the harbour, must have caught his head and badly damaged himself. He may have been picked-up by the Dutch boat, which didn't want the trouble of turning back, so took him on to London. There, he seems to have wandered off the ship, got himself robbed, and then walked into the arms of our men in Limehouse. I gather his memory may come back. The surgeon at the Yard said it might mean an operation, however. A spicule of bone, dislodged by the blow, or something."

And then the conversation turned to more personal things until dinner arrived.

"Everin', sir. Good to be puttin' a sight on ye again...."

Maggie Keggin, the parson's housekeeper, entered with a dish of grilled Manx ham, eggs, and fried potatoes. And then there was apple charlotte and fresh cream.

"As soon as she heard you were coming, she started in the kitchen. You're a great favourite there, Littlejohn."

After coffee, they drew up to the fire and lit their pipes. They chatted of all things which interested them and grew drowsy in the heat of the logs. At ten o'clock, Littlejohn telephoned his wife, Letty, in Hampstead, to tell her of his safe arrival.

Strange, every time he rang up the mainland from the Isle of Man, his vivid imagination pictured the cable crossing the dark, watery world under the ocean. Caverns of rock, weird lights, hideous deep-water fishes, ships sailing over the top.

The talk was continued until past eleven. Parson Kinrade kept leading it into criminal channels. All the cases Littlejohn had been engaged on since last they met. Then, cases before that. They were sleepy when they parted, partly from the heat of the room, partly from the Archdeacon's old port which came from a grocer's shop in Kirk Michael.

"They say one of the bishops got the grocer's grandfather ordering that port a century ago and they've sold it ever since."

And after it all, Littlejohn couldn't sleep. It was either the excitement of a full day or the port which hadn't settled down. He felt like he did when a child and was anticipating some big event on the following day and was too excited to fall-off.

He got out of bed once and looked through the window. The fog was thinner and he could see the trees in the garden, but beyond that, a wall of thick darkness.

The fog-horn on Langness was still blaring in the distance. Otherwise, not a sound, except the crackings of the house, settling down after the day.

The grandfather clock in the hall struck twelve. Only an hour since they'd retired! It seemed more like three or four. The slow strokes seemed interminable. Nine, ten, eleven, twelve. ...

And when the clock stopped striking, the telephone took it up. Only more urgently and swiftly.

Littlejohn slipped on his dressing-gown and went downstairs. The parson and his housekeeper must have been fast asleep. There wasn't a sound from either of their rooms. The Chief Inspector groped for the instrument.

"Is that ... ? Is that you, sir? This is me ... Inspector Knell, sir. Glad you're back."

Good Heavens! His old associate, the diligent Knell, eagerly ringing him up in the small hours, just to say he was glad Littlejohn was 'over' again!

"Sorry to get you up, sir, if you'd gone to bed. The man you brought over to-day ... Mr. Crennell, sir ... Sorry, I couldn't get to the pier to meet you. I was out on a case ..."

Littlejohn played five-finger exercises on the wall with his spare hand to soothe his nerves. *Traa di Lioor.* Time enough!

"... He's dead, sir. He must have wandered out of his house. They found him outside the *Jolly Deemster*, his favourite public house. He'd been shot this time. Right through the head. One or two people heard the shot, but with it being the fifth of November only a day ago and the night being wet so they couldn't let off the fireworks on bonfire night, they..."

"Don't you think I'd better come along and we'll talk it over on the spot, Knell?"

Littlejohn was starved through and this looked like going on for ever and ever.

"Would you, sir? I'd be very grateful."

A hand with a lamp and a froth of whiskers following appeared over the balusters of the stairs.

"What is it, Littlejohn? Anything wrong?"

"Yes, pazon. Finlo Crennell has been attacked again. And this time it's murder."

Before a look of sadness and alarm came to the parson's face, did Littlejohn see a gleam of adventure in the bright blue eyes?

WANT ANOTHER PERFECT MYSTERY?

GET YOUR NEXT CLASSIC
CRIME STORY FOR FREE ...

Sign up to our Crime Classics newsletter where you can discover new Golden Age crime, receive exclusive content and never-before published short stories, all for FREE.

From the beloved greats of the Golden Age to the forgotten gems, best-kept-secrets, and brand new discoveries, we're devoted to classic crime.

If you sign up today, you'll get:

1. A free novel from our Classic Crime collection.
2. Exclusive insights into classic novels and their authors and the chance to get copies in advance of publication, and
3. The chance to win exclusive prizes in regular competitions.

Interested? It takes less than a minute to sign up. You can get your novel and your first newsletter by signing up on our website www.crimeclassics.co.uk

22190994R00174

Printed in Great Britain
by Amazon